THE DRIFTWOOD TOUR

JP Lane

To Lynn,
I hope you enjoy my love letter to music lovers. Craig's character is based on my old drinking buddy from Ontario.

DEDICATION

To my wife and children for their patience, grace, and encouragement throughout this process.

I have seen the carpet of cats and mice playing basketball with my own eyes.

A.P. Lane

TABLE OF CONTENTS

ACKNOWLEDGMENTS

This book could not have been written without the guidance, feedback, and encouragement of the following people. Jamie Fontana, Angela Stettler-Hetrick, Sophia Lane, Yolanda Lane, Todd Lewis, Nick Meraz, Gregg Montgomery, Joe O'Connell, Antonio O'Farrell, Suzan O'Grady, and Jim Stowers. Their assistance included feedback on regional norms, concert venues, musical descriptions, language, and writing structure. The Champagne Mane universe is the brainchild of Gregg Montgomery. Someday they will unite and take the stage – with perfect hair.

INTRODUCTION

The characters, such as Wood, Jesse, Charlotte, Uncle Freddy, Rachel, Olive, Craig, and Atsushi are fictional. Any resemblance to actual people is entirely unintentional and coincidental. Many of these stories come from my own experiences. I watched Santa Barbara in Kazakhstan. I was hit by a car in Tokyo and was taken to physical therapy by the young speedster who hit me, but this story is by no means autobiographical. I never fought off hillbillies or handed anyone an exploding guitar pedal.

There are numerous famous people mentioned in this book, all of which is done in good spirit and to serve the larger story. If I didn't love their music they would not be mentioned. Additionally, my hope is to draw attention to musicians who have not received the accolades they deserve, such as Lloyd Cole, Wayne Hancock, Mark Hollis, The Ronettes, and Shuggie Otis.

The story plays loosely with some of the facts, particularly with the calendar. For example, there was a rock festival in Estonia throughout the late nineties. Public Image Limited played there, as well as Bjork, however, not in the same year. PIL and The Sugarcubes toured together, so we can assume that John Lydon and Bjork know each other. Another example is the Chalmette High School marching band in New Orleans. The high school is real, but mean old Mr. Capois is a fictional band teacher. I hope each student, as well as anyone who finds this book in their hands, enjoys the story.

Cover art: Watercolor by JP Lane. Model, Dean Lane.
Cover Design: Jane Dixon-Smith

LIST OF COVER SONGS

Cover songs played by Wood and/or Jesse (in order of appearance). In Spotify, search for "The Driftwood Tour" and listen to each song when it comes up in the story. This is intended to add context.

Coat of Many Colors – Dolly Parton

Bring on the Night – The Police

Edge of Seventeen – Stevie Nicks

87 Southbound – Wayne Hancock

Tus Desprecios – Selena Quintanilla

Tusk – Fleetwood Mac

Jealous Guy – John Lennon

Till Your Well Runs Dry – Peter Tosh

You'll Lose a Good Thing – Barbara Lynn

Happy Hour – The Housemartins

Slippin' into Darkness – WAR

Creep – Radiohead

The Air That I Breathe – The Hollies

Bayou Teche – Columbus Fruge

I Believe In You – Talk Talk

Jesse's medley

> Bo Diddly – Bo Diddly
>
> Not Fade Away – Buddy Holly and the Crickets
>
> Willie and the Hand Jive – Johnny Otis
>
> I Want Candy – The Strangeloves
>
> Desire – U2
>
> Faith – George Michael

Someone Saved My Life Tonight – Elton John

Half of Everything – Lloyd Cole

Cocaine – JJ Cale

Sweet Thang – Shuggie Otis

I Wish I Never Saw the Sunshine – The Ronettes

I Won't Last a Day Without You – The Carpenters

If You Want to Sing Out – Yusuf Islam/Cat Stevens

PROLOGUE

TOKYO METROPOLITAN HIROO HOSPITAL

November 8, 1998

"You found him knocked unconscious, covered in blood, and the solution was to go to another bar?" The lawyer shook her head and whispered, "For fuck's sake" as she scribbled her notes.

"It seemed like the right thing to do at the time."

Wood opened his eyes, looked out through the gauze, trying to make sense of the small crowd. The faint smell of old people masked with cleaning agents told him he was in a hospital. A searing pain cut through his neck and he felt the hard plastic of the brace scraping against his stubble. How long had he been there? His old friend Craig was speaking with a lady of about 30 wearing a dark blue pants suit. He continued to listen to their conversation, undetected.

The lawyer continued, "How long were you at the bar?"

"Till dawn."

"Till dawn?"

"The last train ends around midnight so you either go home early or stay out until they start running again at dawn."

Wood raised his left hand to get the attention of the only face he recognized, but the handcuffs anchored him to the bed. Hearing the sound of metal on metal, the crowd surrounded him.

A nurse leaned forward, "Okiteru mitai. Watashitachi kikoenai kamo shirenai."

The familiar face said, "I don't know if he can hear us. Hey, Wood, just blink if you can hear me."

5

He blinked and tried to say, "Hey, Craig" but all he could conjure was a painful, garbled mess of vowels.

Patting him on the shoulder, Craig said, "Not so fast. You've been in an accident. This is Nobunaga sensei, he's a neurosurgeon – and this is nurse Nishimori. They have a great medical team and they're going to bring you back to health. Your brain has too much swelling. They're going to put you in a medically induced coma. It will be like a long dream while you heal. I wanna hear all about it when you wake up."

The lady leaned in and whispered. "Nice to meet you, Wood. I'm Sophia Balmaceda from the US Embassy. I'll be your legal counsel. Once you start to feel better, I'll explain how screwed you are."

SECTION 1: DRIFTWOOD TOURS THE US

THE FEATHERDUSTERS INTERVIEW

May 17, 1996

WLCL Radio Station, Louisville, Kentucky

Rachel's childhood dream was to become a rock star. Upon realizing she had no musical talent, she settled on famous DJ, then college DJ, and finally sultry trucking dispatcher. She majored in Communications at the University of Louisville and completed a full two years before leaving to run Hempstead Trucking full time and care for her father. She didn't like the term 'drop out" because it implied a conscious decision that she had not made, as if she had walked into the Dean's office and announced, "I, Rachel Hempstead, being of sound mind and body, do hereby drop out. I bequeath my disgusting book bag to the Biology department." After the required phone calls and letters of inquiry, the university archived her transcripts. Rachel became one of countless students who had been subsumed by all in life that was not academia.

***

The first time Rachel met Wood was when she interviewed The Featherdusters on her show for 93.9 The Ville, the student radio station. He was their new lead singer and, as the newest member, was also ridiculed by his bandmates, particularly by Tommy, the founding guitar player, who wrote all the songs and dictated their every move. The Featherdusters dressed like a typical rock band, with long hair, wrinkled t-shirts, black leather jackets, Doc Martens, bandanas, and chains, as if they were perpetually en route to a rumble that never materialized. In contrast, their new singer looked like he had been kidnapped from the mall, with shoulder-length brown hair, stubble, a collared black shirt tucked into

Girbaud jeans, and black Chuck Taylor high tops.

It was an awkward interview, with Rachel trying to unravel the mystery of this new singer and the others clearly unwilling to let a college DJ shine a light onto someone so undeserving of praise.

"Wood, our listeners want to know how you came to join The Featherdusters."

Before he could speak, Tommy chimed in, "I found him sleeping behind a dumpster toward the end of our last tour, so we gave him a shot. You see, it's a lot for me to write the songs and still give my time to the fans, so I thought I'd let someone else handle the singing. Plus, he sings in a lower register, and I can hit the high notes. It makes for great harmonies."

"Wood, I noticed that you play guitar on some of the songs. Do you also write songs?"

"I taught him some of the songs on guitar, but mostly he sings."

Wood crossed his arms and shook his head slowly as he looked down, frustrated by the slights.

With one last try, Rachel asked, "Wood, are you also from Texas?"

He looked at Tommy as he said, "Fuck Texas."

The freshman studying to be a radio engineer scrambled to press the Mute button before Wood's cursing went out on the airwaves.

Wood's first radio interview consisted of one word, "Texas." Rachel wasn't shocked to read in a music zine a few months later that The Featherdusters and their enigmatic singer had parted ways due to, "Creative differences."

THE DRIFTWOOD INTERVIEW

June 12, 1997

WLCL Radio Station, Louisville, Kentucky

A year later the station manager called Rachel during a commercial break on her show. "Hey, can you give a little airtime to a solo artist who is passing through. He just released an EP and he asked if you could interview him. He specifically asked for you. He goes by the stage name…get this, "Driftwood." She cackled and yelled, "The rock world doesn't need another shitty band name!"

'To be fair, Milli Vanilli was taken."

"And Policy, Grandaddy, it never ends!"

'Stop! He's sitting out in the lobby. Can you bring him a cup of coffee and ask him a few questions?"

She yelled, "Only if you give me a better time slot!"

"Done!"

When Rachel opened the door she was shocked to see Wood sitting there. He wore the same outfit, as if he had been hiding behind a plant for the last year, the only difference being that he held a puppy on his lap. He stood and put out his hand to greet her, "Well, hello again. It's Rachel, correct? I hope you don't mind my new friend, Margaret. I can't leave her in the car. May we come in?"

Could a tall, handsome man with correct grammar and a Basset Hound puppy come in? He could have sold her a vacuum cleaner and a set of encyclopedias.

The interview started with a relaxed and flirtatious feel.

"We have Driftwood in the studio with us. He's the former lead singer of

The Featherdusters and he has recently gone solo. He has a new EP out called 'Take Me to the Trains.' But first, what's with your stage name?"

"People have been calling me 'Wood' since I was a kid, so you can call me that if you prefer."

"I wish our listeners could see your little friend here. Who is this?"

"This is Margaret-the-Basset-Hound. She's my tour bus driver."

"She's adorable. I did a little research on you after the interview with The Featherdusters. Your real name is Thurston Underwood. Was your family the canned meats Underwoods?"

Wood was surprised. "Sounds like you did more than just a little research. I think we're from the part of the family that made typewriters, although I don't know a lot of our relatives back east."

"My grandparents had an Underwood typewriter. Small world."

"That's us, I think."

"You went to Park Tudor prep school in Indianapolis. That's a prominent private school."

"If you say so." Wood shifted in his chair and looked down at Margaret, petting her nervously.

"Let's take a short break. This is 93.9 FM, The Ville." Rachel played an announcement about a change in the university's library hours during the summer break.

"How did you find out all that personal information about me?" asked Wood.

"WebCrawler is a wonderful search engine. I got a little curious after your one-word interview last time – 'Texas!'"

"WebCrawler?" Wood hadn't jumped on the internet bandwagon yet. The only technology he trusted were his Hamilton watch, his guitar effects pedals, and certain amplifiers. Why would he trust the internet, especially now that he knew it revealed personal details about him, offered up to anyone bored enough to search for it?

"And we're back with Driftwood. I noticed there aren't any photos of you on the internet. Is that by design?"

"If people want to come to my show they'll see what I look like. I'm not big on self-promotion. I think Gary Trudeau said that only in America could the unwillingness to promote oneself be viewed as arrogance."

"And yet you're on a radio show plugging your EP."

Wood cracked an embarrassed smile, "Touché."

"This is the title track from his new EP, 'Take Me to the Trains.' Driftwood will be opening up for The Sleepy Jackson tonight at the Palace Theatre."

As the song played, Wood apologized for being a bad interviewee, twice. "I suppose I'm not comfortable with public speaking yet. It's funny because once I'm up on stage you can't shut me up. Like when I was with The Featherdusters. I don't think Tommy liked that."

"I thought the interview went well. Sorry if I got too personal. I've been wondering if the reason you left the band was really artistic differences. Was there a last-straw moment?"

Wood looked up to make sure the "On Air" light was not on, pushing the mic to the side, just in case.

He started his story with an eye roll. "Here's how it went down. We were staying in a hotel and they were acting out their usual rockstar routine of being loud and breaking shit, like they used a Led Zeppelin biography as an instruction guide. So Tommy breaks this lamp for no reason and I told him to pick up the pieces because the housekeeping lady shouldn't have to work harder just because he wants to act like a child throwing a tantrum. I guess I made him look stupid in front of these girls. He told me I should just shut up and sing when he told me to. I said I was going back to my room, where it will look like a human being slept. One of the girls asked to come with me, which made it worse because Tommy was really into her. So she comes back to my room and we ended up drinking a bottle of Rioja and talking all night about…everything. When I came down to the lobby the next morning the tour bus was gone. I never saw the girl again either. Like that Cure song, 'I used to sometimes try to catch her, but never even caught her name.'"

"It's a great song. 'Catch.'"

"So here I am – with Margaret." Wood stroked her long ears as she puppy snored.

Rachel tried to wrap her head around his story as the song came to the final chorus. "I didn't expect to hear that. Maybe you need a publicist to work with your band manager."

"I don't have either. Know anyone?"

"I might."

Soon after, Rachel became Wood's manager, publicist, accountant, bill collector, and confidant.

THE DRIFTWOOD SYSTEM

After a number of hits and misses, Rachel and Wood arrived at a collection of practices that worked in a variety of unfortunate situations. They could withstand the headaches of tour planning, foul weather, hangovers, no-show musicians, even club owners who refused to pay. It was a repeatable system, while giving fans the feeling that you couldn't predict what would happen at a Driftwood show. It was controlled chaos and fans came back even though they had played the town only a year before. Rachel kept meticulous post-gig notes, always playing the long game, assuming they would return to the region in the years to come.

If an opening band was late or insufficiently obsequious, they'd never get a second chance. The local musician in their backing band who showed up unprepared wasn't asked back and may not even make it on stage that night.

For temporary backup musicians, the gig was their chance to show their chops or gain a new audience, and Wood was happy to make a phone call to put in a good word on their behalf. There was plenty of love to go around for those who played along, but Rachel could be ruthless to those she perceived as trying to take advantage of them.

Wood originally worked with a drummer, bass player, keyboardist, and a young, multi-instrumentalist from New Orleans named Jesse. The interpersonal dynamics of a full band complicated every endeavor, to say nothing of the logistical struggles of traveling with musicians who had other jobs. Wood came to realize that Jesse was a better drummer than the drummer, felt at ease playing keyboards, and could play all guitar and bass parts better than he. The choice to fire the other members of the band and create their duo created musical challenges, yet eliminated nearly all previous headaches.

They had five set lists that differed greatly from one another, making sure not to repeat the same songs in the same town or nearby cities. What truly made their concerts unique was the end, when local musicians and crafts people took the stage to jam on cover songs. Nothing was off limits and selections ranged from blues to gospel, vintage rock to new wave, all of it melding together to become the Driftwood sound. Slow songs were sped up and flowed seamlessly into a similar song by a different artist. Rachel used her encyclopedic memory as a DJ to identify songs that, at least to her, shared similarities in tempo, key, and lyrical themes. Wood and Jesse often arrived a day early to explain Rachel's vision to local musicians and rehearse the setlist.

COAT OF MANY COLORS

Ryman Auditorium

May 21, 1998

Nashville, Tennessee

A quintessential example of this became known as the "Coat of Many Colors" gig. Towards the end of their show, Wood introduced Ms. Mabel

Pinkerton, the home economics teacher from a local high school, who sat at a sewing machine. Jesse arranged an SM58 near the machine's needle, running the microphone through a flanger pedal, making a psychedelic echo as she began sewing. Jesse watched Mabel's foot as it pressed the sewing machine's control pedal, mimicking her movements with his own foot on his Wah-Wah pedal, like Hendrix soloing along with a quilting class.

Wood began to play along with Jesse and Mabel on his acoustic, first slowly, then faster until he was ready to sing Dolly Parton's classic song about her childhood coat, sewn together by an impoverished, loving mother. Jesse launched into a long solo, looking over at Mabel to see how the coat was coming. When she shook her head, "Not yet" he went to a higher octave and added distortion. Finally, with a flamboyant flick, Mabel cut the thread from the coat and triumphantly walked across the stage, holding it up to the cheering crowd before draping it over Wood's shoulders as he played. He looked up, smiling with closed eyes, then brought the song to an emphatic close.

"Thank you, Nashville! Let's hear it for Ms. Pinkerton!" The crowd cheered as she blushed and waved.

"You have no idea how much I want to keep this coat, but I think we should auction it off for Mabel's school program. What's the name of your school?"

"Wilson Central, over in Mount Juliet!"

"Are there any Wilson Central alumni in the house? Yes! We're gonna sweeten the deal. The highest bidder gets to party backstage with us and the opening act, Rile 9 Collective. Hopefully, Mabel will stick around to have a few drinks with us."

She blushed, "I gotta teach in the morning but maybe I'll have just the one!"

The auction raised enough money to buy all of the craft supplies the high school would need, plus a new Yamata Speedway 9000 sewing machine for Ms. Pinkerton.

Payment

As the backstage party began to wind down, Wood met with the club owner in his office to receive payment for the gig, which by all accounts, was musically and visually memorable. It even tugged at the heart strings, a rarity in the rock world.

"Good show, but I gotta tell you, I can't pay the full amount. The contract was for 90 minutes of music, not interviewing a home economics teacher and adjusting microphones. It wouldn't be fair to the other bands who honored their contract." The owner braced himself for one of the many versions of a tantrum he was used to witnessing. To his surprise, Wood quickly counted out the half payment and said, "This is disappointing. You'll hear from my management in the next day or two."

The next morning, he reported what had happened to Rachel.

"Sounds like he needs a little prodding. I'll take it from here."

"I'll call you from the next hotel. Thanks for your help."

As the club owner arrived the next day to work on payroll checks, he noticed a large refrigerator truck blocking the club entrance. He made a mental note of the name, "Hempstead Trucking." As he pulled out his keys, he felt something cold press against his neck, followed by a quick series of electric shockwaves racing through him. His body pulsated and collapsed on the ground and he felt the warm liquid run down his leg as he pissed himself at the entrance to his club. His vision glazed as tears ran down his face. Half unconscious now, drooling, and unable to move, he strained to focus on the figure standing above him, holding a cattle prod against his chest.

The club owner smelled the stench of his burnt neck and tried to mumble something, but could not form a sentence.

"Got nothing to say? Let's see if this helps you remember your ATM number." The Teamster slid open the back door of the refrigerated truck, revealing a horror scene of beef carcasses, dangling from hooks.

"I got a spot picked out just for you! Meet your new friends." He picked him up, climbed up and hoisted his limp body until the hook caught under his jacket collar. The sleeves cut into his armpits as the weight of his body pulled him down. The driver pulled down the door and latched it, returned to the cab, and called out to Rachel on the CB. "Sweet Pea, you there? This is Tweety. Over."

"This is Sweet Pea! Whatcha got for me, darlin'?"

"The Push Pop is in the icebox. How long should he reflect on his sins?"

"Well, he did pay us half, so not too long. You need to be in Des Moines by tomorrow morning."

"10-4 Sweet Pea. I'll take it from here." The trucker pushed in a Deepak Chopra cassette and dozed off to the soothing sounds of his mellifluous voice, reassuring him that everything in his life was exactly as it was meant to be and reminding him to commune with nature.

The simple, yet highly effective prodding-and-refrigeration technique concluded the Driftwood system. Since the truck drivers took the money and funneled it back to Rachel there was no direct connection between the lack of payment for the concert and the nightmarish crime that followed. For all the club owners knew, it was a loosely connected coincidence. They refused to pay Wood then got robbed by someone else the next day. For those with higher powers of logical deduction, a causal relationship between Driftwood, cattle prods, and refrigerated trucks emerged over time, spreading a rumor throughout the small world of club owners that if you booked Driftwood for a gig, payment in full was expected, and, above all, be polite.

BRING ON THE WHITE WINGED DOVE

The Vogue

June 13, 1998

Indianapolis, Indiana

During their pre-gig phone call, Rachel sounded excited to explain her plan for the encore. "I found some great local musicians to sit in towards the end and I think the encore is going to be one for the ages."

Wood was intrigued, "Really? Let's hear it."

"Listen, I'll play the first few seconds of this song and you tell me who sings it." She hit play on the CD.

Wood could hear guitar strings muted with the left hand going through a chorus pedal, "Got it. 'Edge of Seventeen' by Stevie Nicks."

"That's what I thought you'd say! It's 'Bring on the Night' by the Police. So you start with that song and play for 3 or 4 minutes, then Jesse does a solo and you break it down to that muted guitar part and everyone sings, 'Just like a white winged dove' and it goes into 'Edge of Seventeen.'"

"Wow. That could work. Can I leave out the part about seducing a seventeen-year-old boy?"

"Yeah, just keep singing the chorus and jamming, but check this out. You blend the choruses from both songs into 'Bring on the white winged dove…'"

For Wood this was a bridge too far. "No way! I'm not blending the lyrics, and I'm not throwing bars of Dove soap into the audience or releasing doves from a cage!"

There was silence. Dejected, Rachel said quietly, "But I already booked the dove lady."

Sighing, "What dove lady?"

"She releases doves at weddings and she's affordable. It's simple. She'll be off to the side of the stage, she will release the doves while you're playing, the crowd will be in awe of what they're seeing and hearing. They'll go to work the next day saying, 'You should have been there!'"

"Why do I feel like I'm going to regret this?"

"Wood, you'll regret *not* releasing doves."

"How does she get the doves back?"

Rachel thought for a moment, "I guess they're like homing pigeons and just fly back to her house. Let her worry about that."

"This is an indoor venue!"

Big sigh. "Sugar, you're trying to control everything again. Just let her worry about it. She doves this all the time. Get it?"

"I don't want to laugh at jokes right now."

***

"The Dove Gig" would be seared into Driftwood lore for years and combined a highpoint in performance creativity with a nadir in audience relations. A week after the show, an article from the Indianapolis Star reported that the doves were still stuck in the rafters. As with all bizarre stories, it was picked up by the AP and published in papers everywhere.

Rachel read the article to Wood over the phone, which included quotes from the club owner, the regional PETA spokesperson, and the dove releaser, who blamed it all on Driftwood.

"The club manager released an 18-pound cat into the rafters, which began methodically preying on the doves, leaving blood and feathers strewn on the stage and dancefloor, mixed with a layer of bird droppings. As the huge feline reached for the final dove it lost its balanced and plunged to its death.

In closing, Reid wept, saying, 'I told Driftwood it was a bad idea, but he waved the contract in my face and said he'd sue me! All I want is my Sharon back.'"

Wood said, "I never even met the lady. And who the hell is Sharon?"

"I guess that's the last dove," Rachel replied.

In a fleeting moment of respect, Wood whispered, "She recognized that the last dove was Sharon."

Rachel tried to redeem herself, "I knew she was a weirdo from the start. She should have known not to release them indoors! Besides, who becomes a dove releaser? You don't tell your kindergarten teacher 'I want to be a dove releaser when I grow up' and end up in the Governor's mansion!"

Wood consoled her, "It's cool. We were trying to make something special happen and it got away from us. We'll just deal with this head on. Can you write up a simple press release saying that we love all animals? I'll make a point of having Margaret on the stage with me for my next few shows."

"Thanks, Wood. I like it. Who doesn't love a Basset Hound?"

"That's true. Margaret can bust out her Basset diplomacy. This will all blow over. As my friend from New Zealand used to say, 'Today's newspaper wraps tomorrow's fish.'"

Wood, Margaret, and Jesse drove to the next city together. As they approached the entrance to the backstage they were greeted by a throng of protestors and a few reporters. They looked down and politely made their way through the crowd, being sure not to instigate any trouble. Margaret sniffed at the crowd and howlbarked. Glancing up, Jesse saw an old couple dressed as doves, holding signs that read, "Sharon is not your bitch!" and "Neither is Margaret!" Other signs read, "Free Sharon!," "Free Margaret!," "Driftwood = SHAME!," and the required, "John 3:16."

Jesse said, "If I ever meet Stevie Nicks or Sting it's gonna be awkward."

They did their sound check without issue and returned to the motel, avoiding the protesters by slipping out the main entrance. Later, they walked across the street to a large store to buy snacks, Jack, and 9-volt batteries for the effects pedals. Looking up to the rafters, they counted 12 birds of varying species, over 20 helium-filled balloons and a dangling piñata. Jesse shook his head, "Well I'll be dawg."

TUS DESPRECIOS

Pabst Theater

June 24, 1998

Milwaukee, Wisconsin

The boys and Margaret-the-Basset-Hound arrived a day early to practice the cover songs with the local musicians. The usual chord progressions and the order of solos made for a smooth performance. The annual Polish heritage festival was winding down and they had convinced Daniela, a talented accordion player on the polka circuit, to stick around for the Driftwood gig. She dragged along her husband Stan, and Gabby, a tuba player.

Jesse flipped through the hotel's TV channels and passed The Cosby Show. Margaret relaxed on the bed, gnawing on a femur.

"Dude, put it back on Cosby. This is the episode where they find a joint in Theo's textbook. See, if I had a dad like Cliff Huxtable, I'd be a better man."

Jesse nodded. "We all would! Plus, Lisa Bonet would be your sister. Dayam!"

"Yeah, but I couldn't make out with my sister."

"Nah, man. Lisa Bonet would be an actress on the set playing your sister. That's kinky. But you'd have to change your stage name. Before we started the show they'd be all, 'Put your Milwaukee hands together for…HUXTABLE!!!'"

"Nah, I'd use the KISS intro. 'You wanted the best and you got the best! The hottest band in the world...HUXTABLE!!!'"

Jesse laughed into the bong, splashing filthy water all over the hotel floor. Holding his stomach and coughing toward the ceiling. "The crowd be yelling, "HUX – TA – BLE, HUX – TA – BLE!" He went silent. "Dude, check out the ceiling. It's like popcorn."

"That's why it's called 'Popcorn Ceiling.'"

"Well, what'll they think of next? I got the munchies. Wanna get some lunch?"

***

The little restaurant had a few locals drinking coffee and smoking. A dark bar down the hall had a jukebox with George Jones singing that he stopped loving her today. The loud crack of a cue ball broke open a billiards game. The waitress came over, "Hey guys, I'm Lisa. Can I start you off with something to drink?"

"Jack and Coke, please."

Jesse thought for a moment, "I'll have a pint of Leinenkugel."

Wood handed back the menu, "So, Lisa, what are your two favorite dishes?"

"Right now we have a special on the fettucine alfredo and..."

"No, what are two things that *you* personally like?"

She had never been asked that before. She snapped out of her work trance and smiled. "I like the beer battered trout and the Reuben sandwich."

"I'll have the Reuben. Thanks."

"How about for you?"

Jesse squinted and scratched his head, staring at the menu like a Neanderthal trying to solve a Rubik's Cube.

"I'll come back with your drinks."

"I hate ordering when I'm high. Too many choices."

"You need to try my method. Ask her what her two favorite foods are then pick one. Works every time."

"Why don't you just ask her for one option?"

"Because then she'd only say beer battered trout, which sounds kinda sketchy. If I don't order it, she feels stupid. I try to leave people feeling better than when they met me." He looked out the window at the lake. "It's a gift."

"She could have recommended the steak and lobster, so she gets a bigger tip."

"Nope. They still have to pay for their food. If she could afford that she wouldn't be waiting tables."

Jesse had the dry and uninspired fettucine. "Either I have cotton-mouth, or this was made with sawdust."

Wood basked in the glory of his sensuous, dripping Reuben. "I'm trying to find the adjectives to describe the culinary spectacle that is this sandwich. Want a bite?"

"Don't rub it in." Jesse moved his lumpy pasta around the plate, hoping his fork would imbue it with flavor.

"Not to mention the pickle." Wood held up the wedge to the light, twisting it, inspecting it for clarity like a diamond. "It's flawless. Locally sourced, I'm sure." He shook the pickle in Jesse's face. "Look at it, Jesse! You could've had the Reuben." Wood channeled his gravelly Marsellus Wallace voice and tapped the pickle against his temple, "At the next restaurant you might feel a slight sting. That's pride fuckin' witchoo. Pride only hurts. It never helps."

"Okay, Mr. Pulp Fiction. All you're missing is the band-aid on the back of your neck."

***

As they approached their room, they saw that the door was propped open with a cleaning cart. They heard singing in Spanish, soft and perfectly on key. They stood on either side of the door listening and watching her from behind. Margaret was on the bed sleeping as the lady cleaned around her.

"Si vieras cómo duele perder tu amor
Con tu adiós te llevas mi corazón
No sé si pueda volver a amar
Porque te di todo el amor que pude dar"

She noticed the bong water on the carpet and stopped singing.

"Ay, estos cochinos imbeciles fumando su mota! Que asco! Mugrosos pendejos!" Just then she sensed someone was there and turned around. "Oh! I'm sorry, sir. Five minutes, please. Almost finished."

Feeling like voyeurs who had just been caught, they ran into each other and shuffled down the hall. Wood turned to Jesse, "That's the most beautiful voice I've heard in a long time."

"Voice? That's the most beautiful woman I've ever seen. Perfect skin, and that tight uniform barely holding in that onion booty."

"Onion booty?"

"So fine it brings tears to your eyes."

Wood shook his head. "It never ends with you."

"We should ask her to sing with us, or just have her stand on stage. Then I'll propose to her and move to Milwaukee."

"Jess, she barely speaks any English. How's that gonna work?"

"It's music, we'll make it work. Remember the Roxy Music song, Avalon, with the lady singing at the end?"

"Of course, everyone knows it."

"That singer is Yanik Etienne. She's Haitian and didn't speak a word of

English. When Roxy was recording the album in the Caribbean, they heard her singing in the next studio – just by chance, like today. They asked her to sing on Avalon and now that song is a classic."

Back at the room, Wood tried to convince her that he was famous while Jesse apologized. Pointing to the floor, "Lo siento por el bong water."

Wood pointed at Jesse, "He did it, but lo siento too. You have a very beautiful voice. It's perfect."

She looked confused and uncomfortable. Just then another cleaning lady arrived and said, "Oye, apurete, estamos atrasadas. Listen guys, we got a lot of rooms to clean."

"Sorry. Can you tell her that we're having a big concert tomorrow night and we would love for her to sing with us? We're playing with some other musicians here from a polka band…like German accordion music." Wood and Jesse played imaginary accordions with their hands. "We're practicing tonight at the Pabst Theater, and the concert is there too." Wood handed her the address. "Maybe we can do a song that she likes."

The lady looked at the address and raised her eyebrows. "The Pabst is a big place. I'll explain it and we'll see."

A few hours later they found a Selena CD slid under the door with a post-it note that read, "Tus Desprecios."

***

That night in the freezing hall, the musicians stamped their feet to warm up and discuss the order of solos. Daniela was clearly the leader. The music gods, in their sadistic humor, decreed that Gabby - all 112 pounds of her - would play the tuba while hulking Stan got to beat out life's frustrations using two skinny maple wood sticks. They ran through "87 Southbound" when Marisela walked in with a man. She was wearing jeans, a red sweater and hoop earrings.

"I'm Marisela. He's my husband, Luis." she said, motioning to him. He shook hands with Wood and a dejected Jesse. "Nice to meet you."

"Where are you from?"

"Mexico…Oaxaca."

Turning to the band, Wood said, "Everyone, this is Marisela and her husband, Luis. They're from Wahaka!" She's going to play a song with us. We listened to it back at the hotel and worked out the chords. It's pretty simple." He handed the charts to Daniela, who studied them with Gabby.

"Why didn't you tell us earlier?"

"We didn't know if she'd show up. Anyway, she's incredible. You'll see."

Daniela said, "Yeah, these chords are straightforward. What the hell, let's give it a whirl!"

Wood hit the microphone a few times to make sure it was on and handed it to Marisela, whose eyes darted from person to person, wondering if she was being accepted. Jesse played the chords a few times on keyboard. Wood and Stan came in on guitar and drums, then Daniela added accordion. Gabby picked up her immense tuba and breathed the oom-pahs into the song. Marisela looked around the hall as the song blasted through the sound system, infusing life into the old theater with sonic vibrations.

She sang timidly at first, but when she belted, "Que me estás, clavaaaaaaaando!" the whole band looked at each other smiling and shaking their heads.

As they were packing up their instruments, Marisela asked Wood. "The tickets…how much?"

"Oh yeah! Please, bring your friends!" He grabbed a stack of tickets from his bag and handed them to her.

Jesse said, "It was lovely to see you again, Marisela." Luis stared a hole through him.

***

The next night's gig was positive and raucous, buoyed by the city's festive mood that week. Wood introduced the Polka band, who played the last few Driftwood songs.

"This next song is by Wayne 'The Train' Hancock. It's called '87 Southbound.'"

Jesse quickly pulled lederhosen over his pants and put on a festive, German hat while Wood spoke the song's intro. Pointing at a lady in the crowd:

> "I caught you with him.
> On those damp, slick, sticky satin sheets.
> Then I packed my things and then I hit the streets.
> 87 Southbound…to San Antone!"

The song's Tex-Mex feel lent itself perfectly to the accordion and tuba. The crowd loved it and a variety of Polish and German dance jigs broke out as the band joined in. After a big ending, Wood said. "Thank you. I'd like to invite a special guest onto the stage. She lives here in Milwaukee, but she's come all the way from Wahaka, Mexico. Please welcome…Marisela!"

She walked onto the stage wearing a purple dress covered in sequins. Her long black hair was curled down over her shoulders, easily the most beautiful thing ever associated with a Driftwood gig. A group of family members and workers from the hotel went crazy near the side of the stage. One of them handed her a bouquet of red roses.

She looked to the crowd and said, "Esta canción está dedicada a la memoria de Selena Quintanilla, nuestra diosa, quien nos dejó demasiado temprano. Se llama 'Tus Desprecios.'" She motioned for the band to start the song.

The band was surprised by how many people understood Marisela. Backstage, after a flawless performance, Daniela said, "Marisela, I just have to say, you are so beautiful. I thought ol' Stan was gonna have a heart attack!"

"Oh, thank you!"

"Here's my card. Please call me. I've been wanting to add a few mariachi songs to our setlist. Or just call if you need a friend in Milwaukee."

"Thanks. We call them 'Norteños.' I will call you."

After two years singing for Daniela and Stan on the Polish and German festival circuit, Marisela began singing every weekend for a mariachi and Norteños band, bringing a steady income for her family. She quit cleaning hotel rooms. Noble work, but no longer needed.

GUN STREET GIRL

Louisville, Kentucky

Wood walked into Hempstead Trucking with Margaret, who immediately got along with Misty, the hulking Mastiff who guarded the yard at night.

Rachel smiled, "Hey, Wood! I'm wrapping up some loose ends. Have a seat. I just made some coffee over there if you want some."

Wood sat down and perused the magazine offerings, observing Rachel silently as she answered the phone, filled out invoices, gave orders over the CB, and used every psychological tool at her disposal, which included flirting, playing dumb, and intimidation.

"Now Sleepy, you know I can't marry you, but if you get that load to Fresno by nightfall, I might let you buy me a drink when you get back."

"Bucky, I'm just a little ol' Kentucky gal. I cain't figure out them newfangled refrigeration systems like you cain. You gonna have to figure it out for yo' self!"

"Chiclet, put that bitch of an inventory clerk on. OYE CABRONA, SI NO ACEPTAN NUESTRA CARNE, VOY A PARTIR TU MADRE! ESTAMOS?!" All of this while adjusting the circular fan with her foot. Wood wondered if he she had multiple personalities, like Sybil with a CB radio.

Two truckers walked in, one obese, the other only morbidly so - two sumo wrestlers dressed for a rodeo. Rachel continued to talk on the CB and motioned for their paperwork. She scanned it quickly, signing and stamping each page as she continued her conversation.

"Oh, sorry Sleepy. I thought you were a lady at the warehouse. Got my wires crossed there."

Finding an error on the invoice, she circled it, shook her head "No" and passed it back to one of the truckers, whispering, "That shit ain't gonna fly. Have a seat, honey."

"Quit your sweet talkin'! I'll talk to you soon, Sleepy!"

Rachel put the CB microphone on its cradle and sighed. "This gal's gotta tinkle." She wore a red plaid shirt, tied at the bottom. Her jeans probably fit perfectly at some point in the distant past, but now her ass was desperately trying to liberate itself. Wood observed the two truckers lean over to watch her walk down the hall.

"Goddam, I love coming in here. She's put on weight, but she looks even better."

"I always make a mistake on my paperwork so she has to explain it to me. Where I come from, we call that 'country dumb.'"

"Damn, boy, you ain't as ignorant as you look." He glanced over at Wood, who was reading an article in American Trucker about the importance of yoga and back stretches.

"Hey, man, you turning in your paperwork?"

"No, just waiting to talk to Rachel."

Rachel came out of the bathroom and looked at the biggest trucker, "What are you still doing here? Your paperwork's good to go. Get moving!"

"Oh yeah, I guess I can leave."

She explained the invoice error to country dumb, who said "Uh-huh" over and over as he checked her out.

"I can't keep explaining this to you. You show up at a highway weigh station with this Mickey Mouse paperwork and they're gonna detain your ass. Got it?"

"Yes, ma'am. I'll figure it out eventually." He winked at Wood and walked out, holding the door open for an older gentleman.

***

"Oh, hey daddy."

Rachel's father looked Wood up and down. "I guess you're the rock star."

Standing to shake his hand, "Nice to meet you, sir. Why didn't you think I was a trucker?"

"Because you're skinny. Jesus, boy, you look like you could use a home-cooked meal."

"Yes, sir. I would appreciate that very much."

"I didn't mean *our* home. Can't you get one of your groupies to cook something? One of them is bound to know her way around the kitchen."

"Thank you for the advice, sir."

Rachel looked embarrassed, like a boy was picking her up for the prom. "Daddy, you're being a pain!"

Beneath Wood's wrinkled clothes and groggy demeanor, Rachel's father sensed good manners and a certain nobility. Calling him "Sir" didn't hurt his chances. Rachel's father threw out a small olive branch. "It was nice to finally meet you, Wood. Rachel enjoys keeping her connection to the music industry and the extra money sure helps. We appreciate that."

"Thank you, sir. I'd like to take Rachel out for a bite to eat- if that's okay with you."

Rachel was mortified. "I'm 30 years old! I'll just head on back to Walton's Mountain while you two decide my fate!"

"Sweet Pea, he's just trying to be a gentleman. Your mama was never this moody. Anyway, you kids do what you want."

"Don't wait up, daddy!"

Wood went back to the hotel, showered, shaved, and ironed a white shirt. He put on dark trousers, Chukka boots and a navy-blue sport coat with a white pocket square. Not a bad look, given the choices at hand.

***

When he came back to pick up Rachel, she was embarrassed. "I didn't know you were going to get all gussied up in your Sunday best. Now I feel underdressed."

"You look beautiful. Do you think Margaret will be okay with Misty?"

"Oh yeah, those girls will be fine. If someone tries to rob the place they'll lick 'em to death."

When Wood opened the car door for her she remarked, "Aren't you old fashioned."

"It's just a habit. My Mom was big on etiquette."

Rachel asked, "Where do you want to go?"

"I asked around and found a place I'd like to try. You probably know it. It's called Jockey Silks Bourbon Bar in the Galt House Hotel. Sounds cool."

Rachel had been there before on a date she preferred to forget. She was relieved that Wood didn't trigger her date night pet peeve of a man who didn't make plans, assuming that it was gentlemanly to let her decide everything. She worked hard all week managing a trucking company and caring for her father. Did she have to plan the date, too? Of course, this wasn't a date. She and Wood were business partners, but it seemed to hover in the grey area all night.

Jockey Silks had just enough lighting to highlight the displays that boasted what Kentuckians held dear, horseracing and bourbon. With deep mahogany wood and dark leather seats, it invited people to drink, smoke cigars, and talk over appetizers. It was the kind of bar where business deals got done.

The server came over, "Can I get something started for you?"

"Jack and Coke, please." Wood immediately sensed his signature drink was sacrilege in the land of bourbon. He corrected himself. "What are your two favorite bourbons?"

"Personally, I like Elijah Craig and Pappy Van Winkle, but, of course, nobody can get Pappy's."

"Then I'll have the Elijah Craig. Neat, please."

Rachel added, "I'll have a Blanton's. We'll start with some truffle fries and fried green tomatoes."

The waiter brought their drinks and they toasted to continued success. The bourbon went down smooth, maybe too smooth for a business meeting. They ordered another, just to be sure.

Wood smiled and said, "I loved watching you do your thing today. You have an entire army of truckers all over the country wrapped around your finger. I learned all your little tricks today. Playing the dumb brunette, flirting, logic, threats. I was impressed."

"Oh, there are more tricks where that came from! Most of these guys are lonely. They want to do a good job. They just need some help."

"Remember that guy who couldn't figure out his paperwork?"

"I call him Jethro. Dumb as a sack of rocks."

"Well, he's 'country dumb.' I learned that expression today. He's got a crush on you so he messes up his paperwork so you have to explain it to him each time.

"That *is* country dumb. That sneaky bastard."

"Shit, they *all* have a crush on you with your sultry DJ voice. I don't even want to guess how many of them are thinking of you at some desolate truck stop at 3:00 a.m."

"Gross! I think I've counted nine times that I've been proposed to – only once face-to-face though."

"The CB proposal. Nice!"

"I guess we both have jobs where we're adored from time to time."

"Maybe you're right."

"Can I ask you a serious question?"

"Sure."

"What do you want?" Rachel observed Wood's reaction. His eyes met hers then quickly looked down at his bourbon, which he lifted to his lips, took a healthy drink, and motioned to the waiter for another.

"I'm not sure I follow you. What do I want from life?"

"Maybe we can start with your career since I'm your manager. The reason I ask is because sometimes I propose ideas to push you into the spotlight, to sell more records, play at bigger venues, and you shy away from that. I'm not mad. Really, I'm not, but if I knew what you really wanted from your career I think we'd both be happier."

This abrupt shift to serious questions about his career startled him, but it was a fair question. Wood thought for a moment, knowing that his answer would influence both of their lives.

"Here's the deal. I want to be big enough to keep writing music that is taken seriously, sell enough CDs to renew my contract with the label, and play enough gigs so that I never have to do anything else. Can you imagine me trying to sell insurance or wait tables to pay the bills? Music is all I know - and I don't mean that romantically. It's the only trade I can do. I feel lucky. It's brought me money and some notoriety. On the other hand, I like being able to walk through a mall and not be recognized. Now and then someone does and that's fine, but I never want to be mobbed by people because they think they know me."

Rachel nodded. A lot of his decisions made more sense now.

Wood continued. "I knew this French guy who had a little restaurant in Indy, a bistro. It was incredible and it got great reviews, a line out the door, the whole thing. So naturally, everyone pressured him to expand. They'd say, 'If this restaurant is so great, why isn't there a whole chain?' That's a very American attitude. But all he wanted was his little restaurant. He made plenty of money and had a good life. Get this - he closed at 7:00 p.m. every Saturday night. Can you imagine a restaurant that's closed on a Saturday evening? One time I asked him why. You know what he said?"

"What?"

"I like to watch TV with my wife."

Rachel laughed. "What a cute couple."

"Right? Eventually, he just closed the restaurant and they moved back to France. He made his mark, made his money. That's a good life."

"That's what you want to do?"

"Not exactly. That was his life, but I have a lot of respect for a man who lives on his own terms. If I end up playing Wembley someday, that's great, but I'm happy with what we've been able to accomplish so far. You've been amazing."

"Thank you. What about your shows? Do you want to keep doing them the same way? You play similar sets of songs, but nobody knows how the show is going to end."

"True, but they're also expecting that kind of gig from us. Even a band like the Grateful Dead is predictable. Their fans know what to expect, even if every show is different. If the Dead played disco for three hours people would freak out."

"Are you sure? I would pay to see the Dead play disco for three hours."

Wood reluctantly agreed. "Actually, that would be badass. Okay, it's your turn to bare your soul."

"What do you mean? What do I want out of my career?"

"Sure, or out of life. The first time we met, you were a college DJ. Did you go to college to find yourself?"

"Yeah, but in the end I just found myself back at the Bursar's Office paying for more classes that didn't relate to my life. Once daddy got sick my heart wasn't in it so I dropped out. It's funny how life derails you, then the bent train tracks become your new path. If it goes on too long you can't even remember what your original dreams were." Rachel paused and looked across at Wood, who sat listening intently. "I'm sorry. I didn't mean to lay all that on you."

"Don't apologize."

Wood paid the tab and they left to walk along the Ohio, looking across the river into Indiana. A long barge passed slowly in the night, heading to its rendezvous with the Mississippi.

Wood noticed that Rachel was shivering. He took off his sport coat and put it around her shoulders. She turned around to face him. Even with a healthy buzz she knew it would be a bad idea to kiss her client. Wood looked into her eyes, turned, and walked with his hands in his pockets, trying to conserve his heat. Rachel latched her arm under his.

"Wood, I still don't know very much about you. Were you born in Indianapolis?"

"I was actually born in Bloomington. That's where the university is."

CHARLOTTE UNDERWOOD

1963

Bloomington, Indiana

Charlotte Underwood chased her dreams in the renowned Indiana University School of Music, reaching for a lofty degree held high like a delicate glass object that would be dropped, shattering at her feet as she was beginning to grasp it.

It was 1963, her senior year as a classical Piano Performance major, and she was preparing for the final exam that would determine if she possessed the skills to confer a degree upon her. In a moment of impetuous inspiration, she chose Rachmaninoff's Piano Concerto No. 3 in D minor, convincing herself that having the gumption to choose the complex piece would impress the three professors who were to judge her performance. She soon came to regret her decision.

As she struggled to learn the piece, an enigmatic young piano teacher, Dr. Menders, offered to help. They agreed to meet in one of the practice rooms. By this time, she could play the piece, albeit deliberately, it was the feel and the difficult finale where she struggled. He asked her to play it like Debussy.

"You want me to play Debussy?"

"No, Charlotte. Play the Rachmaninoff as Debussy would have played it. You won't pass if you just press the correct keys in the correct time. You need to perform it with the intended feeling of Rachmaninoff, so we'll practice it with the feel of other composers then come back to him."

She closed her eyes and attempted to channel the French composer as she played.

"Better. How would Beethoven have played it?" With each composer he listed she continued playing the Rachmaninoff in their style. He shouted over the grand piano, "Now Vivaldi! Now Brahms! That's too slow! Faster! Now Satie! I said Satie, not Debussy again!" When she got to J.S. Bach she was overwhelmed and stopped playing. She slumped her shoulders, staring at the keys as her eyes filled with tears. Charlotte saw the keys and sheet music blending together into strange geometric shapes.

"I know it's frustrating," Dr. Menders sighed. "Let me show you." He removed his coat and sat on the bench beside her. "Did you know Bach fathered twenty children? *Twenty!* Can you imagine him playing with all those kids running around? 'Honey, come get these brats!'" She giggled through her tears, listening to Dr. Menders play faster and faster, pounding on the keys like a cranky German with twenty children. She put her right hand on the keyboard and began playing along with him. When their hands touched, they stopped playing, gazing down at their interlaced fingers on the keyboard. The vibrations of the final notes settled into the walls, fading into a profound silence. As they ripped each other's clothes off, Charlotte wondered how many other musicians had made love in that room, designed to be soundproof with a locked door and no windows.

The next two months were a whirlwind of secret encounters, flirtatious phone calls that went into the night as they discovered each other. They hid anonymous love poems around campus for the other to retrieve.

He called, "Go to the phone booth in the lobby of Ballantine Hall and turn to page 242 of the yellow pages" then hung up. Charlotte rushed there, thumbed through the pages, and found a sonnet in his handwriting. At the bottom of the sonnet he had written, "Don't forget your change." She was confused for a moment then pushed her finger into the little door of the payphone's change holder. She pulled out a delicate gold necklace with a treble clef pendant. She clasped it around her neck and moved to catch the reflection in the chrome pieces of the phone. She rifled through her purse to find a dime, turning the rotary numbers clockwise in a frenzy and giggling as they glacially returned to their positions.

Her classmates noticed that something was amiss and remarked that a less attractive student might not receive as much personal guidance from a professor. One night, drunk at Nick's English Hut with her friends, she reached for his arm as he passed. He turned, startled, and she ran her fingers through his wavy hair. He meandered through the crowd to a booth with two older professors, who looked at him, then across the room at her. One of her friends yelled above the din, "Are you crazy? We'd all like to sleep with him, but he's our professor!"

His life came crashing down. The department chair shouted accusations, provoking a full and unexpected confession. Being a relatively new professor with neither tenure nor allies, his firing came as a shock to no one, and the department resumed its daily activities. Graduate assistants and other professors flowed seamlessly in to teach his classes, telling confused students that he was ill.

After Dr. Menders dusted himself off, his applications for teaching jobs elsewhere were ignored. Phone calls to music schools were rushed to a close. He quickly grasped that the rumors, now exaggerated, were already following him. He hired a lawyer who specialized in wrongful terminations and informed the university of his intention to sue.

The university, with its existing legal team and financial war chest brought to bear, would have certainly won the case, but at a high cost to its reputation. In their destruction of the professor, the pyrrhic victory would have revealed that protocols were not followed and that a series of lines had been crossed by more than Dr. Menders and Ms. Underwood. It would have revealed that the department chair, unduly influenced by a similar scandal in another college, fired him without speaking to anyone or documenting the conversation accurately. There were no witnesses to the professor's confession, which he now denied. There was a chance that the prominent Underwood family would be dragged into the scandal, with its own legal team revealing disconcerting truths in an effort to restore its reputation.

The settlement Menders received from the school was generous and he moved back to Chicago without telling Charlotte goodbye. Without wondering how all of this might affect her. She received no support; financial, moral, or otherwise. As she began to show, she was discouraged from attending classes. Pregnant students didn't exist in 1963. They went away. Classmates whom she had considered to be friends spoke with her begrudgingly, avoiding eye contact, as if their fate would be engulfed by hers. Unable to practice due to morning sickness, she informed the department that she was canceling the Rachmaninoff concert.

The semester ended and students abandoned Bloomington for the Christmas break. After years of arduous study, Charlotte Underwood's academic status culminated in a simple "I" on her transcript:

"Incomplete"

Thurston Frederick Underwood was born on November 21st, 1963, the last day of modern American innocence. The following day, the maternity ward, generally an upbeat place with the hope that new life brings, was dark, depressing, and frantic. Doctors and nurses crowded around a small TV, crying as the news of the Kennedy assassination came in.

Left alone in the room, feeling Thurston's soft breath on her chest, Charlotte whispered, "Someday you will receive everything that was stolen from me."

LOUISIANA

July 1998

Wood and his sidekick, Jesse, drove to Louisiana with Margaret-the-Basset-Hound. Jesse hadn't seen his family in months and told them in advance that they had an upcoming gig in New Orleans. The Hayes family home was old, but large enough to fit their five children, with a spacious backyard. It took 10 minutes to meet everyone and it wasn't long before Wood was confused about who was connected to whom, all he knew was that everyone was loud, happy, and that he was the only white person there.

Two of Jesse's aunts approached him. "Wood, can you settle an argument for us? We both brought potato salad and we need you to tell us which one tastes better. Whatever I bring, my sister says she got confused and brings the same thing, just to show me up. Go ahead, tell us which one is the best."

This was a social nightmare. Wood reluctantly accepted the fork from her outstretched hand and tasted both intently, closing his eyes for effect. "Well, they're both better than any potato salad I've had in my life…so I think you're both winners."

"Nice try. They're quite distinct from each other – one of them has to be better."

"Okay, well, again…they're both perfect, but I think the extra paprika in this one kicks it up to another level."

As one aunt proclaimed, "Wood, you're gonna fit in just fine around here!" the other was walking away shaking her head.

Jesse's uncle leaned in and whispered, "That's been goin' on for ages. I learned to keep my mouth shut years ago."

There were too many people to fit inside the house, so they set the food on long tables in the back yard. Walking down the steps, Jesse's grandmother held onto Wood's arm and whispered, "Would you like to say grace?"

"Oh…I'm very honored, but I'd rather not, if that's okay with you."

"I understand, sweetie. I just wanted to offer."

They all stood in a circle on the grass and joined hands in silence as parents shooshed the little ones. Jesse's father spoke in a booming, deep voice. "Lord, we thank you for bringing us together on this beautiful day. We are so grateful for bringing Jesse back to us safely and to meet his friend, Wood. We ask that you follow them along their journey and keep them free from sin and all anxieties. Please, Lord, bless this food that we are about to receive, that it may nourish us and help us to be humble as we enjoy your bounty. We thank you for your many blessings. Amen."

"Amen."

They sat down and started passing gumbo, crawfish, both potato salads, short ribs, rolls, cornbread, candied yams, string beans, and corn on the cob. Wood hadn't eaten that much in years. When there was a lull in the conversation, Jesse's older sister Shauna spoke up.

"Our entertainment at the prison fell through so I was hoping you could come play for the ladies on your way back up north. It's in St. Gabriel, only about 45 minutes away. You probably passed it on your way here. These ladies just sit in their cells all day. After a while they start to go stir crazy. You'd be helping us out. You cool with that?"

Wood picked at his food. Despite the perceived highwire act of a Driftwood show, they were well planned, rehearsed, and somewhat predictable, at least to him. He didn't like curveballs, but sitting at the table with the whole family waiting to hear his response, he replied, "We would be honored, right Jesse?"

"Yeah, we'll make it work, sis. Thanks for inviting us."

Shauna beamed. "Thank you! Okay, you're gonna go through security. It ain't gonna be like some stadium security where they think it's cute when they find your coke."

Jesse said, "Now hold up...I ain't takin' no rubber glove up my booty."

Jesse's grandmother interjected, "Please, not all of this filthy talk at the table!"

Shauna lowered her voice and leaned toward Jesse. "They'll be cool because you're with me, but if they so much as find a little roach of your Mexican dirt weed, I will hogtie your black ass myself."

"Choctaw."

"There you go with your heritage noise again! Don't get cute cuz I ain't playin.' You make me look bad and I'll tell Mr. Capois."

The table fell silent. All life vanished from Jesse's face as he heard the name.

Wood said, "Mr. Capois, the band teacher, right? I called him the other day. We're gonna jam with Jesse's old marching band at our gig."

Jesse's brain was exploding, "Are you kidding me? Why would you call Mr. Capois?"

Wood was surprised by Jesse's reaction. "I thought you'd be happy. At first, Mr. Capois didn't make the connection but he remembered who you were. He said it would be a nice reward for the seniors to play on stage, so it won't be the whole band. He was a cool old man."

After dinner they cleared the table and brought out desserts. The two biggest men at the party, either of whom could have been linemen for the Saints, walked up, each holding a pecan pie. "Wood, could you taste these and settle an argument for us?" Wood closed his eyes. There was silence, then twenty hands pointed at him and fell over laughing. "Did you see his face?! That is NOT cool! Aww...poor Wood! He's never coming back here again!"

Wood fell asleep on a lawn chair. Margaret had eaten all of the same dishes and slept at his feet. He woke to hear Jesse's father managing a dispute between two of the male cousins. Putting his hands on their shoulders, "You young men need to work this out. You borrowed his boombox and someone stole it. Now you need to pay him for its value."

"But it's not my fault someone stole it!"

"Well, you shouldn't have left it in plain sight on the damn porch!"

"I'm not paying him."

Jesse's father persisted, "What would a real man do - make excuses or take responsibility?"

Stammering for a moment, he whispered, "Take responsibility."

"You're going to pay him and that's that. Understood?"

"Yes, sir."

Wood walked over to Jesse. "I like your dad. He holds everything together. I wish I had a father like him."

"Yeah, here and at the church. It wasn't always easy to live under his roof, but I appreciate him when I come to visit."

"I'm heading to the hotel. You coming?"

"No thanks, man. I'm staying here with family. I'll get a ride there tomorrow."

After saying their goodbyes for a half hour, Wood and Margaret drove down the road and pulled behind the drooping branches of a weeping willow tree to sleep off their food coma.

"Be careful around here, Margaret. This is the bayou - we're part of the food chain."

VOODOO CHILE

Wood checked in at the St. Louis Hotel in the French Quarter and took Margaret out to have a look around. It had been a few years since he'd been in New Orleans but not much had changed. The same college jocks were vomiting into a bush while their girlfriends screamed at them. He walked down the street with a plastic cup of Jack and Coke, nodding to revelers as they strolled, looking up at the architecture.

"Driftwood!" A drunken scream rang out as he cringed to hear his stage name. "It's heeum!" Two college-aged girls with heavy southern accents ran up and began peppering him with questions. "When are you putting out another ayelbum? Is Jesse with you?" One of the girls knelt and fed snacks to Margaret, who gobbled up her offerings. "We came to town to go to your show, but it's sold out!"

"Yeah, sorry about that. I mean, I guess it's a good thing."

"We drove all the way from Oxford. We go to Ole Meeuss."

Wood reached in his bag, "Here are some tickets, and a few extras for your friends."

"Oh my god! Thank you! Would you take a photo of us?" The girls followed the rules of Driftwood fandom, where it was frowned upon to try to take a photo *with* Wood. The correct protocol was to have him take a photo *of* you, with his smashed thumb in the bottom left corner of the frame, revealing that it could only have been taken by Driftwood. He handed their little Nikon back to them and gave them each a hug.

As Wood and Margaret distanced themselves, he looked back to see the girls pointing at them to a group of college kids, who began walking their way. "Come on, Margaret!" he yelled. They turned down an alleyway, hung a left then a quick right, and ducked into a small shop behind a moving truck.

The darkness of the shop was in stark contrast to the light of the late afternoon, and it took a moment for their eyes to adjust. They took in a bizarre scene of curio shop detritus: burning incense, old postcards, dozens of candles, chicken feet, skulls, sage, framed images and statues of Catholic saints, masks, skeletons, bottles of rum, and long peacock feathers. A boy came from behind the counter, bent down to pet Margaret, then rising, took Wood's hand and led them through a curtain of beads to an even darker back room, where an old woman sat, as if she had been waiting a lifetime for a gangly man and his confused hound to enter her voodoo shop.

"Please sit," she said, motioning to a cushion on the cement ground across from her.

Still dazed to find himself there, but obliging, Wood sat down. The boy placed a white handkerchief on Wood's head, tying it from behind. He put another cloth on Margaret's head, tying it below her jaw so she resembled a housewife, glancing up at Wood as if to ask, "What the hell kind of mess have you gotten us into now?" The boy scratched behind Margaret's ears then gave her long strokes down her back.

"How does this work?" Wood asked. "Are you going to read tarot cards or something?"

"You think too much. It's not good for you. I can assure you that none of this will *work*, as you say, if you don't at least try to believe. Are you a believer?"

As a boy, young Thurston had watched "In Search Of" with Leonard Nimoy religiously and counted himself a believer in numerous things that could neither be explained nor understood. He believed that there was, in fact, "something" out there. Many things. As a boy, he looked out his bedroom window in utter fear, waiting for the immense silhouette that could only be Sasquatch, who had left the Sierra Nevada mountains, traversed the US (undetected), found his way through the streets of Indianapolis (undetected), only to arrive at young Thurston's bedroom window. What would happen next was anyone's guess. He had always feared that Bigfoot was not the benevolent, misunderstood creature that Nimoy had portrayed, but was there to tear him limb from limb. Why would Bigfoot choose little Thurston? Did it matter now that his bedroom was drenched in blood?

Bigfoot played a recurring role in Wood's list of childhood fears, fed by a steady diet of TV shows and disaster movies. These included aliens, Brazilian killer bees, tidal waves, earthquakes that cracked open the earth to reveal its molten core, the occult, myths and monsters, snipers in football stadiums, not to mention the undisputed threats like Soviet nuclear missiles, teachers, girls, and whatever was in that Scottish lake. As for voodoo, Live and Let Die was his favorite Bond movie. It had everything; blaxploitation, Jane Seymour, and villain Baron Samedi in his top hat, laughing maniacally into the camera as the credits rolled.

Was Wood a believer? Shit yeah, he was.

She sat on a cushion opposite Wood. "I will summon a Lwa, one of the voodoo spirits, to possess my body and reveal your truths. First, this will require a sacrifice."

Wood grabbed Margaret. "Please, not the dog."

She smiled and whispered. "Money works just fine."

"Oh. I don't carry much cash," as he emptied his pockets. He handed her a twenty, a one, some change, and a guitar pic.

She placed the twenty in her bra, threw the coins and the pic on the floor, and held the dollar bill over a candle until it burned. Taking sand from a jar, she made a fist and began sifting it down onto the floor, forming geometric shapes that connected to each other. It began to take the shape of an alien formation that can only be seen from high above the earth. Reaching for a bottle of rum, she took a long swig and swallowed it, groaning. She took a second drink, held her forearm under her chin and spat rum on the sandy configuration. She poured some rum on the cement and lit it with a wooden match then passed the bottle to Wood, motioning for him to drink. He took a long swig and stared into the flame. The boy handed her a machete and she began hitting the flame with the steel blade, rhythmically, as she chanted loudly in sounds Wood could not comprehend.

The boy handed a small drum to Wood and began hitting a tambourine, matching the machete beat of his grandmother. Wood joined in with the drum as he continued to stare into the flame and her chanting became louder and coupled with sporadic, convulsive shakes. This went on for a time until they entered a trance. She stopped singing and shook violently for a moment, slowed and whispered in a low tone, "You will be at death's door. Death comes from the right." She repeated this over and over, then began shaking less and hitting the machete softer and slower. The boy, knowing that the spirit was leaving her body, stopped playing. Wood followed suit. There was silence before she opened her eyes, gazed into the last flicker of the fire, then up at Wood with a sense of confusion, as if she had just walked into the room.

Looking into her eyes, Wood whispered, "What did all of that mean?"

"I don't know. I wasn't here. That was the Lwa speaking through me."

The boy revealed one of the reasons he was present. "Nana, the Lwa said this man will be at death's door…and that death would come from the right."

"Is there anything you can do to prevent it?" asked Wood.

"I'm sorry, but I cannot. It is part of your path between this world and the next. It needs to happen for you to grow."

"Dying is going to help me grow?"

"If that is your fate, there is nothing any of us can do, but we can try to cleanse you, if you will allow me."

"Um…yes, please do."

"We will perform a Lave Tet and a Garde. These are not to be done on the same day, but I sense you are passing through town. We shall do what we can and hope the Lwa are in a forgiving mood."

The boy helped Wood to lie down. Margaret snuggled against him. He covered them both with a white sheet up to their necks. Margaret poked her snout out and yawned, as if a voodoo ritual was part of her daily beauty regimen. The woman poured water over their heads as the boy rubbed herbs into Wood's hair, then smiled as he rubbed more herbs into his new friend's fur. Next, the woman took a knife and cut light slashes into Wood's forearms, rubbing herbs into the bleeding wounds, humming softly with her eyes closed. She placed a hand on each of their heads, gripping tightly, shaking Wood and Margaret.

"Now rest."

When they awoke, the woman was gone. The boy escorted them out to the street, now dark. He kneeled to hug Margaret, who licked him about his face. Wood handed the rest of his concert tickets to the child.

"Thank you, my friend. You can scalp these on Bourbon Street."

TUSK

Civic Theatre

July 10, 1998

New Orleans, Louisiana

On the way to the hall the next afternoon, Wood started to light up.

"Put that shit out!" screamed Jesse. He snatched the joint out of Wood's mouth and threw it out the window, something he had never done in his life.

"Dude, what the hell is wrong with you? You are not yourself."

"Nah, man. You're not gonna be yourself once you come into the presence of Mr. Capois. I can't believe you called him."

"I thought you'd want to see your old band teacher. He seemed cool on the phone. A little stern but, what do you want, he's a band teacher. Come on, relax! It's a nice reward for their seniors after being in the band all four years."

Mr. Capois was a direct descendent of Francois Capois, famed Haitian military commander who helped the slave population to rise and take control of the island, defeating French military commanders and beheading wealthy aristocrats along the way. Haiti was the only Caribbean nation to be forged by former slaves and it was Mr. Capois' intention to continue the family code of discipline and honor, in the form of a high school marching band.

Jesse spoke in a rapid-fire description, "He's been the band teacher since, like, the 1800's. We endured screaming and marching in humidity, torrential rain, blazing sun. One time we practiced during Hurricane Bonnie because it was only a Category 1. We called him "Mr. Bonnie" behind his back for a while, then he found out and made us practice in the heat with no water. Brothas and sistas were passin' out left and right!"

Wood laughed. "I thought dealing with Tommy from the Featherdusters was bad. This dude is way more hardcore."

"Oh yeah. We had cats join the Marines, come back telling us it was easier than being in Mr. Capois' band because there was less marching, and the drill instructors didn't yell as much. Armed forces recruiters were hanging around like groupies because we already had the skills they wanted; Marching, carrying heavy objects, crying silently, triage."

"Yeah, but you never got shot at."

"This is New Orleans! Of course we got shot at."

"Wow. The Marines also lasts four years. At least you would have been paid and got free meals."

Jesse shook his head, "Why did you have to say that?" Looking out the window, "Shit, man. I just realized I was a Marine…for free."

"Well, I'd like to talk to him."

"You don't talk to him, you listen. He's a poet warrior in the classic sense. I could tell you that he said he was gonna kill me."

"Why did he say he was gonna kill you?"

"Because I took his picture. He said, 'If you take my picture again, I'll kill you'…and he MEANT IT!" Jesse held his hands around his head to convey a profound level of consciousness.

Glancing over, Wood asked, "Have you seen Apocalypse Now?"

"No. Why?"

***

When Wood and Jesse got to the Civic Theater, the marching band was already inside and warmed up.

"It's good to see you again, Mr. Capois."

"You're late. This must be Mr. Underwood. You're the one babysitting our lost sheep, Jesse."

Wood attempted to sing Jesse's praises. "I don't know what I would do without him. He plays everything from drums to keys, guitar, even the bone sometimes. Plus, he writes all the charts for other musicians who jam with us. You taught him well, sir."

"Well, well. Sounds like my wise tutelage made a difference. My joy is only surpassed by my shock."

Jesse told the kids to huddle up, "Now listen, we're gonna play a song called 'Tusk' by Fleetwood Mac. They recorded the song with the USC Trojans marching band. The drums go crazy in the middle, but we're gonna have all instruments playing whatever the hell you want to play, not just the drums."

This was anathema to everything Mr. Capois stood for. "Excuse me? I don't think some cacophonous headbanging is going to please anyone. This band prides itself on discipline and we're going to keep it that way!"

Jesse strained to reason with an unreasonable man, "Sir, you said yourself it would be a fun reward for these seniors. Lord knows they've paid their dues." The band had never seen anyone argue with Mr. Capois. They shifted their feet, wiped their foreheads, and stared down at their instruments.

"And playing with a unified sound is how we're going to keep it."

Wood interjected, "Mr. Capois, do you mind if I ask you a technical question about a song we've been working on?" They walked over to look at some charts and lyrics. Wood stroked his ego, pretending he couldn't understand the changes in time signatures.

With their band leader distracted, Jesse lowered his voice and gave the musicians a pep talk. "I don't care what Mr. Capois says. In the middle of the song I want you to take out all your frustrations on your instrument. Divorced parents, your dad in jail, school bullies, homework, Mr. Capois. Let it all out, ok? I'll signal for you to stop, then we'll all come back together and finish the song. I'll point at each of you for your solo. Be ready! Once Mr. Capois sees it go down he'll be cool with it. You're about to graduate so just have fun!" The kids nodded and smiled.

***

The gig went well. As Wood looked out across the audience he saw the boy from the voodoo shop atop a man's shoulders, which he assumed was the boy's father. He pointed at him, "Hey, little man! I see you!" After they finished "Take Me to the Trains," Wood and Jesse donned their honorary Chalmette High School marching band caps, "We're gonna finish up with a little surprise. This song is called 'Tusk' by Fleetwood Mac."

Wood hammered out the first two measures in a looped recording by strumming his acoustic and muting the strings. This created a recurring rhythm over the sound system and he began playing chords over the top as he and Jesse harmonized,

> Why don't you ask him
> If he's gonna stay?
> Why don't you ask him
> If he's going away?

As Jesse came in with the iconic bassline, the marching band started playing from the lobby of the hall, then marched through the middle of the shocked crowd, which parted to let them pass. The majorettes twirled batons, screaming "Tusk!" along with Wood and Jesse. The band high stepped their way up a makeshift staircase and onto the stage. Drum Major Dominique Haskins performed a back bend, nearly touching the ground with her cap, then rose and flipped her mace high above the stage, catching it to cheers from the crowd. Owl mascot Minh Nguyen did a backflip off a Marshall amp and continued doing cartwheels across the floor as the majorettes, led by Julia Boudreaux, launched flags to each other high across the stage as the drums and horns added power to the song.

Mr. Capois, proud son of New Orleans, a guiding hand to countless students, died on August 20, 2005, just days before Hurricane Katrina struck. His death was a blessing, as he could not have tolerated seeing his beloved St. Bernard Parish destroyed when the levees broke.

TILL YOUR WELL RUNS DRY

Louisiana Correctional Institute for Women

July 12, 1998

St. Gabriel, Louisiana

The next morning they drove to the prison. Jesse looked over at Wood.

"Why are you so quiet? Hung over?"

"Nah, it's just…I had an experience the night before the gig, when you were at your parents' house."

"What kind of experience?"

"Margaret and I were running through the French Quarter to escape some fans and we went into some lady's voodoo shop, just by chance. It could have been a door into anything, a café, a travel agency, a souvenir store, but it was a voodoo shop. And this trippy old lady and her grandson did a ritual on us. We even slept there."

Jesse paused, then could no longer contain himself. "Bwaaaaaaaaaahahahaha. Dude, those people are everywhere in the French Quarter, telling drunk tourists what they wanna hear. Let me guess, she said you were on some long journey, right?"

"Something like that."

"And you believed that shit because it was all about you. See, if they feed our ego we'll fall for it every time. That's why we only read our own horoscope, not anyone else's. 'Yo, read Sagittarius!'"

"I used to read my girlfriend's horoscope."

'But that's only because you were curious how *her* horoscope might affect *your* life. Did you read hers after she dumped you?"

"No, but this was different, man. This voodoo lady wasn't trying to be dramatic. She didn't want a lot of money, just something for a sacrifice. She didn't care what I thought and didn't make any promises or say she was going to save me. She told me I would be at death's door."

"Yeah, that's because someday you *will* be at death's door! We all will. The minute before you die you'll whisper, 'She was riiiiiiiiiight.'" Jesse slapped his knee. "Wood, you are too much!"

"Dude, you can laugh all you want, but this was different. You weren't there."

"You and your mysteries, Wood. Did the killer bees ever arrive from Brazil? Did Sasquatch show up at your bedroom window?"

"I'm not gonna tell you my secrets anymore if you're going to ridicule me. Anyway, she said my death would come from the right."

Jesse paused, "Well, that's specific. Did she say what it meant?"

"She couldn't because she was no longer in the room. She was being possessed by a...a Lwa. A voodoo spirit."

Jesse's entire demeanor changed. "A Lwa possession? Okay, I don't mess with that shit. Do *not* mention that to my sister when we get to the prison. Shauna hears that and she won't let us in."

"Look at you, so desperate to get into a prison when so many are trying to escape. Speaking of these lady prisoners, your sister said we're gonna meet some of them, like Johnny Cash at Folsom Prison."

"Yep. It'll be cool to hear their stories. I'm sure there are some cuties - and they haven't had sex in forever. Even you could get laid in there."

"I do just fine. Should we be worried? I don't want to get shanked with some ice pick made from a license plate."

"Nah, man. We're only meeting with the women who haven't gotten into trouble. No fights, no contraband in their cell. Most of them shouldn't even be in there."

"What do you mean they shouldn't be in there?" asked Wood.

"They get into drugs and all the crimes that go along with it - dealing, robbery, prostitution. About 80% got mixed up with a bad dude they felt sorry for. 'Nobody understands him! I can fix him! He just needs a loving woman!' Next thing you know she's committing the crimes that he would be committing if she wasn't there."

Jesse's clemency speech struck a nerve in Wood. "How can you say it's not their fault? It all comes down to their choices. Nobody else robbed that liquor store, she did! It's her face on the security video, she got caught and goes to jail. End of story."

"That may be the end of the story for this fictional woman you just made up, but it ain't the beginning of the story."

"I'm saying nobody forced her to commit these crimes."

"How can you be so sure? This is my point! People get coerced into all kinds of shit when they grow up in poverty."

"So, you think she's not guilty if she can blame it on some thug, a dude she *chose* to hook up with? Nice, Jesse! You don't actually believe that."

"Wood, you are from a diff-er-ent world. You haven't spent one day in a public school, have you? You've had opportunities those women will never have. Look the fuck around you, man!" Like a deranged tour guide, Jesse pointed out Louisiana's poverty as they drove down the road. "Shacks, liquor stores covered in graffiti, cars on blocks! Check this out, an engine hanging from a tree! A playground basketball court with no rims! Wood, if you can't even see what is right in front of your face then I can't help you, brother. I really can't. Maybe that's what that lady meant by death coming from the right…from your right-wing bullshit!" Jesse shook his head and looked out the window.

They drove in silence until they arrived at the prison.

***

Shauna met them in the parking lot and made sure they passed the most critical portion of the security check – Shauna. She was impressed that they had cleaned up a little.

"Someone got his ears lowered."

"Just a little trim," said Wood.

Margaret yawned and gave a protest bark as a prison guard waved the wand around her long, Basset Hound physique.

"Archie's gonna go crazy when he realizes he's got a lady visitor. Maybe we should put them in the conjugal visit trailer. That old Bloodhound is gonna keel over!"

Wood massaged Margaret's long ears, "Please don't. She's still recovering from a voodoo cleansing."

Margaret and Archie ran around barking at each other as if they'd grown up together, carrying out their hound ritual of sniffing, howling, and licking. Archie, named after the loyal Saints quarterback, Archie Manning, was a Blood Hound with the Saints' fleur-de-lis on his collar.

Shauna said, "The inmates love ol' Archie, that is until he finds contraband in their cell. Then they say their loser boyfriend is gonna bring a pit bull to get revenge. You'd think he'd be a little more energetic after sniffing all that coke. His nose doesn't work like it used to but he improves morale. I've arranged for you to meet with some of the ladies in the cafeteria.

As they walked through the main artery of the prison, cat calls echoed off the walls, a blend of propositions, reverse misogyny, comments about their bodies, and the time-honored inmate tradition of yelling just to yell. Arms reached through the bars at them from both sides.

"Look at that fine piece of ass!"

"You wanna be my bitch, baby?"

"You wouldn't dress like that if you didn't want it."

During a brief break in the noise they heard, "Wassup, Jesse?" He looked around but couldn't decipher the trajectory of the sound, then looked down and continued walking to the cafeteria.

Shauna went over the ground rules. "I'll be here the whole time unless I'm transferring them to and from their cells. Try to resist the temptation to ask what crime they committed. If they offer it up that's cool. Finally, everyone's got a sob story so do *not* agree to do anything for them."

As they met with the ladies they found them to be nice, and appreciative that they agreed to play a concert for their entertainment. Most of the inmates explained their court cases and the argument between Wood and Jesse resurfaced during the breaks, when Shauna brought each group back to their cells.

Jesse shook his head. "See? That jackass of a husband got her addicted to drugs, then they both had to start breaking into houses to support their addiction."

"Do you hear the words coming out of your mouth, Jess? They *had* to break into houses, like the police forced them to go on a crime spree?"

Each story that supported one of their respective arguments led to a glance between the two, as if to say, "I told you so." Jesse said, "We're supposed to be here for these ladies, not to settle some stupid debate. We're being assholes."

Wood conceded, "Yeah, you're right."

The next group asked questions about their lives as traveling musicians and the freedom to wander anywhere in the world that their tour might deposit them.

"Do you have groupies that do whatever you want?"

Wood smiled, "I try to avoid people like that. At first it feeds your ego, then you realize that some of them have a screw loose. One lady found out where I lived and was following me around. I didn't even know until the police told me. I found an envelope that said, 'Your Mine' on my windshield with a bullet inside. I thought it was Jesse playing a joke on me."

The ladies laughed in shock.

Jesse laughed, "Nah, man. I know my grammar and punctuation!"

"Is it true you won't take photos with your fans?"

"I just don't enjoy it very much. One time I said that I would be happy to take a photo *of* them, not *with* them. Then I put my smashed thumb in the corner of the photo as a joke so they'd know it was me. That photo ended up in a magazine and it became a thing, like you can only call yourself a *real* fan if my thumb is in the photo. It's ridiculous, but I like it that way. I can walk around without being bothered most of the time. If you make the cover of Rolling Stone, that's one thing, but once you're on the cover of People or Newsweek, *everyone* knows who you are and your life goes haywire. I try to avoid that." He held up his demolished left thumb for their inspection.

"Oh, you poor baby. Let me kiss it." Jesse and Shauna rolled their eyes, like a synchronized eye-rolling team, linked by their shared DNA. The inmate kissed Wood's thumb a little too long, all the while staring into his green eyes, lost in a world where she and Wood were the only people in the prison. "How did you get this owie, baby?"

Wood pried his hand from her grip, inspecting it closely, like he hadn't noticed his own thumb in years, "Umm…smashed it with a hammer." He never told the truth. His thumb was the last finger on the piano keyboard as his mother slammed down the heavy mahogany lid during a lesson of Bach etudes that he struggled to play accurately, splattering blood everywhere and deepening his hatred of her piano lessons.

The inmate started kissing his thumb again, this time with her tongue, as she stared at him.

"TIME'S UP!" barked Shauna, putting a stop to the creepy romance before it could take root.

"But it was just getting good! I promise I'll come to one of your shows when I get out. Okay, baby?"

"Ummm…sure, I'd like that," said Wood. He whispered to Shauna, "When does she get out?"

"With good behavior, Ms. Innocent here will be following you around like a Deadhead in 2035."

"What was her crime?"

"She murdered a singer." Shauna paused for a moment then couldn't contain herself. "Just messin' with you!" Jesse nearly fell off the bench laughing with his sister. "Did you see Wood's face?!"

"Jesus. What is it with this family? Always messing with me."

***

Shauna brought in the last two ladies. "Got a few stragglers here. They were working in the shop."

"Wassup, Jesse?"

"Gina!" he beamed. "What are you doing in here?"

She laughed, "Long story!"

Jesse gave her a hug and kissed her on the cheek. "Let's get caught up." They walked across the cafeteria and sat at a distant table, laughing, and reaching across to touch hands and flirt.

The remaining woman didn't look old enough to be in prison. A slender girl of no more than 18, she half-smiled and looked at the ground. "I didn't plan on talking to you alone, sir."

"Lucky us. Please, have a seat. My name is Wood. What's yours?"

"Aliyah."

"How's your day going, Aliyah?" He cringed. Every question seemed inappropriate to ask an inmate, like asking terminally ill cancer patients how they're feeling.

"It's going well." She looked down at the table. "I hear you're a good musician. I was good at music too. Good at a lot of things. Honor roll, I was in GATE because I was Gifted and Talented."

"That's impressive. Hopefully, you can get back to the things you love someday." Cringe. He couldn't help but ask why she was in prison.

"When I was 15 my mom died so I went to live with my uncle. He got custody somehow. I realized quickly why she never took us to meet him. His house was always full of shady people. Doing drugs, dealing, hiding stolen property, fighting all the time. I just stayed in my room. Then he took the lock off the door and started to…he started to visit me at night.

Then one night he was on top of me in the dark and I heard my uncle's voice downstairs. I realized it was one of his friends on me. The next night it was a different friend. Sorry, I didn't plan to talk about this, but you asked."

Wood stared at the table, trying to make sense of the kind of man who pimps out his own niece. He asked, "Did you tell anyone?"

"I didn't know a soul in Iberville Parish. It was summertime and I planned to tell a counselor once school started. One night they got really drunk and he called me down to the living room, I guess to show me off. He was waving his pistol around, trying to act like a tough guy. I saw where he hid the pistol and the next day I put it under my pillow. That night they had a party and made me do shots with them. I hadn't even tried beer yet. I pulled myself up the stairs, threw up and passed out. A while later I felt someone heavy on me. He was trying to rape me, but from behind this time. I was drunk and wanted to die. I pulled the gun from under my pillow, pointed it behind my head and pulled the trigger."

There was a long silence and she finally looked up at Wood, who sat motionless.

Searching for something to say, "I think your uncle was an evil man who deserved to die."

"The man raping me wasn't my uncle – he was a Baptist preacher. My uncle testified against me to keep himself out of jail. I was tried as an adult and all the papers called me, 'The Black Widow.' They appointed a lawyer for me, but he knew the preacher that I killed. They all went to high school together. I'm trying to get another court date in a different parish."

"Time's up," said Shauna, softly. Showing her only moment of sympathy, she put her hand on Aliyah's shoulder. "These gentlemen have to get ready for their concert, okay, hon?"

Wood gave Aliyah a bear hug and said everything was going to be alright, one of many lies he told at the prison.

***

In the quad, Jesse yelled into the mic, "Alright ladies, for our last songs we need a drummer up here!" Dozens of hands shot into the air. He laughed and squeaked in his highest falsetto, "I wanna try drumming! Nah, we need a *real* drummer." They laughed and pointed at a woman holding her hands over her face. "Get up here, sister! You can do it."

They all cheered as Wood helped the lady onto the makeshift stage. She sat behind the drums, twirling a stick in one hand. Pointing at her, Wood added, "I got a good feeling about her! Now we need a few backup singers. Anyone sing in the church choir?" He pulled up a few ladies and handed them each an SM58, whispering, "If you don't know the words, just repeat what we sing a second later." They laughed and nodded.

Jesse shouted, "Now I only trust one person on bass and that's my big sister, Shauna. Come on, sis, don't be shy!" The prisoners laughed and chanted, "Shauna, Shauna!" after finally learning her first name. She smiled and pulled the Fender jazz bass over her head, playing a few quick scales. "This whole concert was Shauna's idea so you ladies be nice to her when you see her on duty, okay?"

Archie and Margaret relaxed on some amps, gnawing on T-bones, and enjoying their VIP seats.

Jesse played the keys while Wood started singing John Lennon's "Jealous Guy." He felt a tug on his trousers and looked down to see Ms. 2035 singing back to him, commenting as he sang, increasing her grip with each line.

"I was feeling insecure" (It's okay, baby!)

"You might not love me anymore" (You know I'll always love you, honey!)

"I was shivering inside" (I'm nervous too, baby doll!)

"I didn't mean to hurt you." (I know you didn't!)

"I'm sorry that I made you cry." (I deserved it, baby!)

"I didn't want to hurt you." (We'll hurt each other, sweetie!)

"I'm just a jealous guy." (Oh I'm jealous too, baby!)

For a moment, Wood appreciated a system that would keep her out of his life until well into the 21st century. Just then, he spotted Aliyah in the crowd, a girl among women, shaking her head, giggling at his predicament.

He pointed at her, "I see you, Aliyah! Stay strong!" Their eyes met and she held up her fist, smiling.

As the song came to an end, Wood continued playing the chords as Jesse addressed the quad. "I hope we got some reggae fans up in here. This song is called 'Till Your Well Runs Dry' by Peter Tosh! He used to jam with Bob Marley." He came to the edge of the stage to rescue Wood and sang,

> You said that you loved me
> And that's no lie
> You break every promise
> You win every bet

Bending down to hold 2035's hand.

> You never miss your water
> Till your well runs dry
> So tell me, tell me

Wood signaled for the band to come in.

> What you gonna do
> When your well runs dry?

The quad was hopping as ladies danced with each other and swayed to the reggae rhythm. As the song ended, Jesse said, "We got time for one more song, ladies. Thank you for giving us your love and attention. We love you too! Now I got a big surprise for you. I didn't know my old friend from high school choir was um…one of this fine establishment's distinguished guests. Get up here, Gina!" The crowd laughed and chanted, "Gina! Gina!" as Jesse helped her onto the stage. "Now this lady can sing! We're gonna play a song that we learned in choir and that our band plays for the encore if an audience has been great, and you ladies have truly warmed our hearts! It's called, 'You'll Lose a Good Thing' by Miss Barbara Lynn."

Wood and Shauna started playing the song on guitar and bass. The drummer joined in.

Jesse turned to face her. "But first I gotta ask you, Gina. Why did you reject me back in high school?"

The ladies in the quad erupted in laughter as they watched the romantic tension blossom. Gina bent down, shielding her face in embarrassment. Now armed with a microphone of her own, she replied, "Cuz you was skinny and didn't look like you was gonna amount to anything. Maybe I'll reconsider now."

"What do you think, ladies?"

The ladies cheered and laughed. Someone yelled, "Give him a chance, Gina!" and the band launched into the classic R&B song.

Gina sang,

> You know I love you
> Do anything for you
> Just don't mistreat me
> And I'll be good to you
> Cuz if you should lose me, oh yeah
> You'll lose a good thing

Jesse added,

> I'm giving you one more chance
> For you to do right

Wagging his finger at her,

> If you'll only straighten up, Gina
> We'll have a good life

Everyone joined in,

Cuz if you should lose me, oh yeah
You'll lose a good thing

***

As dusk settled on the quad the guards began shuffling inmates back into the depths of the prison, quickly and, in some cases, pushing them along as they laughed and sang.

Wood stood at the front of the stage watching Aliyah, the last inmate standing across the quad. She blew him a kiss and walked into the darkness of the prison with Shauna. Jesse was already wrapping guitar cables and putting effects pedals into gig trunks, wheeling them to the edge of the stage.

"Hey, Wood. I'm gonna head home with my sister and spend some time with family. I'll make my way to the next show, okay?"

"That's cool, brother. I'll see you there. Tell Gina I said hi."

Jesse blushed after his real reason for staying was revealed.

***

Wood and Margaret drove through the countryside at dusk. "That girl never had a chance, Margaret. Who knows what she could have become? How is she gonna get out after killing a Baptist preacher? She hid the gun under her pillow – that's premeditated murder."

Margaret looked out the window and barked at a magpie, flying briefly beside them before peeling away into the dying light. "Even if she gets out, what kind of relationship is she gonna have after being raped by a bunch of creeps? It's going to take one understanding man to help her work through all that." Aliyah's future had more questions than answers, more problems than solutions.

Wood pulled over, disillusioned with a system that could never save every Aliyah. He stood next to the van crying as the sun crashed below the silhouette of the bayou.

He pulled himself together and continued driving. "Margaret, you ever wonder why your life has delivered you to a certain place and time? Sometimes I wonder if I should've finished college. Check out this story.

SCHOLASTIC APTITUDE, PART I

Spring, 1981

Indianapolis, Indiana

It was a lazy Sunday afternoon in Indy. The spring semester was getting into full swing and Wood was pouring himself into new music. Quitting the high school basketball team freed up his time to focus on listening to new albums and trying to write a few rudimentary songs. Uncle Freddie showed up at the house, which was unusual for someone they only saw at holiday functions. Wood's mother asked him to come have a talk with them at the dining room table. Knowing how much her son hated talking about his future, she broached the subject delicately.

"Thurston, darling, I asked Uncle Freddie to stop by so we can talk about how you're doing academically. I got your report card from the fall semester and it doesn't appear that the situation is improving. How are you going to get into a good college if you don't apply yourself? You've got the end of your junior year then your senior year will be a blur of homecoming dances, the prom..."

Feeling blindsided, Wood became defiant. "Maybe I don't want to go to college."

"Now don't start that again. Getting a degree is your best chance to secure a good future for yourself. I don't see you as the military type. What else would you do?"

Uncle Freddie touched his sister's arm to signal it was his turn to try to talk sense into his nephew. He spoke slowly but firmly. Maybe addressing him by his nickname would endear him to his uncle. "Let's all be honest with each other, Wood, your grades are mediocre at best. If you don't get it together you won't be accepted into a decent school. Now that time is running out, we think that getting a high SAT score is the only way to make up for your grades."

"Uncle Freddie has found a tutor for you. A lovely girl from a prominent Zionsville family named Yvette. She aced the SAT, absolutely *aced* it. She's studying philosophy at Butler, just down the road, and she's agreed to tutor you."

Mulling this over, Wood asked, "What if I don't like her? I mean, just because she's academically smart doesn't mean she can explain it to me. Maybe she's a horrible tutor."

Charlotte tilted her head to the left, dropping it with a condescending lift of her eyebrows. "Now, dear, you are not her first pupil, and I don't think you're in a position to negotiate. She's got quite a resume for someone her age. Could you just give it a try?"

Wood was reluctant to go along with their plan, simply because it wasn't his, but decided that going through the motions would be easier than arguing. His staunch resistance to being tutored dissolved immediately when he opened the door and saw Yvette standing on his porch the following Saturday afternoon. She had long black hair and wore glasses. Her clothes were standard college garb…jeans, a Butler sweatshirt, and Doc Martins.

***

The first session was awkward. Yvette was used to students being nervous, particularly teenage boys. She made jokes and familiar references to remind Wood that they weren't that far apart in age and that she had also lost sleep over the SATs, just like him. "Thurston, remember that we're both juniors, just in high school and college."

"Only my Mom and Uncle Freddie call me 'Thurston.' Everyone else calls me 'Wood.'

"Sounds good. Wood it is."

So...I guess you're drinking age now."

"Yes, although you won't find me in the bars."

"Are college parties crazy, like on Animal House?"

"Sometimes they are. When people start acting like idiots I head for the door."

"So how did you get this gig tutoring me?"

"I put up some fliers and I got a call from your uncle. I had to go meet him in Carmel to interview for the job, which seemed pretty formal for a tutoring gig."

"Yeah, he lives in Carmel. Uncle Freddie loves to golf and he also has a condo in Carmel, California, so our family has to say he's either home in CARmel, Indiana, or he's out in carMELL, by the sea. My Mom always says it with a grand flourish, like, 'Frederick, darling, are you going to the rodeo in CARmel or the ro-DAY-oh in carMELL?' Uncle Freddie is strict but he's been good to us."

"Your mother sounds funny. I thought she was a little stuck up at first, but she's cool."

"Our family back east is pretty stiff. It's like she can't let go of those high-class manners. She's constantly on her piano students about their posture and manners. I don't think it's about piano at all. She's just standing firm against the decline of society, one little kid at a time.

"Yeah, sometimes I hear her yelling in the other room."

"She can be funny if you don't piss her off. We avoid each other for the most part."

Changing the subject as they ran out of time, "Have you thought about colleges you'd like to apply to?"

"Probably IU, Notre Dame, maybe some places back east like Bates or Wake Forest."

"Purdue?"

"Purdue is a great school but my mother went to IU so she'd disown me if I even applied. Uncle Freddie went to Wabash. He says it's the Harvard of the Midwest, but everyone says that. Vanderbilt is the Harvard of the south! We're the Harvard of the northwest! Do you think the students in Massachusetts say they're the Harvard of the Harvard?"

"True. It is a big game, but so is life and you have to play along. You could try to go to Butler."

"Nothing against Butler, but it's just down the road. If I attended there I'd probably stay right here living with Mom."

Looking around Wood's bedroom, Yvette remarked, "Careful what you wish for. Looks like you've got a pretty sweet gig right here. Your mother leaves you alone, no bills to pay, a nice stereo, Penthouse magazines, you can play your music and study."

"I never really thought of it that way."

As the tutorials progressed, Wood and Yvette became closer. He put in extra time during the week, not wanting to disappoint her the following Saturday. Uncle Freddie had arranged a bonus system based on Wood's score. She was incentivized by his success, although she never breathed a word. Knowing that keeping Wood engaged correlated with the time he put into his preparation, she wasn't above wearing tight shirts, showing cleavage, or sucking on the end of her pen as Wood tried to form a sentence. Her last lines of each tutorial session were always sexual cliffhangers meant to tide him through the week until their next meeting. "Let's stop here. If you study extra-long and hard, we'll work on something special next week…together." Wood's mother couldn't grasp what kind of magic brew this girl was serving up, but it seemed to be working.

TUSCALOOSA STARTS WITH A T

July 15, 1998

Cottondale, Alabama

Jesse called Rachel from the hotel after their gig in Tuscaloosa. "Hey, Rachel, it's Jesse. You got a minute?"

"It's one o'clock in the morning! What the hell is wrong with you?!"

"Is it that late?"

"Yeah, dumbass! This better be important."

"It is. Remember how Wood gets the TV remote when we play in a city that starts with the first half of the alphabet, like **A**tlanta, and I get the remote when it's from the last half, like **W**ichita? We just played in **T**uscaloosa, so it's my night to get the remote, but he's trying to steal it because our *hotel* is in **C**ottondale. He's pointing out the window at the sign. So, is it the name of the town where we had the concert or where the hotel is located?"

"Really? You guys get high, argue over the remote like kid brothers, then call me, like I'm your mother?"

"Well, now that you put it that way."

"Okay…it's the name of the town where you had the concert. Roma locuta, causa finita!"

"What does that mean?"

"Rome has spoken. Translation - don't fucking call me at one in the morning to settle an argument about the TV remote."

"Dang…sorry. It won't happen again."

"It's okay, Jesse. I'm just sleepy."

Wood motioned for the phone.

"Here's the thief himself." Passing the phone to Wood, "Tuscaloosa starts with a T. Remote, please!"

Taking the receiver, Wood chuckled, "Sorry about that. I told him not to call."

Rachel sighed, "It's fine. How was the show?"

"It was good but I'm dehydrated. They had this row of lights right above our heads. I felt like a hamster in a terrarium with a big weed lamp shining down on me. The crowd always digs it when I drip sweat."

"Damn. Drink some Gatorade."

"I will. Anyway, can you find a good defense attorney in New Orleans? Make sure they're from the city, not the sticks."

"Did you get in trouble down there?"

"It's not for me. It's for someone I met."

"What was the crime, drunk driving?"

"Murder. It's a long story. I'll call them and explain the situation if you can find a good one."

"Will do." Rachel changed the subject. "Remember when we were brainstorming ways to bring in more income? The record company has a new distributor in Europe and their rep contacted me. He was really jazzed about trying some new ideas so I sent over a few of your singles."

"I didn't know we had a new distributor. Which songs did you send?"

"'She Saw Me Coming' and 'Palace.' I figured they both cover your style at different points in your career. Anyway, they put 'She Saw Me Coming' on a compilation CD. It's getting a lot of air play and selling really well, especially in Italy."

"Interesting. I wonder why it's selling in Italy."

"Who cares! It's #27 on their chart and rising."

"Thanks for taking the initiative. What should we do next?"

"Y'all need to wrap up your tour dates and get your asses to Europe! I've already contacted some people that I know from a music industry convention I went to. I'd rather have gigs in the towns with people I trust. You and Jesse can do a mini tour this time and see how it goes. The promoters can hook you up with some local musicians to sit in."

"Sounds like a plan! We play University of Georgia in Athens tomorrow then we'll head back." Looking at Jesse, "That's Athens with an A!"

"The first gig is going to be in a cute little seaside village in England. It's where The Housemartins came from. Remember that band?"

"Oh yeah. Great band."

"I've been talking with a promoter there. The town is called Hull. I guess that's where they build yachts. How cute is that?"

"I'm sorry, did you say 'Hull'?"

***

Wood heard voices in Japanese and he felt a sting in his arm. He opened his eyes just enough to see Dr. Nobunaga inserting a new IV. Through his eyelashes he saw Nurse Nishimori turning the nob to adjust the drip. The doctor smiled and patted him on the shoulder, saying, "Okay okay…back to sleep."

SECTION 2: DRIFTWOOD TOURS EUROPE

DRIFTWOOD   **0**

HULL   **4**

The Tower

July 22, 1998

Hull, England

When Wood and Jesse arrived at The Tower, they were immediately offered drugs by a man mopping blood from the floor. They couldn't have known it would be the high point of the evening. Backstage they milled around with Fonda 500 but couldn't understand the local dialect. The turnout wasn't bad, a few hundred at least. As Wood, Jesse, and local drummer, Tony, took the stage, they heard screaming from the left. Jesse shielded the stage lights from his eyes just in time to see a woman kneeing a man in the balls without spilling a drop from her pint, clearly something she had done before.

They launched into the first song and for the first 20 seconds the mood seemed to lift as the jangly guitars came through the sound system. Once the crowd realized they were playing "Happy Hour" by Hull's The Housemartins the boos and beer began raining down on the stage. Wood made it through the first verse. As Jesse joined in to sing, 'It's happy hour again' an unopened bottle of Grolsch struck Wood in the mouth.

Dazed from the impact, he paused for a moment, then heard a high-pitched ring as his brain morphed into enraged psychosis. He scanned the crowd, barely discerning shapes, finally settling on a collection of fingers pointing to a smiling man who was giving him the backward peace sign. Wood threw off his Les Paul, which landed on the stage in a cacophony of feedback. Jesse and the drummer kept playing as Wood performed a stage dive. The crowd parted politely, allowing him to faceplant at their feet. The man reached down, grabbed Wood by the collar, and punched him repeatedly in the face. This was the moment in every brawl when Wood realized that no one had ever taught him how to fight. Wood pried the hand from his shirt and began screaming in falsetto as he formed fists with his thumbs tucked inside, thrusting his arms in the general direction of anything in front of him. His opponent looked perplexed at first, then kicked Wood in the stomach. Just as the man moved in for the crescendo headbutt, Jesse landed in front of Wood, now doubled over in pain. The man held up his arms and yelled, "What the fack you gonna do?" Jesse knocked him out cold then helped Wood to the dressing room.

The crowd, having realized the show was over, began yelling, as if some form of protest was required, then returned to drinking their pints. Wood and Jesse found a way out of the club in time to witness a naked man running down the middle of the street, covered head to toe in shaving cream. Thursday in Hull.

Rachel called them at the hotel the next morning. Wood mumbled incoherently then handed the phone to Jesse.

"What's wrong with Wood?"

"His mouth doesn't work. I think he swallowed a tooth, hopefully not one of the important ones."

"What the hell happened?"

"They didn't like the Housemartins cover we played. We didn't even make it through the song before they attacked us. At least back home fans would have had the common courtesy to finish their beer before throwing the bottle. Not in Hull!"

"Dang. Do you think they hated The Housemartins or your version of the song?"

Jesse sighed. "We'll never know."

"It's such a sweet little song from a sweet little band. I thought Hull was a seaside village, like on TV."

"This place should be called Hell. We're getting outta here before they find out where we're staying."

"How much did you get paid?"

"Nothing."

"Don't worry. They just need some prodding. I'll find out if there are Teamsters in England."

"We only played for 50 seconds. Face it, Rachel, the show was a wash."

Wood tried to feel which tooth was missing by pushing on his cheek, then moaned as he opened his mouth. Inspecting him, Jesse reported, "Good news. His tooth is still there, it's just pushed inward."

"Which tooth?"

"The one on his upper left side. The doggy tooth."

"Poor baby. Is he going to be able to sing at the next show?"

"Yeah, he's tough. It was mainly a blow to his ego, but to be fair, he looks like shit, too."

"Did he at least get some good licks in?"

"I guess you've never seen Wood fight. It was a cry for help. Listen, we gotta bail."

"Call me when you get to the next town!"

Wood examined the pink foot-shaped outline on his pale tummy. "You didn't need to say that to Rachel. I didn't have a dad or brothers around to teach me how to fight. You know that!"

Jesse felt guilty. "Listen, the combination of never backing down while not being able to throw a punch is not a sustainable plan, brother."

"So I should just let people throw beer bottles at me for the rest of my life?"

"Nah, man. I'm gonna teach you how to win a bar fight, or at least 40% of them."

"Those aren't good odds."

"Neither is screaming like a castrato while flailing your arms with your eyes closed. Come stand in front of me."

Wood walked over, formed his special fists, and raised his arms.

"First off, your thumbs go on the outside!" Jesse helped Wood make a proper fist. "Now, here's the situation. It's midnight in the bar and things get heated with a drunk loudmouth."

"Usually it's a frat boy whose girlfriend wants to take me home."

Jesse rolled his eyes. "Who wouldn't want to take you home? The process is simple. You say something so insulting that he goes nuclear. Always insult the mother because she is the jugular in every male culture on the planet. For example, he calls you a fag and you say, 'Your mother didn't think I was gay when I was banging her last night.' That's when he'll try to punch you in the face."

'How do I know he'll punch me in the face?'

"When a man goes Neanderthal, he just wants your head gone."

"Makes sense. That's how I felt last night."

"Most people are right-handed so we're playing the odds here." Jesse threw a slow-motion haymaker with his right hand and instructed Wood to duck. "See how I'm twisted to my left and off balance after I missed your head? Now look at my torso. It's a buffet of organs just waiting to be clocked. You're gonna punch me as hard as you can in my liver, which is already overworked from the heavy drinking." Jesse motioned to the proximity of his vital organs. "Even if you miss, you'll probably hit my kidney or solar plexus."

"I get the idea."

"When you throw a punch the power comes from your legs, not your skinny arms. Imagine you're throwing a baseball."

"I can't throw a baseball. What about pushing a Marshall amp?"

"That'll work. Just push that amp with your legs. Lean into it and your arm is going to follow your torso."

"Like this?" Wood lunged forward in slow-motion, adding a Six Million Dollar Man face as he threw the first real punch in his life, connecting softly with Jesse's stomach.

"That's good. Now stand up straight because once the pain registers in my brain I'm gonna curl over, down and to my right. That's when you clock me with another right to the jaw. Two punches and it's over – one to the torso and one to the jaw. Lights out!"

"Shouldn't I throw a left?"

"Let's imagine your left arm has been amputated for now."

"What happens after I throw my second punch?"

"Usually, people have jumped in to break it up by that point. Idiots hang out with other idiots and their girlfriends. Intervening is part of their role."

Wood, grasping the complex beauty of pugilism, the sweet science, began to reenact the fight from the night before. Ducking and punching all around the room, saying, "Duck, liver shot, stand up, jaw! Duck, liver shot, stand up, bam!" He turned to Jesse with a newfound confidence, "What if I duck, but he aims lower than my head?"

"That's when you get knocked out."

THE OLD NICKEL HOTEL

July 26, 1998

Amsterdam, The Netherlands

Back at The Old Nickel Hotel after the show at the Melkweg, Wood was visited by the concierge.

"Hello, Mr. Driftwood. Sorry to disturb. We received a message from the US embassy. They will be sending someone to meet you in the hotel bar at 11:00 a.m."

Confused and buzzed, Wood asked, "Am I in trouble?"

"It's not something they typically reveal, sir."

Wood handed him a tip and closed the door.

Jesse was flipping through a variety of porn options on the hotel TV. "I thought *I* was kinky, but they got some twisted stuff on here."

"You know that Rachel goes through our expenses, right? She's gonna know if you order that."

"If this rock star thing doesn't pan out I can fall back on a career as an adult film star. Just gotta come up with a great name."

Wood laughed, "Let's hear it."

"Jesse the Pool Boy."

"Dude, half the pornos involve a pool boy. You can do better than that." Wood raised his voice to a sexy feminine timbre, "I have all this suntan lotion, but I can't reach my back. Pool boy, can you help a lonely widow?"

"See, that script writes itself. Alright, what kind of porn star would you be?"

Wood paused long enough to trick Jesse into thinking he hadn't considered a career in porn. "Got it. The tennis coach."

"Can you play tennis?"

"Not a lick, but I could buy a racquet at Goodwill."

"True. And what would you call this masterpiece?"

"Wimbledong: New Balls."

Jesse nearly fell off the bed laughing. "There is no way you haven't thought about this before!"

Wood blushed and nodded, "Long and hard."

***

The next morning, Wood and Jesse drank coffee on a red leather sofa downstairs. The dark wood and intricate patterns of the Moroccan carpet lent an old-world ambience to the bar.

Speculating why the government would want to speak to them, Jesse said, "I'll bet this is about what happened in Hull," as he admired the deep mahogany ceiling. "That shit follows you, man."

At 10:55 a lady in a pants suit and hair tightly pulled back in a bun entered the bar and began scanning the room for someone looking like a malnourished musician. This described a significant demographic in Amsterdam. "Hello, you must be Driftwood. I'm Janine Greeley from the US embassy. May I sit down?"

Motioning to the chair, "Call me Wood. This is Jesse, my," he hesitated, "…my music associate."

The lady looked at Jesse, "How do you do. Are you an American citizen?"

"I'm a proud member of the Choctaw nation, but I hold an American passport, if that's what you mean."

"Okay…super. I'll cut to the chase. As you know, the Berlin wall came down and the Soviet Union has collapsed. Those former members are their own nations again and we're trying to build relations with them in any way we can. There's a huge festival in Estonia called 'Glasnost Rock.' We'd like you to be on the bill. I found your tour schedule and it would work logistically. We'll pay for the flight, hotel, meals, and your normal concert fee." She slid over a folder containing an agenda and various documents.

Taken aback and still waking up, Wood said, "I'd have to talk to my manager about it. This is out of left field."

"Rachel is already onboard. She faxed back the signed contract this morning. We just have a few requests on behalf of the US State Department. Obviously, don't do anything to embarrass our country. We noticed that you finish your shows with cover songs. We were hoping you could play something patriotic like 'Born in the USA' or…"

Jesse spoke up, "We only embarrass ourselves, and that's usually unintentional. Do you really want us to sing about a screwed-up Vietnam vet?"

"Is that what the song is about? Anyway, I'll let you decide what to play. Just don't embarrass us. In the folder you'll find your contact in Tallinn and profiles of the local musicians you'll be…jamming with. I think that's the term, jamming?" She strummed a few air-guitar notes. "They're talented musicians and have been vetted by our people there. Someone from the embassy will be there to brief you on the situation."

Wood opened the folder to see a black and white photo of a stoic, chubby grandmother in a fur hat glaring back at him with piercing grey eyes.

Sitting up in her chair to see what Wood was looking at, Ms. Greeley chuckled and said, "That's Galina. She was a sniper in Afghanistan. Now she plays bass!"

"I need to get back to the embassy. Break a leg!"

Before they could respond, she was gone.

Sighing, Wood asked to no one in particular, "Why would they ask Driftwood? What the hell are we gonna play in Estonia? Maybe we should do our take on a Russian composer."

Jesse said, "Dude, all they do is listen to classical music and stand in lines! You think they're going to be dazzled by our ham-fisted attempt at Tchaikovsky? You'll regret it."

"Yeah, you're right. Maybe some country songs?" Answering his own question, "No…they'd be expecting that."

Smiling, Jesse said, "I got it, man. I didn't wanna resort to the nuclear option, but desperate times, desperate measures. We're gonna drop the funk on these mofos."

Wood tried to drink his coffee without spitting it out, wiping his chin with his sleeve. "Like what, 'More Bounce to the Ounce?'"

"Nah, man. This means WAR, with a capitol W."

Wood smiled, "I like it. Lowrider?"

Jesse shook his head slowly, his diabolical gears grinding, "'Lowrider' is too fast. Any decent musician can play fast, but it's hard to get into a groove and play slow. We're playing 'Slippin' into Darkness.' I have it on a CD in my bag."

Pondering the cruelty, Wood whispered, "Damn, Jesse, you're cold."

"Fire with fire, man. When do we fly out?"

Shuffling through the documents, Wood found the tickets. "Shit, we need to get to the airport!"

HOLIDAYS IN ESTONIA

When their plane landed in Tallinn, Wood and Jesse were greeted by a young lady holding a Driftwood sign written on a piece of cardboard. She spoke English haltingly, "Welcome to Estonia. I am Maria. I am DJ and promoter…helping with festival. I can take you to your hotel, help you find food, take you to practice place."

"Nice to meet you. Thank you."

They drove through the city, which was a mix of Soviet-era grey and gingerbread houses straight out of Sweden or Bavaria. There was some graffiti, but the city was generally clean and busy with people shopping and going about their daily affairs. Maria got them checked in to the hotel, informed them she'd be back at 10 a.m., then disappeared. They felt lost as they made their way to their room. Jesse picked up the remote, "Ah yes, I believe Tallinn starts with a T, does it not?" He held the remote close to his heart and turned on the TV. He flipped through the channels; the offerings included a news reporter standing next to a cow, a fuzzy basketball game, Little House on the Prairie in gibberish, and the show he settled on, a documentary featuring an eye operation.

"Dude, this place is already trippin' me out."

The phone rang, they looked at each other. Maybe Maria had forgotten to tell them something. Wood picked up the receiver, "Hello?"

"Hi, Wood. This is Don Bainbridge from the US Embassy. I'm down in the hotel café. Could you come down here? Leave Jesse in the room." The phone went dead.

Jesse asked, "Who was it?"

"Uh…it was Maria. She's down in the lobby with our itinerary. I'll be back in a bit."

"Cool. I'm gonna watch them fix this dude's eyeball."

Wood's gut feeling that their reason for being sent to Estonia was more than just a desire to spread goodwill was confirmed when he met with Mr.

Bainbridge, who had a folder containing the same contents. He was decidedly less chipper than Ms. Greeley and got to the point.

"Thanks for meeting with me, Wood. It sounds like Janine got you up to speed." Pointing to the sniper's photo, "This is Galina. She did deadly work in Afghanistan and we believe she's still working with the Russians, for the right price, that is."

"I thought the cold war was over."

"That's adorable. After the wall came down the former Soviet republics have been more chaotic and dangerous than ever. People are struggling to make ends meet. Galina is a great bass player but, apparently, that doesn't pay the bills."

"Tell me about it."

"You're not in any danger, but we'd like you to help us out."

"Listen, Mr. Bainbridge, I love all this James Bond stuff. This is all really intriguing, but it's not really my thing. I just got my ass kicked in Hull the other night."

"We know. That's why you're perfect. You're a fellow musician, nonthreatening, you can drink with her, have a jam session, try to get inside her head."

"What are the chances that she'll kill me?"

"I'd say pretty low, maybe 30%."

"That doesn't inspire confidence."

"Listen, this is off the record. The Russian mafia has her on the payroll to perform hits. Lately, we haven't agreed with a few of those hits. So unless the mafia is after you, you've got nothing to worry about."

"Why would they be after me?"

"Believe me, they're not, although you're on everyone's radar. Your latest song is quite the toe tapper. 'She Saw Me Coming'…great tune. I love the guitar solo."

"Are you a musician, Mr. Bainbridge?"

"I dabble a little. I brought my Strat over with me but mostly it just sits there."

"Look at you!"

Mr. Bainbridge pushed a small bag across the table, "We'll keep it simple. Get to know Galina and give her this as a sign of your friendship." Wood pulled out a BOSS effects pedal.

"Interesting. She steps on it to get a better sound and it blows her all over the stage. I like it, but Jesse and I will be on the same stage."

Smiling, "Not quite. It's a fully functioning chorus with a tracking device. We've noticed that she tends to perform her hits on the same nights that she has a gig. And if we want to blow her to smithereens it will do that, too, but we control that. Don't worry."

Sensing there wasn't any point refusing, Wood took the pedal and stood up to leave.

"One more thing. Don't trust 'Maria the DJ', or whatever she's calling herself these days."

"I'll be careful. Can I tell Jesse about all this?"

"What do you think?"

"Sorry I asked."

SLIPPIN' INTO DARKNESS

Maria met them in the lobby the following morning and drove them to the practice facility, the band room at a local university. She introduced Wood and Jesse to the band.

"Nice to meet you. I am Markko, the drummer."

"Maria…keyboard. Hi."

"Jaan." He smiled and held up his trumpet.

"Hello. My name is Juhan. I am trombone player. This my sister, Kersti. She play saxophone."

Jesse smiled and said, "I was also in a band with my sister…for our church."

"Oh wow! Yes, very fun."

Maria pointed to the last member, a sweet, grandmotherly lady who stared back at them without any facial expression. "This is Galina, our bass player. She is mother of the group." Galina nodded her head slightly.

Maria pointed to her watch, "I must go to concert venue. I will be back in maybe three or four hours, okay?"

"You're not staying to translate for us?"

"Markko and Juhan speak some English. Besides, you have sheet music. Break legs!" Their linguistic lifeline rushed out the door.

Wood said, "We have sheet music and a CD with the songs we will play, but first, let's get to know each other." He motioned for everyone to pull their chairs in a circle. Within a few minutes it was clear that young, cheerful Markko had the strongest grasp of English.

"We all from Tallinn, but Maria from small village. She study music in Austria so she speak German but only little English." Maria smiled and pinched her fingers to show just how little English she spoke. She had blonde hair, high cheek bones, and eyes of a color Wood and Jesse had never seen before. If Debbie Harry from Blondie had mated with a timber wolf they would have spawned Maria, the gorgeous, sweet organ player.

Jesse asked while air drumming, "So Markko, do you have a favorite drummer?"

"Clyde Stubblefield. He was James Brown drummer."

"I was not expecting that! You learned from the best." Wood gave him a thumbs up and patted him on the shoulder. "Do you have any questions for us?"

Juhan asked, "What's mean ACME?"

Jesse smiled and looked confused. "Sorry, what do you mean?"

After some discussion in Russian, Markko explained. "It is animation of desert doggie who chase a fast bird everywhere and try to blow him up with dynamite, but the doggie never catch him." Sniper grandma Galina smiled and said, "Beep Beep!"

Wood laughed, "Oh, The Roadrunner! That's right…they always delivered boxes with ACME written on them. I forgot all about that. Yeah, we loved that show when we were kids. I don't think ACME means anything."

Jesse pointed at Wood, "He is the desert doggie. I'm the fast bird." Wood and Jesse suspected that they might connect with their new friends over their love of family and music, maybe their shared nightmare of growing up under the impending doom of a nuclear fallout, but never The Roadrunner.

Wood stood up and said, "Let's get started!" They passed out the sheet music and played "Slippin' Into Darkness" while they read along. Markko, having studied James Brown grooves for years, was a quick learner and immediately found the rhythm. Classically trained Maria grasped the musicality of the song but struggled with the percussive feel. Galina's bass line hummed along rigidly. The horns were accurate, but it all sounded so tight. After a few minutes, Wood signaled for them to stop. Turning to Markko, "We need to loosen up."

Jesse added, "It sounds like they took the members of WAR out back and beat them with canes."

Markko said, "Let me try something." He walked across the room and began pulling open drawers and cabinets, finally yelling, "Yes, here you are." He turned around with a bottle of vodka in hand and grabbed some teacups next to a large samovar. The eight members of the makeshift band stood in a circle, finished off the bottle of vodka, then listened to the song again. They closed their eyes and clapped along with the groove, swaying while they channeled the rhythm.

After the song they returned to their instruments and hit Play. They sounded like a different band, looser, grittier, unbothered by minor errors and missed notes. Galina added a few slaps and pops to the bassline. Maria moved her head from side to side as she remembered that the piano is a percussion instrument. Wood already knew the song, which freed his mind to daydream about a future life with the elegant Maria.

SANTA BARBARA

The band was fully engulfed in a collective groove when Galina suddenly stopped playing, jumped up, put down her bass and tapped her wristwatch. Markko put down his drumsticks and ran over to a small television, turned it on and manipulated the antenna with his left hand while slapping it to life with his right. The remaining members of the band formed a viewing gallery. Galina positioned her chair with the best view and turned back to see Wood and Jesse, still standing with their guitars, looking at each other in confusion. Motioning for them to join her, she yelled, "Santa Barbara Forever!" They put down their instruments and sat on a small sofa next to Galina. Markko worked his magic and cranked up the volume. The soap opera started with cheesy 80's Casio synthesizer and a montage of photos of beautifully tanned people in tuxedos, polo players riding ponies, Spanish missions, the ocean, and palm trees, lots of swaying palm trees. Galina turned to them excitedly, "Santa Barbara!" They didn't know what they were looking at and shrugged their shoulders, shaking their heads at her in confusion. Markko said, "Santa Barbara is biggest show. Everyone know it in Russia, Estonia, Ukraina, Romania...is from California. You know it?"

"No. Sorry."

Markko and Galina cocked their heads in disbelief, then returned to the screen. Just below the volume of the overdubbed Russian they could hear the English conversations. A woman wearing a sequined dress and perfectly feathered hair spoke nervously into a telephone. Something was horribly wrong and her expression revealed that there was nothing she could do to set her fate on a new course.

Markko explained, "She is Eden. Very beautiful but...many problem."

Just then, a handsome man wearing a tuxedo entered from behind, walked up and put his arm on Eden's shoulder, reassuring her with his equally perfect tan and feathered hair.

Markko continued, "This man name Cruz. He wanted to marry Eden but on wedding day, big fire at church. So they no marry. Also...he is spy."

Maria smiled and cupped her hands to form a small bowl shape, "I have little kitten name Cruz."

Wood leaned over to Jesse, "Bro, what the fuck are we watching? We need to practice!"

Jesse turned and whispered, still staring at the screen, "I love it. The budget for hairspray alone must have been..." A movement caught his eye and he realized that a small crowd had gathered behind them to watch the soap opera. A janitor sat on the ground looking concerned for Eden in her sequined dress. Next to him, an attractive young cleaning lady rested her chin on her mop handle, dreaming of living in scandalous Santa Barbara, where everyone was perfect, but whose destinies were imperfectly intertwined with the other gorgeous people in their orbit. A place where homes were palatial and regal, where maids followed closely behind to recover the tiaras and bowties that were flung across rooms in passion, jealousy, and rage. A place with no need for worn-out heaters in the winter.

***

As the credits rolled, the crowd dispersed and the musicians returned to their instruments. Wood remembered his special gift from the embassy. Pulling the chorus pedal out of his bag, he handed it to Galina. "This is for you. It's for your bass." Galina stood staring at it, but did not reach out to touch it. Realizing that he would have to facilitate the transaction, Wood removed Galina's bass cable from the amp and plugged it into the new pedal. Next, he found an extra guitar cable in his guitar bag, plugged it into the other side of the pedal and back into the amp. He walked across the room to put on his guitar. "Tell her to play and then step on the pedal to hear the difference." Once this was translated Galina began playing, but was clearly reluctant to step on the pedal. Wood walked over to her. She took off her bass, handed it to Wood, pointed to the pedal and said, "You first." She walked across the room and stood behind a standup piano, "I want to hear sound like audience hear." Wood played and Galina ducked slightly as he stepped on the pedal. They were both relieved to hear a beautiful and lush sound come through the amp. The pedal improved her bass tone – and nobody even got their leg blown off.

***

Back at the hotel, Jesse mused in disgust. "I feel so cheated. Growing up in the cold war we thought they were brainwashed, and yet all those years Santa Barbara was kept from us. I wonder if it's on VHS. If not, I'm writing a letter to Blockbuster when we get back! Oh yeah, Jesse's gonna watch him some Santa Barbara!"

"Simmer down. Name one other soap opera you were into."

Jesse held out his arms, "Like sands through the hourglass, so are the Days of Our Lives. I watched it every day with my nana. You met her at the barbecue."

***

The next day the band tackled the Driftwood songs. As a supporting band, they were expected to play for forty minutes, definitely within the band's reach. Galina fully embraced her chorus pedal, with every bassline now a wall of sound. Wood tried to think of ways to talk with Maria, but every effort to speak with her involved an additional person to translate. His German vocabulary included the standard Hogan's Heroes vernacular – no help there. He thought he caught their eyes meeting for longer than normal, although his wishful thinking had let him down before. While they practiced "Palace," Wood glanced over to see Maria looking down at the keyboard, her blonde hair hanging down over her face and swaying as she nodded her head to the rhythm. He saw her eyes raise to watch him. She smiled, although it could have been from relief that the songs were coming together, that their setlist might actually work in front of thousands of concertgoers. He decided not to push his luck.

***

Glasnost Rock Summer Festival

August 1, 1998

Tallinn, Estonia

Backstage at the festival they were treated like royalty, enjoying the catering and a variety of drinks. They met the other bands, as equals. Across the room, Bjork was talking with John Lydon. She laughed and slapped him on the arm. The Estonian bandmates would have been content with getting backstage, let alone play onstage. They were starstruck when Jaagup Kreem from Terminaator started joking with them. Wood and Jesse were used to this scene, although it reached a higher level of stardom than even they were used to.

Maria came over holding a clipboard and pretending to know about concerts, "It's time!" Jesse gave everyone the same advice he gave the St. Chalmette Fighting Owls marching band; "If you get nervous, play louder, not softer."

They all took their places and looked out over a sea of people that rose up a hill, creating a natural amphitheater, easily 100,000. They listened to the introduction, specifically for the last word as their cue to start, "Driftwood!" They kicked off with the trusty "Take Me to the Trains" with its mid-tempo distortion-fueled intro, like a train rolling down the tracks. If they could get through this they'd be on their way. Galina could have kept her new chorus pedal on top of the amp – she had no intention of stepping on it to quiet her wall of sound. It served to cover minor errors. With Jesse's guitar playing locked in with Markko's beat, a lot could go wrong and still sound right.

After the song ended, Wood yelled, "Spaciba! Mnye zavut Driftwood!" He knew it was wrong but crowds always appreciated the effort. They launched into "Palace," "Drenched," then "How Could I Blame You?" As he played the opening chords to "She Saw Me Coming" the crowd recognized the song and cheered. When they got to the chorus they noticed people waving their hands in the international gesture for beating off. Jesse and Wood looked at each other, then at the rest of the band, who laughed and shrugged. Maria and Kersti blushed.

They finished with "Slippin' Into Darkness," which was so slow, plodding, and funky that Wood vowed to never doubt Jesse's judgment again. Galina had the decency to turn off the chorus pedal. She dropped into a solid groove with Markko. The horn section sounded percussive and when Jesse sang, "When I called to my brother" the band sang "Whoa whoa whoa whooooooooooooa" before stopping on a dime with the snare shot, "Who never said their name. Yeah!" - and came back together in the groove. The stadium was grooving and with the hardest parts over, the band jammed and enjoyed their moment of fame. They were playing with house money.

To Jesse's recollection, they were the only group at the festival to drop some funk. He was always proud of that.

Backstage they all hugged and laughed, the improbable became the possible, transcendent, triumphant. Maria walked over to Wood with an older couple who were smiling and shaking their heads. "This my mother and father."

Wood beamed, "Zdraztvuytye! Maria is a beautiful organ player...piano player. I mean...she's great."

Awkward moment completed, the parents smiled and wandered over to chat with the bandmates who understood them. Maria stayed. She reached into her coat pocket and pulled out a locket, opening it to reveal her photo inside. She stood on her toes and clasped it behind Wood's neck, her cheek brushing against his. She whispered, "Thank you, Mr. Wood." She kissed him on the cheek then slowly on his lips. She looked embarrassed and walked quickly to join her parents as they left, blowing him a kiss as she disappeared behind the curtain.

Le Temps de L'Amour

France

In their hotel room in Paris, Jesse came out of the bathroom raving about the bidet. "Only an advanced culture like France would use a bidet. I feel like a new man. I wonder if I can have one sent back home."

Wood smiled, "I'm sure you'll figure out a way. By the way, thanks for everything you did in Estonia. The band, the arrangements, the funk. It all came together."

"Thanks, man. Good job leaving Maria alone. Some girls are meant to stay innocent. You're old enough to be her father. She needs a younger man, like me."

"I am *not* old enough to be her father. Maybe an uncle. She gave me a locket with her photo in it. I was getting the vibe from her but I wasn't sure. I guess I still got it."

"I guess you do."

"I need to call Rachel. She should be awake by now." Wood called the front desk and asked them to connect him to her work number and charge it to his room. "Good morning, sunshine. I'm calling from Paris. How's your day going?"

"Fine. Just drinking coffee and yelling at truckers. You know the drill. How did it go in Estonia?"

"It was…unexpected in every way. Remind me to tell you about Santa Barbara sometime. How's Margaret?"

"She's great. I brought her to the office with me. She's under my chair gnawing on a bone."

"That's good. We're getting ready for our gig tomorrow, but we haven't heard from anyone yet."

"That's because I have some good news. The single is selling like crazy and the show sold out so fast that they're moving it to a bigger venue. The new hall is called Le Trianon. One of their people will contact you. It's in Montmartre so you should be pretty close. Another band is playing there tomorrow night so that will give you some time to check out Paris."

"That's great news. How are we doing financially?"

"Great! We got a hefty sum from the state department for the Estonia gig. The single is selling well."

"I wonder what it is about that song that connected with people. I suppose everyone has been dumped and felt tricked before."

"Who *cares*! Can you put Jesse on the phone? I'm going to tell him the good news."

Jesse smiled and looked out over Paris as he listened. He hung up the phone and announced, "Rachel said I could get my own room! With my *own* remote and my *own* bidet."

"You've earned it. I'm going to go check out the neighborhood. Want to come along?"

"No thanks. I'm going to get settled in. I'll let you know which room they put me in."

**

Wood walked through the 18th Arrondissement. He stopped in at Le Consulat café, ordered a croque monsieur sandwich and a glass of Cotes du Rhone – the perfect culinary pairing for people watching. How many famous people had sat there and watched the world go by? Van Gogh, Picasso, Hemingway, Bowles? It was always bittersweet to see lovers walk past, especially when they were being giggly and foolish. Wood could always tell the new couples by how giddy they were.

He bit into the sandwich. The bread crunched then gave way to flavors of black forest ham and the bite of Dijon softened by melted gruyere cheese. While still chewing he drank the Rhone, its cool acid taking the sandwich to another culinary level. He chewed as he watched two lovers laugh and kiss. Would he trade this meal for that love? It was a tough call. Somehow, he didn't feel deserving of both.

He paid his bill and wandered until he came to a dusty record store. Above the counter a crooked chalk board announced upcoming concerts. Towards the top he read, "Driftwood avec Kwicherbichin– Le Trianon – 7-8." Pointing to the board, Wood asked, "Excusez-moi, avez-vous le nouveau chanson du Driftwood?"

The young lady chuckled, rolled her eyes, and replied, "Ah, oui! C'est ici." She walked to the imports section and handed him a compilation CD with an Italian title. He bought it with a pack of Gitanes and walked to the top of Montmartre, sitting on the grass in front of Sacre-Coeur basilica. Tourists and lovers strolled the grounds, taking photos of the city. He lit a Gitane, took in the view, and tore the plastic cover off of the CD, opening the liner notes to find his song. His Italian was rusty, but the title's translation said it all:

SHE SAW ME COMING - IL MASTURBATORE

His lyrics, written years before while drowning his sorrows after being dumped, fit perfectly into the linguistic error.

I thought I was alone

Just my own hand to guide me

Shaking to the bone

Never meant to give her the key

She walked into my life

And stormed out in disgust

Now I'm chasing her down

And I know that I must

Try to explain

Save my name

Because, yeah, yeah, yeah, yeah

She saw me coming (Chorus)

He closed his eyes, "Ah shit!"

Wood jogged back to the hotel, reciting all of the curse words he knew in a variety of languages. At the front desk he asked which room Jesse was staying in. "Excusez-moi...en quelle chambre est mon...bandmate. Mon ami, Jesse."

"Jesse's new room is the same number as your room, but one floor above. He went out maybe twenty minutes ago. By the way, I love your funny song. We listen to it in the break room."

"Merci beaucoup."

Wood went to his room and called Rachel.

"What's wrong, Wood? You never call twice in the same day."

"Can you grab the CD with She Saw Me Coming on it?"

"Okay, you want me to play it?"

"No, look at the lyrics. I found out why it's a hit."

Rachel shuffled through a stack of CDs. "Got it."

"Whoever translated it into Italian totally screwed up. It's been distributed all over Europe on a compilation CD. They're calling it 'Il Masturbatore' over here, like some beat-off song!

Rachel glanced through the lyrics then screamed, "Oh my God! Wait till I tell my dad. That's hilarious!"

"It's not funny."

"I disagree. This is the funniest thing I've heard in years – and I have a CB radio. The lyrics match perfectly. 'Just my own hand to guide me/Never meant to give her the key.' That's amazing."

"I meant the key to my heart! Everyone knows that. I'm a serious musician. I'm an artist!"

"Relax, honey. I'm here. How did you figure this out?"

"When we were playing in Estonia the crowd was doing this little dance. I thought they were line dancing at first, like cowboys with a lasso, but they were motioning like they were masturbating. Everyone was laughing and trying to sing along. I'm never playing it again."

"Now hold on there, tough guy. As your manager, it's my job to remind you that this song is on its way to being a big hit, maybe your biggest ever. The reason you're in Europe is to support this song."

"This is a nightmare. Weird Al will probably do his own version."

"Nah, he couldn't improve on this train wreck. Actually, it's like a train wreck pulled over to watch this song go by."

"Thanks, I feel better."

Rachel slowed her voice and went into night-DJ mode. "Listen to me, Wood. We'll do some damage control. Just keep your cool and inform people that the song was never meant to be about that. Explain that the expression is about being tricked."

Wood's breathing started to slow along with Rachel's voice. "Okay, I like that plan."

"It will work, just breathe, honey."

He closed his eyes and matched her breathing until his pulse slowed. "I guess I shouldn't take myself so seriously."

"That's the spirit."

"Thanks for helping me calm down."

"It's one of my many talents. I just have one question. When you wrote the song, were you holding the pen with your left hand?"

"I hate you. I actually hate you."

She sang the chorus as he hung up the phone, "Because yeah, yeah, yeah, yeah, she saw me" click.

***

He called Jesse's room to tell him the news. No answer. Maybe a glass of wine and a hot bath would calm his nerves. He ordered a bottle of '94

Alsace Riesling, an omelet, and pomme frites from room service then drew a bath. It helped, but the song lingered in his head - lingered out there, finding new radio stations, listeners, DJs, and dancers by the hour. He smoked a Gitane, stared at his long toes at the end of the bath, and floated the bottle in the water, buoyed by the warming Riesling.

He whispered, "What if I died right here in Paris, like Jim Morrison?"

When his fingertips turned to prunes and the Riesling was gone he dried himself and collapsed into a deep, restorative sleep. No turning over, no checking the time, only darkness and bizarre dreams until the following morning.

He awoke feeling refreshed after a ten-hour catatonic sleep, determined to deal with the situation with a positive attitude. He called Jesse, to no avail. Where the hell was Jesse? Wood took the stairs to the next floor to find his room. As he came up the stairs he saw a man opening the door slowly and entering. He was dressed like he'd been to a rave, with the paper bracelet still attached to his hand. His hair was messy and he had a scruffy beard. Was it the right room? He stood outside the door listening to muffled words. There was no mistaking Jesse's laugh. He went downstairs to eat breakfast then returned to his room and called Jesse again. This time he answered, but sounded nervous. Wood tried to hide his annoyance.

"What have you been doing, man? I've been trying to get in touch with you."

"Hey, Wood. I tried to call your room last night, but nobody answered."

"I went to bed early and slept like a log."

"Ah ok. I went out and found a club. Did some drinking and dancing. Paris is a cool town. Check this out, the DJ was playing some drum n' bass music then mixed in your single over the top. People knew the song!"

"Yeah, I heard it's the summer hit. More on that later. Anyway, we have an extra day before the gig. Want to check out the city? I want to show you the Musee d'Orsay."

Jesse stumbled through his explanation, "Yeah, maybe tomorrow. I'm feeling under the weather. I think I'll catch up on some sleep and watch TV."

Wood was tempted to call his bluff and ask him who was in his room, but decided that it wasn't his business. He wasn't Jesse's father.

"Okay, get some rest. I'll talk to you tomorrow."

***

Wood took a taxi to the Musee d'Orsay, convinced that seeing some art would inspire him and settle his nerves. He always held that we should seek inspiration from every corner of the creative world. Musicians should visit museums, painters should attend the symphony, writers should seek out architecture. Hemingway, no matter how busy, always put down his pen to go out into the world, returning to write with new stories and inspirations, often involving a drunken bar fight.

Wood had always preferred the Orsay to The Louvre, since attending one summer with his Mother and Uncle Freddie. He found his Mother's favorite painting, *Jeune femme en toilette de bal*, by Berthe Morisot. He remembered Uncle Freddie walking around tsk-tsking and saying, "Yes, but what does it *mean*?" to no one in particular, until he came to one of Degas' equestrian paintings. "Now that's a painting," reassuring his prejudices that the western world was superior to all others. Plus it had horses. Wood's favorite painter was Paul Gauguin, who left the world he knew to find the exotic life of Tahiti, or his version of exotica.

It worked. He walked out of the museum, not with inspiration, but the perspective that his music, his art, would someday be adored, mocked, or forgotten altogether, entirely unaltered by his own opinion of it.

***

LE TRIANON

August 7, 1998

Paris

The following evening, Wood walked backstage at Le Trianon and observed a sumptuous spread of culinary delights and drinks. A group of young men and women walked past him with a member of the staff. He observed the scene without interrupting, as they seemed to be frantically solving an important problem.

"See? There are sodas, beer, wine, and Evian, but where's the Perrier? We *specifically* asked for Perrier! Do you understand me?"

Flustered, the young staff member replied, "Ah…oui. I go buy Perrier?"

"Oui!" When he yelled "Merci" it sounded like "Mare – sea."

As the young lady whisked off to find Perrier she shot a glance to Wood, rolling her eyes. The band took notice of him standing there.

"Whoa, I think it's him." They formed a semi-circle and spoke to him reverently. "Are you Mr. Driftwood?"

"Call me Wood."

"Mr. Wood. We love your work. We have a cassette of tunes we like and you're always on it. Can we see your thumb?"

Wood held out his famously smashed left thumb for their silent adulation.

"We just released our first CD. Do you have any advice for us?"

"Advice? Yeah, quit your bitchin'."

"Yeah, that's the name of our band, Kwicherbichin."

A young lady in pig tails and a plaid shirt said, "Cool, he knows our band!"

"No…I said QUIT – YOUR – BITCHING! I've watched you belittle some hardworking lady who is simply trying to make you happy so you can have a good show. You didn't even attempt to speak her language, which is insulting. Believe me, if you never get booked here again it will be because you berated their employee. She has every right to tell management that you're not worth the trouble. So my advice is to either change your attitude or change your band name, because you can't call yourselves Kwicherbichin, then bitch about not having Perrier!"

Humbled, they looked at the ground. One of them summoned the nerve to whisper, "Maybe we should have a band meeting." Wood observed their dynamic, shocked at their poor decision-making skills.

"It's going to be a lot easier for us to change our name than change our attitudes. We should go back to calling ourselves Trippy Longstockings."

"Oh, I like that! Then we can have our Perrier and eat it, too."

Wood couldn't contain himself any longer, "That's not the point!" He paused to gather his thoughts, realizing that he was becoming their impromptu band manager. "Okay, let's start from the beginning. You're not special. None of us are."

"We're not? Dang."

"You should have stopped listening to your mothers years ago. Do any of you speak French?"

They pointed to a shy girl with a brunette bob who had yet to speak, "Candace minored in French."

"Good. While you're in France, Candace does all the communicating with the hotel, the concert venue staff, and the crowd."

"But she's the drummer! She can't talk to the crowd."

"It doesn't matter." Pointing to her, "Candace, you're in charge while the band is in France. Got it?"

Candace beamed at the possibility of finally having some power. She nodded, "I'm ready to step up."

"Excellent. Where are you going after France?"

"Germany."

"Okay, does anyone speak some German?"

Pig tails spoke up, "My dad was stationed there. I understand quite a bit. I'll make it work."

"You're in charge in Germany. You get the idea." Wood felt guilty about giving them a dressing down and wondered what unfortunate alignment of planets brought these brats together. "How did you all meet?"

"Boarding school in Rhode Island."

Sighing at the insurmountable wall they would have to climb, Wood said, "You need a band manager."

"We had one but she always told us to shut the fuck up, so we fired her."

"You need to beg her to take you back."

"Okay, we'll call her tomorrow. Thank you so much for setting us straight, Mr. Wood. Can we be your opening band in the future?"

Without having heard a single note of their music, "I don't know if our sounds really match, but I know the perfect band for you. They are always looking for someone to take on tour. I'll even make a call to their manager for you."

"Really? Who?"

"The Featherdusters."

"You would do that for us? We love them!"

They took the stage with renewed energy. Candace sat at the drums and greeted the crowd, "Bon soir, Paris! Nous sommes Kwicherbichin!"

The lead singer immediately reverted to complaining, "Before we start, can you turn the lights down just a shade."

"A little more."

"More."

"Now up a tad."

"Up."

Pigtails protested, "Now my light is too low."

"Up a little. How do you say 'smidgin' in French?"

Jesse walked up, observing stage side with Wood, who shook his head and recalled the perfect Hoosier expression, "Trying to help them is like watching two monkeys hump a football."

"How's that?"

"Pointless."

***

In the dressing room, Wood confronted Jesse. "Where have you been these last few days? I thought we were going to hang out."

"I think I just needed some time to myself. It's nothing against you."

"Do you have something to tell me? Because if there's anything going on that's going to affect us as a band then I need to know."

"What's the big deal? I'm not keeping anything from you. You're not my father!"

"I was hoping you would be open with me. Who is that guy that went into your room?"

Jesse stared at Wood. His face offered nothing while his mental gears hummed, searching for a plausible answer. "I met him at the nightclub that I told you about."

"Is he your dealer? Because if it's weed or ecstasy, I don't care, but if you're going back to that hard shit I can't deal with that. Rachel and I stuck by you when you had to clean up your life but we're not going down that road again. Whatever is going on, I need to know the truth."

"I get it. I talked to him at that club and he asked if I needed a connection, so I'd be set for the rest of the tour. It's just like you said, some weed and a little X. We did a few lines together but I didn't buy any. I stayed in my room the next day to sleep it off. I'll catch The Louvre and the Eiffel Tower next time we're here. I appreciate your concern, but you don't need to worry."

"Cool. That's all I needed to hear. Anyway, I wrote up this set list. I was thinking for the encore we could do that Hollies tune we talked about."

"Nice! So we start off with Radiohead's 'Creep' then transition to The Hollies?"

"Yep. We'll just do the first verse and switch." Wood sang, "I wish I was special. You're so fuckin' special…BUT, all I need is the air that I breathe and to love you!"

"That's dope. The whole crowd's going to be singing that they're a creep, then we throw the curveball. I love it."

"Should we switch back to Radiohead?"

Jesse considered it for a moment, "Nah, man. Screw those one-hit-wonders. Let's stick with The Hollies."

***

FRÉJUS AMPHITHEATER

August 12, 1998

Côte d'Azur, French Riviera

Jesse sat at the café table outside, looking out over the Mediterranean, the salty morning breeze coming off the coast. A handful of sailboats were anchored nearby. The French Riviera, heaven on earth. When the waiter approached, Jesse said, "Un café, s'il vous plait."

He heard a soft voice to his left, "Not bad. Are you American?" He turned to see a lady in her mid-forties in a light blue summer dress. A Harlequin Romance with Fabio dressed as a pirate, shirt ripped open, rested face down on the table.

"How did you know?"

"The shoes. I can tell where anyone is from by their shoes." A couple walked by, she turned her head to motion toward them and whispered, "Italian." They began speaking Italian and Jesse smiled.

"That's quite a talent. Where are you from?"

"Originally from Alabama. We live in Lyon now. We come down to the Riviera once a year on vacation. My husband and daughter are sleeping in."

"Small world. I'm from Louisiana. I never thought I'd come across Crimson Tide fans in the south of France."

"We're Auburn fans!"

"I stand corrected. War eagle!"

"War eagle all the way, baby! Louisiana, huh? I guess that explains your French."

"I know some Cajun phrases. They probably cringe when they hear me speak."

"Believe me, they appreciate the effort. Just start out in French and they'll usually switch to English, but if you start barking out orders in English, you're gonna get what's comin' to you."

"I'll keep that in mind. I'm Jesse, by the way."

"Wendy. Nice to meet you."

"How did you end up living in France?"

"My husband came here on business a few times. He brought me along to a conference and I was hooked. His company had an opening in Lyon and we never looked back. We go back to Alabama just to make sure they still treat us like second-class citizens, then we come back. We don't have to deal with that here."

"Really? No racism?"

"Actually, I take that back. If I speak French with no accent they think I'm an immigrant from Senegal or Cameroon and I might get rude service. If I add a little Yankee accent they want to be my friend, like they finally get to hang out with Josephine Baker. It's a weird dynamic, but I'll take it."

"It's sad that you have to dumb down your accent to get treated better."

"Colonialism. They all raced around the world sticking flags in the ground and they still wonder why their subjects speak with an accent." She smiled at her own rant. "Sorry. I'll get off my soap box."

"Don't apologize! I'm right there with you. We're all just trying to figure out who we are. Our family is Black and Choctaw. There's probably some French mixed in there, too."

"Don't get me started on heritage. We hired an expert in genealogy and after all this research she came to a dead end in 1821 with an ancestor named 'You'. We were like, 'His name was 'You'?"

Jesse furled his eyebrows, "You?"

"According to the records, the plantation owner died and left the estate to his daughter. She decided to sell off the slaves, but she didn't know their names so she wrote down what she heard them being called. '*You*, pick faster! *You*, fetch me some water!' '*You*, don't even think about touching that gun!' She sold him and wrote 'You' on the Bill of Sale."

Jesse shook his head, "It's a crazy world."

"Yep! So, what are you doing here?"

"I'm in a band. We're playing at the Roman amphitheater tonight with a few local bands. I don't have any tickets on me, but if you write your names on this napkin I'll put you on our guest list."

"Thank you! Our daughter is fifteen. We'll see if we can drag her along. Everything we do is an embarrassment to her so she just stays in the room watching 90210 in French."

"Tell her that Luke Perry came to one of our shows. He was a good guy."

"That ought to get her attention!"

"I hope to meet her and your husband tonight! If you'll excuse me, I need to find my bandmate."

***

Backstage in the dressing room, Wood was pacing nervously. "Remember the Roxy Music video that I had? We're about to play on the same stage. Can you believe that?"

"I know, brother. It's crazy."

Wood tried to calm down by noodling around with an accordion that was hanging on the wall. He handed it to Jesse, who immediately displayed his proficiency.

"I didn't know you played."

"I can get by. If you play piano you pick it up pretty fast."

"Do you know any Cajun tunes? I think people would like it."

"Yeah, I know 'Bayou Teche.' That's a ¾ Waltz in b flat. Pretty straightforward. We used to visit my aunt and uncle out in the middle of nowhere and there were always instruments just sitting around. After a while it just seeps into you. I don't remember the words though."

"That's fine. Let's just start the show playing it for a few minutes to get the crowd going, then we'll transition into She Saw Me Coming."

Jesse was surprised. "I thought you were boycotting that song."

"I've decided to embrace it. Can you explain to the crowd what's it's really about?"

"I can try."

"Maybe we can get them to stop doing that crazy little dance."

"It's the hit of the summer, Wood. I'm telling you, when you got the next Lambada, you just ride the wave instead of trying to hold it back with a broom."

"I guess dancing is never a bad thing."

"That's the spirit."

Someone knocked on the dressing room door. Wood opened it to see Wendy, her husband, and their teenage daughter.

The girl smiled and asked, "You met Luke Perry?"

"Um…who? Oh, the guy from that TV show? Yes, we did. He even took a photo with my thumb!"

Toward the end of the show, Wood said, "I'd like to sing this next song to a good friend of mine. It's called, 'I Believe in You' by Talk Talk. He looked over at Jesse as he sang the words of the slow song.

> Hear it in my spirit
> I've seen heroin for myself
> On the street so young laying wasted
> Enough, ain't it enough, crippled world

A time to sell yourself
A time for passing
Spirit

***

After the show, Wood rented a van and headed for Italy, driving through the night, through Cannes, Nice, the famous casinos of Monaco and into Italy.

After a long silence, Jesse inquired, "Why didn't we just fly to Florence?"

"Because God knows what kind of contraband you have on you."

Jesse shook his head, "It's just airport security. We'll check in our bags and walk to the gate. Unless there's a dog around we're fine. What's the big deal?"

"I don't want to chance it."

FIRENZE ROCKS FESTIVAL

August 15, 1998

Florence, Italy

Wood called down to the front desk and asked them to make an international call to Rachel.

"Hi, Rachel. We made it to Florence with no problems."

"That's great. How was France?"

"It was good, but something is going on with Jesse. I think he's using again. He's been acting strange. I caught him with a drug dealer in Paris. He fessed up to it, but only after I grilled him. He was better in Fréjus though."

"Damn, after everything we went through. Can you put him on the phone?"

"He got another room again so it's harder to track him down. He totally ditched me in Paris."

"Poor baby. You had to finish all those bottles of wine by yourself and whatever floozy you hooked up with. Anyway, the record is selling like crazy and they want to do an interview with you. A reporter is going to meet you in the lobby at 3:00 this afternoon. Her name is Alessandra."

Wood closed his eyes, "What is she going to ask me?"

"How should I know? I didn't tell her that anything was off limits, but she'll probably ask about the hit song - this is a chance to explain what it really means. This is a good thing, like we talked about."

"Did you tell her that I'm camera shy?"

"Yes, I did. She said not to worry. She was cool."

***

The first thing Wood saw when the elevator doors opened to the lobby was a TV crew setting up lights and microphones. A beautiful woman, inexplicably wearing a black leather jacket in the summer, sat at a table looking over her notes. Maybe they were filming a TV commercial. He could always sit in the café and wait until the reporter showed up.

Their eyes met and she jumped up, walking towards him quickly, holding out both hands. Her eyes were dark pools that stared straight into one's soul, detecting both truths and lies, the last kind of person he wanted grilling him with questions. He turned around to escape into the elevator. The doors had closed and she was upon him. "Mr. Driftwood, thank you for the interview. Very nice to meet you. My name is Alessandra Montieri from Rai TV."

"How do you do? What's with the cameras? I thought this was a magazine interview."

She talked as she gripped his arm and pulled him to his seat, the way a mother stealthily guides an unruly child through a church of onlookers. Assistants plastered his face with makeup as she made small talk to ease his worries, gesturing to the statues and plants in the lobby in the hopes that a glimpse of Florentine beauty would keep him from running away. A man placed a device in front of his face to adjust the glaring lights.

Wood gestured to the TV camera, "Is that on?"

"No, don't worry."

"Because the little red light is on."

"So we will speak in English then they will add Italian letters to the bottom later on."

She began speaking to the camera. He recognized some of the Italian and all of the English words that she threw in for good measure, like "Cantante di The Featherdusters," "She Saw Me Coming," "summer hit," and "DJ."

"So, Driftwood. Your hit song is huge here in Italia, especially in dance clubs. They even have a little dance. How this success make you feel?"

He paused and gathered himself, sitting up straight, feigning a half-smile. "Well, it has been a surprise, to say the least. The song came out years ago in the US and we recently added it to a compilation CD here in Europe. I want to be clear that the song is not about...we have an expression, like if you buy a car and they trick you we will say that they saw you coming. This song is about a woman who tricked me. So...she saw me coming."

"She trick you into being a masturbatore?"

He could feel his face becoming hot as he stammered for an answer, "No, she didn't even trick me. I was just naïve and sad when I wrote the song, but I'm happy that it's a hit."

She cocked her head sideways and tried a different angle, "There was a recent article by a feminista professor who say you are a sexist because the song is only about male sexuality and ignores the woman's needs."

"It's not about sexuality at all! I mean, it's about a relationship, but it's all a big misunderstanding."

"The Vatican is calling for the song to be banned from Italian radio. Did you know that?"

"The Vatican knows the song?"

"Yes, but some priests love it, so it has caused a...come se dice, a controversy."

"Well, I can understand why the priests like it on many levels." He needed to exit this interview as smoothly as possible. "Thank you so much for your time. I need to warm up for the show. Devo riscaldarmi."

Alessandra looked at the camera. "Driftwood has to..." she winked, and added finger quotations, "warm up! Hmmm...che cosa significa?"

Wood stood up, removed the lavalier microphone from his collar, wiped down his face with a towel and retreated through a corridor of paparazzi flashbulbs, jumping into an elevator as the doors were closing.

Wood jogged down the hall and knocked on Jesse's door, who opened it wearing boxers and an immense towel folded around his head. Rubbing lotion on his arms and torso, he sighed, "Dude, I have *never* had lotion like this. You should try it. It's called Borghese Roma. Very chic."

Wood looked down the hall and closed the door, locking it behind him. He paced the floor, breathing heavily. He observed Jesse's arms, looking for needle marks, and saw none.

"Don't ever become famous here, Jesse! Seriously, be careful what you wish for."

Jesse was undeterred from his beauty regimen, rubbing the lotion liberally on his cheeks, "I mean, this lotion is more than age-defying. It's life-affirming."

Maybe lotion would help calm his nerves. Wood held out his hand, "Okay, I'll try some."

"Nah, man, nevermind. I don't have very much and you don't need it."

"I get ashy, too. You just can't see it, you racist bastard. Gimme the goddamned lotion!"

Jesse raised his eyebrows and spoke in a calm voice. "Wood, I don't know what kind of stress you're under, but you do not need to raise your voice at me. Let's not forget which one of us knows how to throw a punch." Jesse held out the lotion with an open hand.

Rubbing lotion on his face, "Sorry. I just got ambushed by a TV crew. Rachel said I would be safe. Most people don't even know what I look like and now I'm going to be on TV, a feminist professor is talking smack, the Vatican wants me banned. Well, not the priests who sneak off to the goddamned clubs, but the Pope does!"

"If the Vatican is after you then maybe you should stop taking the Lord's name in vain." Jesse allowed some silence to calm Wood's nerves, if only slightly, before placing his hand on his shoulder. "Everything will turn out fine. Now go to your room and get ready for the show. They're sending a shuttle to take us to the festival."

***

They sat in the shuttle behind the hotel while the driver transferred their gear to the back. Getting out, Wood said, "I forgot something in my room." He went to the front desk and implored the concierge to let him into Jesse's room.

The concierge smiled, calling on his mastery in the delivery of unfortunate news. "Mr. Driftwood. You know I am not allowed to let you enter another guest's room."

"Mi dispiace, I completely understand, but Jesse forgot our microphones and effects pedals in his room. He already went to the festival." He slipped the concierge a folded bill and whispered. "E molto importante."

The concierge looked at the bill and smiled, "Just this once."

Wood entered Jesse's room while the concierge waited outside. He searched through Jesse's bags looking for drugs, paraphernalia, anything to confirm his suspicions. He didn't want to go through immigration with Jesse and a bag full of drugs.

He found a stack of Polaroid photos, adding credence to Jesse's secrecy in Paris. The first featured the man he saw entering Jesse's room. He was seated across a café table, smiling. Innocent enough. The next photo showed Jesse wearing a French beret and holding a baguette. Other photos, taken by passersby, showed Jesse and the man kissing in front of the Eiffel Tower, then hugging on the observation deck overlooking Paris. The most damning photo featured them in a park, the man seated on the grass while Jesse rested his head on his lap with a rose in his mouth. An empty bottle of wine, two glasses, and a half-enjoyed wheel of cheese were strewn next to them on a picnic blanket.

***

Wood and Jesse took the stage with the drummer and bass player who had given brief auditions, proving they knew the set list. They started with "Take Me to the Trains," always a strong song to kick off a gig. The crowd cheered and danced, some waving immense flags of the Union Jack, the Italian flag, and a variety of football club banners. "Palace" came off well and they transitioned into "Drenched." The crowd grew restless as they waited for the only Driftwood song they knew. As the song ended, Wood cut to the chase.

"There's been a lot of talk about this next song. Maybe, maybe too much talk. This song is not a masturbation song. This song is She Saw Me Coming!"

The song started off with a driving snare and kick drum rhythm, hauntingly similar to Sunday Bloody Sunday.

The crowd cheered and continued air beating as Jesse did his best Bono impersonation, holding up a huge ACF Fiorentina football flag passed to him from the crowd. Wood and Jesse looked at each other, shook their heads, and laughed. Don't try to hold back the ocean. Just ride the wave.

SECTION 3: SPREAD EAGLE TO THE SKY

THE PLAN

Wood and Jesse met with Rachel at a bar in Louisville to debrief the European Tour and discuss next steps. Wood gave a brief summary of the whirlwind that was Europe, "Aside from getting beat up in Hull it was great. Nice people, espionage, Santa Barbara, museums, great wine and food."

Jesse tapped his finger on Rachel's yellow legal pad, "Lotion."

Rachel wrote "spies," "SB?," and "lotion" in her band meeting minutes. She discussed the financials of the tour. "Hull was a disaster, but Estonia more than made up for it and your expenses were covered. Amsterdam, Paris, and Fréjus sold well, and the festival in Florence was huge. Even the older albums started selling more after that gig. Great job, boys. So now we need to talk about what's next. I think if you can get an album out in the next few months it would sell."

Wood said, "Sounds good. Which studio should we use?"

"Here's my plan. I have a friend who has a house for rent with two bedrooms and a big den right here in Louisville. The tenants just bailed on him so we can get it cheap. You can set up your equipment in the den and write new songs. I know the guy who runs Downtown Recording Studios. He'll give us a deal if we buy blocks of hours and it comes with a great engineer. You can write a few songs, record them, then do some gigs to see the crowd's reaction. Write, record, gig. Rinse and repeat. What do you think?"

Jesse deferred to Wood, who thought it over and replied, "That could work. We'd have to move down here for a while, but we'd finally all be together."

Jesse said, "It might save us time in the long run to do it that way. There are plenty of studio musicians around here, right?"

Rachel smiled, "Oh yeah, and I know all of them. Don't worry, I won't call them if they're not cool."

Wood raised his Jack and Coke, "To the next album."

DO YOU REALLY WANT TO HURT ME?

Jesse and Wood settled into their new Louisville digs. It was an old ranch style house with a long hallway, nothing special but offering everything they needed. Jesse brought his TV from Indy and carried it triumphantly to his new bedroom. He packed the kitchen with his foods of choice, adding blue painter tape to delineate his territory on each shelf. One in particular provided evidence of his Louisiana roots – chicory coffee, pralines, bacon and pralines, tabasco sauce, and an assortment of Zapp's chips. As Wood looked through them he read increasingly hostile messages written with a Sharpie: "Jesse's," "Not Wood's," and "Don't even think of it!"

Wood yelled down the hall, "Hey, man, you don't need to write messages on your weird-ass southern snacks when we're the only ones here! I think we know who brought the blackened catfish seasoned pork cracklins."

"If you were from a big family you'd understand! I'm watching Santa Barbara. Leave me alone."

Wood walked down the hall to Jesse's new bedroom. "Where did you find the video?"

"Blockbuster. Just one more episode and then we can jam. Eden has amnesia." Once crisis in Santa Barbara was averted for another day, Jesse ejected the VHS and switched to MTV. They watched Culture Club's Do You Really Want to Hurt Me. The video started with Boy George in a courtroom with a gallery of people in black face watching him plead his case.

"We should cover that song someday. Maybe leave out the black face."

***

115

Within a few days they had written two songs. The lyrics weren't completed but they could record those tracks later. Having learned from the mistakes of past albums, Wood bought a whiteboard and drew a simple grid with rows for working song titles and vertical columns to check off verse, chorus, bridge, solo, and lyrics. If a song didn't contain an element he wrote an X. Without this simple system they would end up with 20 half-completed songs, cost overruns, and infighting.

CHAMPAGNE MANE

Downtown Recording Studio, Louisville, Kentucky

They brought some basic equipment down to the studio to hear how it sounded, meet the engineer, and talk about their approach to the album. They plugged in and tested mic levels. The house drums and keyboard sounded great. Jesse took a polaroid of the soundboard to replicate it each time they came back.

As Wood and Jesse were packing up, they were greeted by the Champagne Mane entourage. A lady with sandy blonde dreads came in and began preparing the space for their arrival, removing any trace of cigarettes, meat, sodas, alcohol, drugs, and impurities. Other followers brought in Moroccan rugs, incense, sage, water, an air purification machine, hairbrushes for each table, and enough lotion for a bordello.

The door opened with the late afternoon sun silhouetting the three musicians, setting a Biblical entrance with shards of light surrounding their statuesque bodies as they entered the studio. They wore loosely fitting white linen shirts and trousers, landing just below their knees for maximized freedom of movement. Their trademark hair, so perfect, smooth, and long fell down to their waist. Hemp necklaces, woven bracelets and sandals completed the ensemble. They glided in silence.

Jesse stood in awe of the vision, "Do you see it, too?"

Wood was less impressed and continued packing, glancing over periodically.

Their lead singer Johann, pronounced, "yo-HAHN" approached. "Nice to meet you, Driftwood. How's the album coming along?"

"You can call me Wood. The album is coming together nicely, thanks. This is my bandmate, Jesse."

"Oh, we know all about Jesse. The musical genius. It's nice to finally meet you."

Jesse spoke nervously, almost inaudibly, "How are you, sir?"

Lincoln Theatre

September 18, 1998

Columbus, Ohio

"Wake up, butter cup." Jesse waved an immense breakfast burrito under Wood's nose, like smelling salts, rousing him from his post-gig slumber. It was good to be back in the US, where life was more predictable, even when it was bad.

First sniffing, then opening his eyes slowly, Wood smiled, "I don't deserve you, man. Thanks."

"No worries. There's coffee over on the table. We need to hit the road soon if we're going to beat the traffic to Cincinnati."

"Now *this* is a burrito. If the Aztecs had given Cortez and the conquistadors one of these, they would have been friends."

Jesse admired the ceiling as he ate, "I suppose we'll never know. By the way, how are we doing on cash?"

Wood checked his wallet and dropped his head in shame, "I can't believe I did it again."

"You ran up a tab at the bar and left your credit card there again? How many times are you going to do that, Wood? That's why I pay with cash. No fuss, no muss."

"Damn. I'm gonna head over to the club and get my card. I'll be back soon."

***

The morning breeze and sunshine felt refreshing and Wood tried to recall the last time he had been in an old downtown this early in the morning, now that he and Jesse had transitioned their lives to a graveyard shift. The coffee tasted perfect with just the right amount of bite. Life was good. Last night's gig went smoothly. It was an appreciative crowd with good vibes. They played the two new songs, Estonia, Estonia, and Lives Drag On. They didn't include any of their trademark antics, like sewing a coat onstage. Still, it was more than most bands gave, and Wood stuck around to sign autographs and take photos of people and his smashed thumb. Jesse was happy to pose with fans. The club owner was disappointed that they hadn't included their trademark antics during the encore and said he would discuss the payment with Rachel. Wood ignored him, making a mental note that the owner was particularly obnoxious. They'd never play there again if he stiffed them.

As he approached the entrance to the club Wood paused, sensing something was not right. He felt the cold burn of an ice cube on his neck. Just as he began to turn, he felt the world convulsing, shaking uncontrollably with loud clicking noises. He fell to the ground as his body vibrated and he was unable to speak, the scalding coffee seeped under his cheek and he felt warm piss fill his jeans. Everything went black as he returned to a deep slumber on the cold sidewalk.

The trucker put down the cattle prod, picked up Wood's limp body, and hoisted it onto a cattle hook. He slammed down the door and returned to the cab of the 18-wheeler. "Sweet Pea, this is Nightcrawler."

"Hey there, Nightcrawler darlin'! Whatcha got for me?"

"The Push Pop is in the ice box."

"Roger that! Thanks for helping us out. We appreciate it."

"Anything for you, baby."

"Quit trying to butter me up with your sweet talk."

"Can't blame an old Okie for tryin'. By the by, thanks for lending me this book. It's great."

"Chicken Soup for the Trucker's Soul. They got one o' those books for everything."

"I guess so. Anyhoo, you got any special requests for Push Pop?"

"Now that you mention it, this guy was a complete prick. He called me yelling this morning because the band didn't do their usual encore. He called me a 'dumb bitch' and said he wasn't gonna pay!"

"Oh hell no. That ain't gonna fly. I'll let him cool down for a while with his new bovine friends then give him a little more proddin'. How's that?"

"You're after this girl's heart. Let me know how it goes, Nightcrawler!"

"Roger that, Sweet Pea."

Nightcrawler read Chicken Soup for the Trucker's Soul for 45 minutes then went back to check on Push Pop. He pulled up the door. Wood was dangling between two carcasses, drooling. His tears had turned to ice, eyes closed, his skin blue-white and translucent. Was he dead? Nightcrawler pushed the cattle prod against his body, nudging him to see if he was still alive. Wood opened his eyes and looked over, squinting.

Nightcrawler said, "You shouldn't be calling a nice lady a bitch, ya know. You need to pay for your sins. I'm gonna shock your sorry ass like the animal you are."

Wood gathered the last remnants of strength and yelled, "I am not an animal! I am a man!"

Startled, Nightcrawler closed the door, hearing the muffled, defiant declaration behind him,

"I...AM...DRIFTWOoooooooD!!!"

***

Nightcrawler called out in a voice that carried much less bravado than before, "Uh…Sweet Pea. You there?"

"What's up, Nightcrawler?"

"Yeah, ummm…what does this guy look like?"

"I don't know. I've only talked with him on the phone. Why?"

"Cuz this dude's rambling like John Merrick back there, giving me some Elephant Man speech. Are you sure we got the right guy?"

"That's because his brain is scrambled. Let me call Wood and Jesse to find out what this prick looks like. Sit tight till I figure out what's going on."

Back at the hotel room, Jesse picked up the phone. "Hey Rachel, Wood needs to get his ass back here so we can hit the road."

"He's not there?"

"Nah, he went back to the club to get his credit card."

"Oh shit!"

Jesse heard her scream into the CB, "Nightcrawler, abort mission. ABORT MISSION!"

By the time Nightcrawler had taken down Wood's limp body and replaced him with the drooling club owner, Jesse had sprinted to the club. He used his sweater to wipe away Wood's tears and drool, breathing onto his hands and massaging his ears. "It's okay, buddy. Jesse's here. Everything's gonna be alright. I'm gonna get you into the sunlight so you can thaw out, okay?" He picked him up and carried him to a bench where Wood shivered in silence. Jesse entered the club, walked behind the bar, and found the credit card for The Thurston Underwood Family Trust.

***

Jesse drove with the heater on full blast with Wood lying down in the backseat. Margaret licked his face and whimpered as Wood stroked her head, whispering to her as they drove through the countryside. Jesse checked them into the hotel and helped Wood to the bed. Margaret curled up at his feet and looked to Jesse for help. "You two get some rest. I'm

120

going to the club to meet with the backing musicians. Don't worry. I got it covered."

***

YOU GOTTA HAVE FAITH

Bogart's

September 19, 1998

Cincinnati, Ohio

"Hey, everyone. I'm Jesse. We met the last time we came through town. I appreciate you helping us with this gig. I'm gonna level with you. Tonight's going to be a challenge because Wood is feeling…under the weather."

"What's wrong with him?" asked Fernando, the local drummer.

"He's got a touch of the flu and he has a horrible sore throat so I'll be doing the singing. Tonight is about you, so when I motion for you to solo, just go for it. If you get confused, play *louder*, not softer. Here's the set list. I scratched off the new songs so we're only playing songs that you and the crowd already know. I added a few of my own tunes toward the end with the chord progressions. We'll practice those today. How does that sound?"

The musicians nodded as they looked over the charts, trying to absorb the structure of Jesse's songs at the end of the set. With a few stops and starts, the songs came together and they began to groove in a unified sound. Confidence established, they headed to the club for some drinks while Jesse went to check on Wood and take a short nap.

***

Jesse shined that night, feeling the pressure to give the crowd a great experience despite the obvious omission of Wood as the leader. It helped that the backing musicians were solid, giving Jesse room to work the crowd and pull attention away from Wood, who sat on a barstool, strumming listlessly at the side of the stage, partially obscured by a stack of amps.

Feeling the need to come clean with the audience, Jesse said, "Now you might be wondering why I'm singing more than I usually do. That's because Mr. Driftwood himself is still recovering from a bug he caught. We're lucky to have him on the stage and we didn't want to cancel the show at the last minute, so we feel truly blessed that you're being so understanding."

A drunk to the right of the stage, "Ah come on man, that's bullshit!"

"What, you've never been sick before? This is a miraculous night, ladies and gentlemen. We have a man here who has never been sick!" The crowd laughed at the man, who eventually cracked a smile and ceased his heckling. "You may not know this, but I write songs myself and we're gonna drop a few of them on you tonight."

Jesse carried the band along, making sure to show them what he was playing and keeping it simple as they glanced at the chord changes. The songs were slower and more bluesy than the standard Driftwood tunes, sometimes switching to minor keys to add a dark sensibility. He motioned for the band to bring it down, pausing briefly for the effect that silence brings, then exploded into a wailing solo with chorus and distortion pedals screaming through the sound system. The crowd cheered and raised their hands in approval while Jesse soloed on his sunburst Les Paul. Jesse turned around and fell backward onto the crowd, soloing as they moved him around. With a final push he was back on the stage as the audience went crazy. Wood sat watching without playing along, unable to fully grasp what was happening.

Jesse's third song ended and he thanked the crowd. "You're the first crowd to ever hear those jams and we appreciate the support." He wasn't sure exactly how long they'd been playing, but sensed that they needed to add substantial time to the show if they wanted to get paid.

"Now let's get a funky groove going. Give me a Bo Diddley beat and we'll have some fun." The drummer leaned into the 3-2 clave Afro-Cuban rhythm and the rest of the band followed Jesse's lead as he turned around to show them the chords.

"Did you know we could play a bunch of songs just off this beat alone. I need you to sing along with me."

For the next 20 minutes the Diddley jam session transitioned through a number of famous songs, speeding up every few minutes. Buddy Holly and the Crickets' "Not Fade Away" led to "Willie and the Hand Jive," followed by the crowd chanting, "I Want Candy!"

"Y'all are gonna put me out of a job! 'I Want Candy' was written by The Strangeloves back in the day. Bow Wow Wow did a great cover!"

After an extended round of solos from guitar to keyboards and back, they shifted to "Desire" by U2 and finally "Faith." The crowd sang and cheered as Jesse turned around and shook his booty for them like George Michael. "Cuz you gotta have faith, faith, faith!" For the last hour, most of the crowd had forgotten that Wood was there. The energy changed as he slowly ambled to the edge of the stage, standing in front of Jesse, and smiling down over the crowd. Jesse looked uncomfortable for a moment, as if he'd been caught doing something wrong, then smiled and played along with Wood. The Bo Diddley jam took a full minute to come to a triumphant end as Fernando launched a psychotic, Muppet-inspired assault on Zildjian cymbals and double bass drums.

After the gig, Wood mumbled "Good job" to the backup musicians, packed his gear without looking at Jesse, and took a taxi back to the hotel. The club owner thanked Jesse for turning a difficult situation into a memorable event, handing over the envelope, and patting him on the back. "The show must go on! Fucking A, man. You're welcome back here anytime."

Jesse smiled, "Thank you. Listen, the rest of the band really saved us tonight. Can we do anything special for them?"

"Yeah, sure. Here are some drink and meal coupons. Great job! I hope Wood starts feeling better soon."

Jesse took some of the cash out of the envelope and passed it out to the musicians along with the coupons. "I can't thank you enough for tonight. You're all life savers, truly." As he was giving his last hug, he felt a hand on his shoulder. He turned around to see a man in a black leather jacket holding out his hand to greet him.

"Hi Jesse, I don't think we've formally met. I'm Tommy from…"

"I know who you are. How are The Featherdusters these days?"

"The group is on a hiatus. I'm a record producer now. Listen, I was blown away by your songs. We need to talk about your future."

Jesse looked around to make sure Wood had left. "Sure, let's talk."

ELECTRIC KOOL-AID

The next evening, Jesse found two tabs of LSD in a Stone Roses CD case.

"Whoa, I forgot I had these. Wanna trip?"

"I don't know. They might not work anymore."

"Come on! Let's do this." Jesse handed a tab to Wood and put the other in his mouth. They watched TV for a while in silence.

"I don't think it's working." Wood opened the hotel's mini fridge to grab a tiny bottle of Jack and immediately slammed the door before it slimed out into the room. "There's an octopus in there."

Jesse opened the door and grabbed a bottle of water for Wood, holding the door open. "See, there's no octopus. I think water would be a better choice for you tonight." He returned the mini bottle of Jack to the fridge.

They watched the Ren and Stimpy episode where they built a hair ball factory. Stimpy licked all of the fur off of his body, creating a hair ball in his stomach, then spat it out onto a conveyor belt where Ren stamped it "Grade A." Huge dollar signs filled his eyes as their product moved down the line. Eventually, Stimpy ran out of hair and resorted to licking Ren. Finally, with no other options, he licked the hair from a hillbilly's back, who giggled, "That feels purdy." By now Wood and Jesse were laughing so hard their stomach muscles hurt. "I'm gonna get six-pack abs from watching this show!"

They watched another episode about the duo's 36-year mission across the universe to the crab nebula. Both Ren and Stimpy succumbed to the effects of space madness. Wood looked over and saw tears streaming down Jesse's face.

"What's wrong, Jesse?"

"I just realized that we're Ren and Stimpy. I'm Stimpy, the innocent, misunderstood fool. You're Ren, devising evil plans and draggin' me all over the universe."

Wood tried to reassure him. "Hey, I don't have evil plans. You're innocent, brother. You're pure because you haven't been screwed up by the world yet, but you're not a fool. We're both trippin' on acid and it's going to mess with our minds for a few hours. Just breathe and stay calm."

"Sorry, man."

"It's cool. Let's watch something else."

Wood turned the channel to MTV. 120 minutes was on and PJ Harvey was being interviewed.

Wood smiled, "I met her backstage at a festival when I was with The Featherdusters. She thought I was a roadie."

"You met PJ Harvey? What was she like?"

"She was…shy. Very nice. I told her that she was one of the greats of all time. She thought I was trying to hit on her until I mentioned specific songs from the Dry album, like Happy and Bleeding. I said I would have covered Hair but it's too hard to play! Then she warmed up. We only talked for a few minutes before I had to go on. I don't think she'd remember me."

Back from a commercial, the VJ said, "Now we're gonna check out the groundbreaking new video from Champagne Mane. They partnered with controversial film director Pietro DeMarini. This was shot in one take on the island of Ibiza, Spain."

Jesse pointed to the screen and shouted, "We just met those dudes!"

The black and white video started with fog on a beach. In slow motion, three jogging figures emerged from the fog, drifting in and out of focus as the music started, wearing the same white outfits they wore at the studio just hours before. They ran as the sun began breaking through the fog, faster and faster down the pristine beach. By now the music was well into the first verse of the song, but Johann did not mouth the words. They continued running, smiling triumphantly as their perfect blond hair trailed behind them in the sea breezes. There were no close-up shots, just one long take with the camera leading them down the beach.

Wood couldn't take it anymore, "Is this a music video or a shampoo commercial?!"

As the song reached the chorus, three majestic white stallions burst from the fog behind the band, galloping effortlessly until they caught up. The stallions forged ahead, the band laughed and sprinted faster until they reached them, matching the horses, stride for stride. As the song reached the bridge, the video transitioned from black and white to full color, the life-giving Mediterranean sun drenching man and beast uniformly. The band and stallions sprinted in slow motion together, as if they could run for hours. Just as the guitar solo began, a massive wave crashed against a rock, exploding gloriously over them as they ran through the bubbly surf. Johann laughed, shaking his head back and forth in an exaltation of life, in crystalline harmony with nature. Finally, the three bandmates grabbed the blonde mane of each stallion, and, without missing a stride, pulled themselves up onto the beasts, riding bareback as their supple hair flowed past the hind quarters. The video slowly returned to black and white as the steeds, now ridden by Champagne Mane, disappeared into another fog bank. The music credits appeared on the screen as the video faded to black.

Wood and Jesse sat staring at the TV in shock. Jesse shook his head. "That's the most incredible music video I've ever seen. The horses ran past them, but the band caught up to them like it was nothing, then they conquered them in the end…man over nature, like Norse gods."

Wood downplayed what he witnessed, "I liked the cinematography, but I'll take Jacqueline Smith massaging Wella Balsam into her hair any day."

Jesse's frustration spilled over, "Why are you so jealous of Champagne Mane?! They shot that video in one take! Jesus, can't you give them credit for that? And they ran forever without breaking a sweat! Even their name is perfect. If you showed that video to a thousand people and asked them to come up with a name for this new band, there is only one answer they would submit, over and over again."

"Silkience?"

"CHAMPAGNE MANE!"

Wood sighed in frustration. "Let's go for a walk. I'm tripping hard and these walls are closing in on me."

***

They walked around downtown Louisville until they happened upon a temporary carnival in a parking lot. Wood bought some tokens from a carnie. They avoided The Zipper, convinced that being catapulted through the night while locked in a cage might be an LSD nightmare from which they may never recover. The lights and noise of the rides and attractions calmed Jesse's mind, giving him a focal point outside of his racing thoughts.

"Can you hear the lights, Wood?"

"See the lights? Sure."

"No, I can hear the lights. They sound like God."

They challenged each other to the basketball shooting game. Wood won handily. Arriving at the knockout punch game, Jesse encouraged Wood to give it a try. "Alright, let's see if you remember your boxing lesson from Hull. You got this."

Wood planted his feet in an athletic stance and exhaled. He repeated the entire routine Jesse had taught him in the hotel room, whispering, "Duck, body shot, stand up, BAM!" The machine rattled and sang as it tallied its verdict. The screen read, "Welterweight. Not bad!"

Jesse laughed, "Check out Wood! That was a solid punch."

"I had a great coach. Alright, show me how it's done." He put a token in the slot.

Jesse glanced over at Wood and gave a wry smile. In a split second the full weight of his body thrust forward violently, his hips whipping to the left, pulling his torso through the air. His right fist connected flush with the bag as he let out a grunt, sending the machine into a frenzy, blaring a variety of honks, dings, and whistles before declaring:

"HEAVYWEIGHT!"

Wood shook his head, in awe of the eruption of brutality he had just witnessed, generated from someone much smaller than he. "I'll bet that dude in Hull is still playing with blocks after you clocked him."

"I'm not proud of my violence. I'm a peaceful warrior."

***

The noise and energy subsided as they walked away from the carnival and sat on a park bench along the river. Their giggles now gone, they settled into a pure and honest conversation, their subconscious on full display, unmoored from fears of judgment.

Jesse began, "Sometimes I feel like I'm the odd man out. You and Rachel are always on the same page and I'm just along for the ride."

"Interesting. Rachel and I are rarely on the same page when we start, but we tend to get there. We don't agree on everything."

"Give me an example."

Wood thought for a moment. "I don't think it's a good idea for us to send thousands of volts through someone's body then hang them in a refrigerated truck next to beef carcasses because they didn't pay. I honestly thought I was going to die when it happened to me. We don't agree on that anymore."

"Do you believe in karma?"

"I do now. How 'bout you?"

"Oh yeah. One time my sister got her car broken into and my family said, 'Don't worry, karma will get 'em!' I said, 'Maybe that *was* the karma. Shauna, you must have jacked someone over a while back and someone broke into your car to restore order to the universe." Jesse formed a large circle with his finger. A streetlight reflected off his fingertip, the circle hovered in the air for their enjoyment. "Karma wheel complete! Shauna didn't talk to me for a week after I said that."

"See, nobody wants the truth. You were probably right though. Here's some truth for ya. I'm attracted to Rachel. I just don't want to ruin everything we've built."

"It's pretty obvious."

"That I'm attracted to her?"

"Yeah, and that she loves you. Just go with it. If you end up together you can always hire someone else. It's a lot easier to find a manager than a soulmate."

"I don't know! Good managers don't grow on trees!" Wood smiled and looked out over the water. "Love is complicated."

"Tell me about it. I'm gay." Jesse sat mortified at the phrase that had slipped out.

Wood looked over at Jesse, "Yeah, I know."

"You know?!"

"Yeah, sure. But it's none of my business. I'm just confused because I've seen you with so many women. What was all that with Gina at the prison? And that time in Denver when they only had a room with one bed and you were getting' down with some waitress while I was trying to sleep next to you."

Jesse laughed. "The next morning you asked if it was considered a threesome if you were just staring at the wall, waiting for us to finish."

"One of many scars I carry."

Jesse sighed and looked up at the stars, "I guess I'm bi."

"It's cool. Jimi Hendrix was bi."

Jesse was shocked, "Really?"

"It's right there in the song, 'Excuse me while I kiss this guy.'"

"I thought it was 'kiss the sky.'"

"I just made that up. He wasn't bi."

Jesse looked out over the river. "I ended up meeting this amazing dude in Paris named Matthieu. He showed me around the city. I'll never forget it."

"Why did you tell me he was a drug dealer?"

"Because I knew you were suspicious."

"So you'd rather Rachel and I think you're doing heroin than think you're gay."

"Well…yeah. That's the world we live in."

"Society is changing fast, Jesse. I never mentioned anything to Rachel because, again, it's not our business, but you know she wouldn't care."

Jesse threw his hands in the air, "Now I feel duped!"

"Why?"

"I went years wondering if I was gay. Once I accepted it, I went years feeling embarrassed and scared. I thought people like you and Rachel would turn on me."

Wood whispered to himself, "When you let someone be who they are, you let them become who they're meant to be."

Jesse thought about it. "Say that again."

Wood repeated his realization.

"That's a song right there. You should work on it."

"I'll try to remember it."

Jesse stood and paced around for a moment, conscious of what he was about to say. He stammered in a low voice, "Speaking of the band, I'm thinking of going solo."

There was a long silence. Wood sighed and looked up to the stars.

"Did you hear me?"

"I heard you. How long have you been thinking of this?"

"It's always been my dream. Doesn't every kid think of being a rock star at some point?"

"Don't fuck with me. How long?"

"Some things have happened in the last few months that made me reevaluate my life. Musically, I know I have what it takes, but I haven't had the confidence. That gig we did after you got shocked changed everything. I played a few of my own songs and the crowd was into it. *Really* into it. I was interacting with them and being the front man. We got paid in full and I gave some of the money to the backing musicians. Rachel jumped all over my ass about it. That fucking gig would have been cancelled if it wasn't for me. Cancelled! All I wanted to hear was two words – 'Thank you.' I never heard it from either of you. I realized that if you and Rachel didn't appreciate me after something like that, you're never going to. I'm just your employee."

"Sorry. I was still recovering from the refrigerator truck experience."

Jesse continued, "When I spent that time in Paris with Matthieu, I saw another world. He introduced me to some of his friends and I was treated as an equal. I could carve out a life for myself in a place like that."

Wood offered a futile rebuttal, "You're dreaming of a new life after spending a few days in a touristy city. It's not that simple, Jesse. You're not thinking of all the risk that comes along with it. After that nightmare in Hull when we didn't get paid, who do you think ate that loss? You just moved on to the next gig while I had to argue numbers with Rachel. Or the SPCA following my ass around. Was your name on those protest signs? The evening news was all over it, dragging my name through the mud." Wood was no longer speaking to Jesse, but thinking aloud. Kipling seemed appropriate. "To hear your words, twisted by knaves to make a trap for fools."

"What are you talking about?"

"Jesse, you're only thinking of the cool stuff, but it's a business. You would need someone to manage you, and don't even think about asking Rachel."

"I already got that worked out." This was the part of the conversation Jesse hoped he could avoid.

"You have a manager lined up? Who?"

Jesse closed his eyes and whispered, "Tommy."

Wood's mind raced, trying to remember all the Tommys he knew. "Not Tommy from The Featherdusters."

Jesse opened his eyes and stared at Wood, expressionless.

Shaking his head, "Well, that's just perfect! I thought this was about chasing your dreams or making your own money. It's about sticking a knife in my back, nothing more." Wood stood up, slapped his thighs, and began walking back to the hotel. After a few paces he turned around and smiled, "You're about to find out what that dude is all about. We're all just satellites that Tommy uses and now he's pulled you into his orbit. When all this blows up in your face I won't rub it in. I'll just wonder why you didn't listen to me."

***

Jesse didn't come back to the house that night. Wood called Rachel in the morning and broke the news. She was stunned and thought of ways to change Jesse's mind. "I'm pretty sure I thanked him for the Cincinnati gig. Maybe I didn't. Shit."

"We were tripping on acid so the whole night was strange. Maybe he was hallucinating or just dreaming out loud, but I could tell that he'd been thinking about it for a long time."

"Well, you've written your other albums by yourself. You can do it again."

"Sure, but we still have that gig in Lexington in a few days. How do we track him down?"

"He doesn't know anyone in Louisville except us. We'll just have to wait for him to turn up. Don't go anywhere in case he comes home."

***

Jesse had walked around Louisville all night, eventually settling in a diner until the waitress said she was topping off his coffee for the last time. As the city came to life he recognized the neighborhood and found his way to the recording studio. When he walked in he looked disheveled. Champagne Mane was playing and Jesse observed from the booth. They were surprised to see him and smiled. After the song was finished, Johann called him in and gave him a hug.

"It's you! I think the universe is speaking to us."

Jesse smiled, "I saw your video that was shot on Ibiza. I was blown away."

"Yeah, we had fun shooting that. We were just saying that it would be great to have you add a guitar solo to a song that we've been working on."

"The song I was just listening to?"

"No, a different one. We don't have a name for it yet." He called to the engineer, "Can you pull up the one from last night?"

They sat on a sofa and listened to the song. Johann explained the different parts to him. Jesse nodded, easily grasping the structure and feel of the song.

"What are the lyrics about?"

"A little girl who wakes up all alone on a boat that's floating down the river."

"Like rapids?"

"No, slow like The Mississippi, but with a strong current. So she has to decide if she's going to enjoy it or try to get to the shore. Either way, there's no going back."

"Interesting."

"So this is where you would come in. It's not crazy long before it comes back to the chorus."

"Yeah, I got this. Can I borrow a guitar?"

"We've got a Telecaster, a Les Paul, and a 335."

Jesse picked up the Gibson hollow-body. "I've never owned a 335. I'll bet the solo would sound warm on this. Yeah, that could work."

"Go for it!"

The engineer played the song a few times so Jesse could practice, not telling him he was already recording.

He played a sparse, bluesy solo that would accompany a confused little girl floating ceaselessly into an unknown future. There was a distinct moment when he bent the strings to sound like a high voice asking, "Why me?" then announced, "Okay, man, I'm ready to record."

The engineer smiled and spoke through the intercom, "I think we already got it. You made that thing talk." The engineer played the song with the solo over the speakers. Johann and crew high fived Jesse and shook their heads in admiration, iconic blonde manes waving behind them. Jesse took off the guitar and asked Johann if they could talk. They walked to the other side of the large room.

Jesse smiled, "Thanks for letting me play on the song. Listen, I've been wondering if you need another bandmate. I'm leaving Driftwood. I could bring a lot to your band. I'm professional, free to travel wherever. I got a great attitude."

Johann looked at Jesse, searching for something to say. "We're flattered that you would offer, but I don't think we're at your level of musicianship."

"Come on, man, don't flatter me."

"I mean, I don't think you really match the Champagne Mane…aesthetic."

"Aesthetic?"

"Yeah, we have a certain look. Don't take it personally."

"How else would I take it? You don't want a Black man in your group. Fine. Fuck y'all."

Johann protested, "You know it ain't about that."

Jesse got the sound engineer's attention across the studio and yelled, "Yo! If I hear my solo on anything I will sue all you motherfuckers!" The rest of the band looked at Jesse in shock, wondering what Johann had done to set him off.

Jesse walked out of the studio and asked directions until he made it back to the house, went to his bedroom and slept until the late afternoon.

***

When Jesse awoke and walked into the kitchen, rubbing the sleep out of his eyes, Rachel and Wood sat at the dining room table drinking a glass of Riesling. Jesse opened the fridge, took out a half-empty bottle of Gatorade and drained it.

Rachel patted the chair to her left and said, "Come have a seat, hon." She was calculated in sitting between the two men as a mediator, conscious of the dynamic created if Jesse felt like they were ganging up on him.

Jesse sat down, preparing for the conversation he imagined during his meandering journey home that morning.

Rachel spoke in a calm voice, "Wood told me a little about your conversation last night. What's going on?"

Jesse glanced over cautiously, "There's not much to say. I've done a lot of thinking and I've decided that it's time to strike out on my own."

She nodded, taking it in, knowing that each word carried weight. "Let's all be honest, you were tripping on acid. That can alter your judgment."

"All that did was bring up the conversation much sooner than I had planned. Believe me, this has been brewing for a while."

She took another approach, "When someone goes on to the next chapter they're either running toward something or away from something. If you're frustrated with us because you think we don't appreciate you, then we can fix that."

"I'm not running away from anything, but some events have opened my eyes – both good and bad."

"I'm really sorry I didn't thank you enough for everything you did in Cincinnati. I was just wondering where some of the money went. I thought it was a legitimate question at the time."

"That was the last of many straws. I just want to put out my own album and see what happens."

Rachel found an opening. "Why don't you help us finish the Driftwood album, then we'll record yours. Wood can play backing tracks and the album would be your songs, your name. Then we can all figure out what comes next."

Rachel's positive spin struck a nerve in Jesse. "You can't charm me, Rachel. I'm not some lonely trucker you can flirt with to get shit done for you. You're a fixer, I get it, and you're good at what you do. But you can't fix this. I'm going solo and I don't want either of you involved. It's not personal, but if you're both all wrapped up in my album, people will always question if I did it on my own. I need to know I can do it by myself. Just me."

Wood finally spoke up, "Just you and Tommy."

"He's going to produce it and help with marketing. I know you had a bad experience with him, but that was years ago. He's grown up a lot since then."

Wood conceded. "Maybe you're right. I hope it works out for you."

Jesse sighed and struck a conciliatory tone. "I can stick around and help you record tracks in the studio, but I need to work on my own songs, too."

Wood's pride took precedent over his logic. "Thanks, Jesse, but I got this. There are plenty of great musicians around here. I don't need your help."

The three of them stared at the table, pondering their new reality.

Rachel brought up the last order of business. "There's the gig in Lexington tomorrow night."

Jesse nodded, "I'll be there."

SOMEONE SAVED MY LIFE TONIGHT

Opera House

October 1, 1998

Lexington, Kentucky

Jesse and Wood avoided each other and drove separately to Lexington. Jesse had packed all of his belongings into his car so he could play the gig then continue on to New Orleans. Wood brought Margaret to ease the inevitable tension. Backstage, Jesse knelt down and talked with her while massaging her ears. "You've been the best roadie a band could have, even though you never lifted a finger to help. Not one paw! Are you going to be onstage with us tonight?" Margaret howlbarked. "That's settled. We'll set up a microphone for you." She licked Jesse's face as he laughed.

Wood reached out and handed Jesse the setlist. "How does this look? It's pretty straightforward."

"Yeah, what are these blank spots?"

"I was thinking you could play a few of your own songs towards the end."

Jesse was touched. "Thanks for the opportunity and the respect, but I don't want to steal any thunder. Let's just have a good gig."

"Let's do it."

Looking for a few words to sum up how he felt, Jesse said, "You've taught me a lot, I hope we can stay friends."

"I was hurt, then I thought of something my Mother told me. When her piano students would reach a certain level she would send them to another teacher. I asked why she would turn down their money and she said that the goal of a good teacher is to become progressively irrelevant."

"Smart lady, but you'll never be irrelevant."

***

They took the stage in the historic theater, waving to the people in the box seats looking down from the sides. The crowd enjoyed the show, oblivious to the emotions behind every chorus they sang, every shared glance. When they finished the last song, Jesse took off his guitar and threw pics to fans in the front, high fiving them as he left the stage. Wood said, "Let's get him back out here!" The crowd chanted, "Jesse! Jesse!" until he returned, smiling and confused.

Wood had Jesse sit in a chair and said, "None of you know this, but our beloved Jesse has decided to go solo." The crowd went silent, then a few people called out a variety of sentiments, unsure if they should ask him to stay or wish him well. "Anyway, we've been through a lot together and Jesse has saved my bacon in ways I can't begin to tell you. You've probably never heard me play piano before. I'm out of practice, but I wanted to sing this song to send off Jesse with some good vibes. Sing along if you know the words."

Wood sat at the keyboard and played the low intro to Elton John's "Someone Saved My Life Tonight."

We've all gone crazy lately
My friend's out there rolling 'round the basement floor
Someone saved my life tonight
Sugar bear

When Wood sang, "You're a butterfly" Jesse lowered his head and began sobbing.

And butterflies are free to fly
Fly away
High away
Bye bye

***

Wood awoke to a quiet house the next morning. He made coffee and noticed the flashing light on the answering machine.

"Thurston, darling, Rachel gave me this number. I'm coming down to Louisville tomorrow for a few days. My girlfriends and I are going to the horse auction, then we'll watch a few races. I hope we can get together for dinner or something. Maybe I'll finally get to meet Rachel."

CHARLOTTE SOMETIMES

Rachel saw this as a rare opportunity to spend time alone with Wood's mother. Her mind contained a collage of stories, mostly bad, that formed a vague image of who Charlotte might be. It would give her a chance to explain the whirlwind of changes that Jesse's departure brought to their situation in case she sensed tension in her son. Who was she kidding? Their meeting was for selfish reasons. Rachel wanted to peel away the layers of the onion that made Wood such a mystery to her.

She picked Charlotte up at the hotel and drove her to Jockey Silks for an appetizer and drinks. She was surprised by Charlotte's classy, yet youthful appearance, then remembered that she was only 22 when she had Wood. Charlotte wore a baby blue skirt to her knees with yellow heels. Her yellow sweater had a pattern that contained the exact blue from her skirt. She wore a silk scarf in her hair and Jackie O sunglasses. When she got in and shook Rachel's hand she reminded her that these were the hands of a piano teacher. Supple yet strong. A diamond tennis bracelet dangled from her wrist. Charlotte lit a cigarette and cracked the window, resting her arm on the door so some of the smoke was sucked out. Rachel glanced at the cigarette but said nothing. Charlotte began punching the radio presets, looking for a classical station, settling on jazz, glaring at the radio as if it would explain its poor choices to her.

At Jockey Silks, the waiter arrived with their menus. Charlotte pronounced, "Two Pappy Van Winkles, neat, s'il vous plait!"

The waiter said, "I'm sorry, ma'am, but we haven't had Pappy's in ages."

Charlotte tilted her head and stared into his eyes, speaking slowly, "The owner and I go way back. If you'd like, I can show you where his stash is myself."

The waiter stammered, "It's just that…"

"I imagine it's still in the back room behind that old humidor that malfunctioned and soaked his Cohibas."

The waiter smiled. "Right away, ma'am."

Rachel put down the irrelevant drink menu and said, "I can't believe it's taken all this time to finally meet you, Mrs. Underwood."

"Call me Charlotte." Taking in the beautiful décor of the bar, she said, "I've always loved this place."

"You've been here before?"

"More times than I care to admit, dear. My girlfriends and I come to Louisville at least once a year. I haven't missed the derby in ages. There's a horse auction tomorrow. I just love bidding on them."

"You own horses?"

"Oh god no! But there's nothing like an auction. The first time I attended one I met a Saudi Sheik. There were southern gentlemen and wealthy people everywhere. The artist Leroy Neiman was flirting with me and sketching me like a madman. I still have it somewhere." She took a drink of her bourbon and waved her hands to signal the story was not finished. "It's such a rush to bid on a horse. I always bid early and someone eventually outbids me, thank god. One time I bid on a beautiful young filly, just gorgeous! I raised my paddle and nobody else bid. I died inside when I heard 'Fair warning...*sold* to the lovely lady in the sequin dress!' The auctioneer slammed down the gavel like the lid on a casket! *Boom!*"

Rachel put her hand over her mouth in shock. "Why didn't anyone else bid on her?"

"A rumor went around that very morning that she had a heart condition. How the hell was I supposed to hear that when I was doing shots with the Saudi Sheik? So I bought a beautiful filly, paid for with my brother's money."

"Uncle Freddie, right?"

"Yes, dear Uncle Freddie. I called him and broke the news. I could hear the veins popping in his forehead. When he said he was in Carmel I said, 'If you're in CARmel can't you just pop down and pick her up? He yelled, 'No. I'm in CarMELL...by the SEEEEAAA!' as if it were Zanzibar."

"Yeah, his beach house in California. So what happened?"

"The Sheik took her back with him, along with the other horses he had bought. He paid the money straight to the auction house. He turned out to be quite the gentleman and the filly's heart was fine. She went on to have a great racing career – so I gave Freddie a heart attack for no reason. Now I drink mint juleps and watch. I've hung up my auction paddle for good!"

Rachel shook her head, "What a story."

Charlotte lit a cigarette and raised her empty class, getting the bartender's attention and pointing to herself and to Rachel.

Rachel took this pause to change subjects. "I want you to know that Wood is going through a tough time. Jesse decided to go solo and Wood has been struggling to write songs for his latest album. He's doing it all himself. I'm there for moral support but I can't play any instruments."

Charlotte took a sip of her bourbon and clicked the ashes into an ashtray. Looking directly at Rachel, she inquired, "Why are you telling me this?"

Rachel was taken aback by Charlotte's lack of empathy. "I just want you to know. I don't think he would tell you what's going on in his life."

"You're right. He wouldn't. Whenever anything goes wrong he feels like I'm rubbing it in. I've never been an 'I-told-you-so' type of mother, but I've watched him stumble for so long that I have to bite my tongue now."

"Are you willing to see the success he's had? He's toured all over the world and released critically acclaimed albums. You should read the fan mail we get. One young man was going to take his life then discovered one of your son's albums that really touched him. They ended up meeting at a show and Wood still sends him postcards from all over the world, encouraging him to stay positive. That's just one story."

"That's nice to hear. I guess I've always wondered why he still struggles financially."

"He just prefers to keep things manageable. He doesn't want to be huge. Did you know he just returned from Europe?"

"No. He doesn't tell me anything."

"It brought in a lot of money so we're good for a while. Believe me, we have his career where we want it."

"That's a relief."

Rachel and Charlotte finished four bourbons before realizing they were drunk. They left the car and walked to her hotel, locking arms. Charlotte told her about Wood's childhood. "He was such a strange little boy, but cute as a button. Of course, I'm biased. He would get himself all worked up about bigfoot or the bomb. He slept with his light on for years. One time when he was about six I asked him to open the mail for me, just to learn how to do it. He hid under the table and yelled, "There's bills in there!"

Rachel laughed, "I feel that way at least once a week!"

"Then music became his outlet. I was worried that he would get mixed up with the wrong crowd, but mostly he practiced his guitar. I taught him piano for years and I think the discipline that I bring to my profession certainly helped. Eventually he rebelled against me and swore he'd never touch a piano again."

Rachel was tempted to ask about Wood's thumb, destroyed at the hands of his mother for testing her patience during a lesson. Instead she said, "Awww….poor little guy. Did he know his father?"

"No. I've always struggled with that. I was bitter about not getting my degree when I was so close. And his father turned out to be a Grade A prick. We went on a few dates but I didn't want to move to Chicago and he was too selfish to move to Indy. I think he wanted to leave our scandal behind. That followed him around for years. He's married now with children of his own."

"That's sad."

"It is, but life is full of tough choices, especially when a child is involved. Most parenting is about guilt. They don't tell you that part."

Charlotte slowed and turned to face Rachel. "I wasn't going to tell you this, but I need to stop running from the truth." She smiled, "Plus I'm tipsy."

Rachel hoped to hear that Wood was in love with her or that Charlotte had decided to add her to the Underwood Family Trust.

Instead, Charlotte said, "I have lung cancer. We don't know how advanced it is yet, but it's not looking good. I need you to promise me that you will not breathe a word to my son. Not one word."

"I promise. Why don't you want Wood to know?"

"I'll tell him in due time. He'll have a lot of questions so I want to get more information and start my therapy."

Rachel agreed not to tell Wood, then cried as they continued walking arm-in-arm to Charlotte's hotel.

TO LIVE THROUGH YOU

Rachel arrived at the studio in the late afternoon with only a few noticeable remnants of her hangover. Wood was playing with a keyboard part, something Jesse would have handled easily prior to his departure.

"Charlotte and I had quite the night out."

He looked confused. "You went out with my Mom?"

"Yes, she's a fascinating lady."

"She's a lot of things."

"During our tipsy conversation I may or may not have asked her to play piano on your album."

"I'm sorry, what?"

"Yeah…so now that's happening. She'll be here pretty soon."

Wood didn't look angry, just confused, his brain going into a protective mode after everything that had happened in the last few days.

Rachel put her hands on his shoulders. "Just trust me on this one. Please?"

Everything in Wood told him to dispute this, but today wasn't the same day as yesterday. "Sure. We'll see how it goes."

***

The engineer pressed record. "Anytime you're ready."

Charlotte played beautifully, but stopped to remind her son that the chords didn't work. "Going into this F# before the chorus doesn't make sense. How about adding a little more darkness and tension to the bridge?"

"Mother, I know I wasn't classically trained like you. Could you just play the

144

song without dissecting it?"

"You can do what you want, but I know when something doesn't make sense, dear."

"Just play it! We can't afford to rewrite songs in the studio."

She tilted her head to the left, dropping it with a condescending lift of her eyebrows. "You don't appreciate the expertise that I bring. You would have learned music theory if you hadn't dropped out of college, but no, you had to do everything *your* way." She turned to the booth, looking for allies in Rachel and the engineer. "We even hired an SAT tutor for him – a lovely young lady. Smart as a whip! She eventually gave up and we never saw her again. He applied all over the place and couldn't get in because he was lazy. It made me sick. Indiana, Butler, Notre Dame…as if. His uncle pulled every last string to get his old friend to let him into a *very* elite private school."

Wood yelled, "I even applied to Purdon't. And guess what…*I didn't get in. So there's that!*"

Charlotte was livid at his outburst, convinced that he would take her feedback without rebuttal. "You never appreciated me. I drove down here to help you but all you do is lash out at me."

"Maybe my life isn't about you any more than yours is about mine. Did you ever consider that? You're my mother, but I never asked you to live vicariously through me."

"What choice did I have but to live through you? Did you ever consider *that?!*"

Charlotte lit a cigarette, stroked her forehead, and looked down at the piano keys. Her son stood shaking his head. Rachel opened the door and slipped in from the sound booth. She put her hand on Wood's shoulder, whispering, "How 'bout if you take a break and let me talk with her." Wood and Margaret went for a walk while Rachel consoled Charlotte.

Rachel rubbed her back and said in a calming tone, "I know it's hard when you're just trying to help. I really want to hear your ideas about the song."

"I didn't come down here to argue with my son."

"I'm sorry. Could you play your ideas along with the metronome? Just play it how you think the song should be."

The engineer gave her a thumbs up and signaled that they were still recording. Charlotte sighed and gathered herself. With Rachel still rubbing her back, the engineer started the click track and Charlotte played the entire song flawlessly, the way she envisioned it. One take and it was accomplished.

Charlotte stood, hugged Rachel, and held her face in both hands, looking into her eyes. "Thurston doesn't deserve you, but if he ever decides to wise up, please give my boy a chance."

Rachel was startled, "Oh, I think you have the wrong impression. I'm Wood's manager. We're just business partners."

Still holding Rachel's face, "That's another reason I want you in our family. You're a horrible liar." Yelling to the engineer, "Isn't she adorable?!"

Rachel dropped her defenses and said, "Maybe he'll wise up someday."

Charlotte grabbed her purse and walked towards the door. "You're good for him. Hell, Rachel, you're good for all of us."

***

Wood and Margaret showed up an hour later. Calmed by his long walk, he was more amenable to suggestions. Rachel asked him to open his mind and listen to Charlotte's version of the song.

Wood sat down, closed his eyes, and listened to his Mother's playing. He raised his eyebrows at the change before the chorus, smiling as the bridge went to a minor key. When the song ended, he blushed, "She was right. That's it. That's the song."

The rest was easy. Since Charlotte had played along with the drum track, they erased the guitar and bass and recorded new tracks over her piano. A studio drummer came in and laid down a track, which they added to the last half of the song. Wood scrapped the lyrics, writing a new version. *To Live Through You* included lines from their recorded argument in the background, Wood's *"I never asked you to live vicariously through me"* and the feeling of countless mothers, *"What choice did I have but to live through you?"* could be heard, spliced into phrases that echoed through a heavy chorus effect, then as one sentence.

> What choice, choice, choice
> What choice did I have
> But to live through you
> What choice did I have but to live through you

Whenever Rachel thought back on the last time she saw Charlotte, her final words became a source of pride.

> "Hell, Rachel, you're good for all of us."

***

On their drive back to the hotel, Wood picked Margaret's brain on the prospects of a relationship with Rachel.

"Here's how it went down, Margaret. After we came back from our walk, I listened to Mom's version of the song and after I swallowed my pride…well, you were there. Anyway, Rachel goes to the store and the engineer tells me I might want to listen to an interesting part of the recording. He plays it back and I hear my Mom telling Rachel that I don't deserve her, but that she should give me a chance if I ever decided to wise up. Then she says that Rachel is good for me, and good for all of us. Even you, Margaret. And then Rachel says that maybe I'll wise up someday. So - I guess she's into me. I always had a feeling but hearing that recording was like cracking the Enigma code. How am I supposed to play it cool after I hear my Mom and my manager cooking up a plan for my love life?"

Margaret put her paw on Wood's arm then barked at him. "Ruff!"

"You're in on this, too, Margaret? I thought you were on my side!"

***

Rachel and Wood stood in the kitchen, drinking the rest of the Riesling, exhausted by Jesse's departure and the whirlwind that was Charlotte.

He smiled, "I can't believe she played on the album."

"Yeah, it took some doing. She and I had a heart-to-heart. I think she's more conscious of the legacy she wants to leave behind. Wait till she sees her name on the album credits."

"Yeah, definitely. She and Uncle Freddie will get a kick out of it. So that brings us to six songs completed so far. I have ideas for a few more, but that still won't be enough. I was thinking of adding a few covers."

"Any ideas?"

"I've always wanted to do a Hank Williams tune, like Lord, Build Me a Cabin."

"I like it. A lot of people have covered his tunes. The copyright should be pretty easy to work out. What else did you have in mind?"

"I've been getting into this Lloyd Cole CD. You know how you listen to something, forget about it, then rediscover it? Check out this song." He rummaged through his CDs and found "Don't Get Weird on Me, Babe." He pressed play on "Half of Everything" and called out from the living room. "I'll have to dumb it down because I'm not doing string arrangements and all that!" He walked back into the kitchen, the song blaring through the house. "Maybe I'll take out the intro and start it when it's already grooving."

Rachel swayed to the rhythm of the song. "I don't know this album. I had the biggest crush on Lloyd Cole. Now that I think of it, you remind me of a Midwest version of him."

"He's still around doing his thing. I think he moved from London to the east coast. We'll get a drummer and lay down a basic track with me on rhythm guitar. I could add the piano and keys then keep layering guitars until we get it right."

"I love it."

"This line reminds me of you." Wood leaned forward and waved his finger at Rachel, "She's got such a pretty please I never could say no."

She heard the next line about leaving, put her hands on his hips and asked, "Do you want me to leave you? Because I don't want to."

He pulled her closer, "I don't ever want you to go, but we're going to blow it all up if we do this."

She kissed him, "Just make love to me."

***

Rachel woke up to Margaret licking her toes. Wood was spooning her, his left arm draped over her. It was 12:42. She whispered, "I need to go. My dad's going to worry if I'm not there in the morning."

Wood snapped out of his deep sleep and stroked her cheek with his thumb. "I understand. Thanks for coming to see me. I was feeling down after everything that happened."

"Yeah, I hope Jesse's okay."

"We patched things up at the Lexington show, but he still left me high and dry."

"People move on. Oh, don't forget you have that corporate gig in Oklahoma City on Saturday. I can watch Margaret."

"That's right. The propane convention."

"I can book your flight when I get to work."

Wood thought for a moment. "You know. I'm going to drive there with Margaret. Who knows, maybe I'll get a song out of it."

OKLAHOMA

Wood packed up his maroon '92 Chevy Blazer with the usual provisions, including some of the snacks Jesse had left behind. The Blazer was a good vehicle for touring, with plenty of space and rare mechanical problems. He kept a running list on a paper hanging from a knob of things he had hit over the years, which included possums, raccoons, skunks, a barn owl that flew straight at him through the fog, an armadillo, a deer that landed on top of the hood, and five creatures that fell into the "Unknown" category. He changed "Coyote" to "Desert Doggie" to honor his new Estonian friends. Margaret and Wood drove down 65 to Nashville then headed west on 40, through Memphis, over the Mississippi, and into Arkansas.

Wood could have stopped at a motel but he was wide awake. He could either eat up miles or stare at a lonely ceiling all night. That was the best thing about driving alone with Margaret — seeing the countryside and making their own schedule. Sometimes they drove through the night, checked in at noon, did the sound check, then slept until it was time to play the gig. True freedom.

One of his travel hobbies was talking to bored employees at the sleepy gas stations and diners throughout the desolate landscape. He tried the same line on what seemed to be the same pimple-faced kid in every small town.

"So, what's it like growing up in Beaver Junction?"

"It's boring as hell. Our football team is good though."

"So, what's it like growing up in Nimby?"

"It sucks. Our basketball team is good though."

"So, what's it like living in Scalding Flats?"

"It's hella boring. All our teams suck ass."

Even better than getting the lowdown from lonely teens was sharing his thoughts with Margaret. One might think it was because she never judged him, but that wasn't accurate. Her inability to put her feelings into words was her charm. Wood drove with his left wrist over the wheel, gesturing to Margaret with his right. He felt cool that way.

"Margaret, can you believe Uncle Freddie just cut us off like that? 'Not another dime. Not one red cent!' That's how he put it. You see, Uncle Freddie pulled some strings to get me into Wabash, then I dropped out anyway at the end of the first year. Well, dropped out before they kicked me out, if you're getting technical. They said I broke the code of conduct one too many times. I said the code was too long to memorize, but it turns out the Wabash code is only one sentence, and I remember the Dean, my philosophy professor, and my advisor reciting it in unison:

> *The student is expected to conduct himself at all times, both on and off campus, as a gentleman and a responsible citizen.*

Don't look at me like that, Margaret. It sounds easy but when you think about it, that is a pretty tall order! Conduct myself like a gentleman *and* a responsible citizen? On *and* off campus? It was an all-men's college, so how long did they expect me to stick around campus when they didn't bother to put any women there?"

Margaret yawned and gave a loud sigh to signal her disapproval of Wood's lame excuses.

"I sabotaged the whole thing after what he did to Yvette, my sexy SAT tutor. She was my first love! That wasn't cool at all, but there was nothing I could do. I was a teenager. Old Uncle Freddie was livid when I dropped out, and I suppose rightfully so. He was always telling me, 'Thurston, I don't want to *give* you the fish, I want to teach you *how* to fish!' I got excited because I thought we were going fishing, but I don't think Uncle Freddie ever learned how to bait a hook. Turns out teaching me how to fish was just an expression about doing everything myself. Now I know why adults use all those metaphors; if they told it to ya straight you'd get pretty depressed."

Margaret crawled over and put her head on his thigh.

"Then Uncle Freddie tried to bring me into his business and 'Show me the ropes.' By that time I was old enough to realize they were metaphorical ropes. He had so many businesses that I couldn't keep track of it all, but over time the key takeaways – that's what he called 'em – key takeaways - started to sink in. He took the time to teach me, and even though I went my own way when I joined The Featherdusters - which really hurt him - I learned a lot more from Uncle Freddie than I ever did at that college."

Wood looked out at the horizon, trying to conjure an example that a Basset hound could grasp.

"Like one time he picks me up to meet some guy for lunch. On the way there he tells me to keep my mouth shut until he gives me the signal to recite the one line he gave me. I had just rolled out of bed and my hair looked like a bird's nest. So Uncle Freddie's talking to this rich guy about a new software program he had been developing and was looking to take public, he just needed to find a computer genius to crack the code and some investors to fund the project. Uncle Freddie points at me, I point to my temple and say, "It's all up here." The guy signs a check for an advance right there! I learned that when people are really greedy, they'd rather sign up for something they don't understand. I also learned to keep my mouth shut until it was time to recite my lines. When we got in the car Uncle Freddie yelled, 'Hot damn! Good job, kid."

So when I joined The Featherdusters I burned through Uncle Freddie's chances and there just wasn't a relationship we could prop up anymore. I always felt bad that I never got up the nerve to thank him. I know, Margaret, it sounds stupid to get up the nerve to thank someone, but how would you understand? You're a Basset Hound. All you gotta do is eat, sleep, and listen to my problems."

***

They stayed the night near Little Rock, woke up, ate, and continued west on 40 into Oklahoma. They had made good time. Wood leaned across Margaret to pull the map out of his glove compartment. He noticed "Choctaw Nation" just south of them. It was an immense area of land, where they had been settled after walking the Trail of Tears.

"Remember how Jesse was always going on and on about his Choctaw heritage? Well, here we are. I thought it would be flat and dry but there are forests and mountains. It's beautiful. let's go check it out."

They turned south on Highway 2, past Porum. He stopped in at Whitefield Grocery to get gas and snacks. A teenage girl with black hair rang up his items.

"So what's it like growing up in Whitefield?"

"It's dead."

"But your sports teams are good, right?"

She looked at him like he was insane.

Wood said, "Sorry. Are we in the Choctaw Nation?"

"Yep. We're right next to Muskogee territory. Everything south from here to the Red River is Choctaw. 11,000 square miles. Beyond that is Texas."

As they drove south near Robbers Cave the sky became dark and a strong wind kicked up from the east. They pulled over to eat their lunch and walked up to a ridge with a majestic bur oak, its branches providing a canopy of protection from the elements. Wood sat on a large, decaying branch that had fallen and asked, "Margaret, what'll it be? We've got turkey and provolone or meatball." Margaret sniffed the submarine sandwiches and was clearly more excited about the meatballs and marinara. Wood unraveled the wrapping and placed it on the ground. It was devoured before he took the first bite of his own sub. "Margaret, you're eating like a dog! Pace yourself." She relaxed at his feet and breathed heavily, licking the sauce from the wrapper.

Wood looked down into the valley and eyed a group of workers. A tractor moved along with them. It was still windy and the clouds moved quickly over them, their billowing forms creating shapes that Wood tried to decipher. A thunderclap broke the silence and a crooked lightning bolt descended from the dark cloud, nearly reaching the ground below them. He jumped and dropped his sandwich. Margaret let out a yelp as it started to pour. As the workers ran into their trucks, Wood heard them laughing and yelling to each other, though he couldn't make out the words. The tractor driver jumped down and sprinted, leaving his hat to be retrieved after the deluge ceased. The wind whipped through the valley and swaths of rain moved horizontally. Wood held Margaret and laughed at the scene. He stroked her stomach and spoke in her ear. "It's just a thunderstorm. We'll be okay." Within ten minutes it was over and beams of sunlight shone down through the clouds like spotlights on the valley below.

They walked back to the Blazer, Wood shook the rain from his hair. "Wasn't that something? Thank God we were under that oak tree or we'd be soaked. Alright, let's get to Oklahoma City."

SPREAD EAGLE TO THE SKY

Rain tumbles down on this valley
Still bearing names
Ghosts and Choctaw remains
Clouds move slowly
Over lands wanting replenishment

Old cars roll through barren farms
Nowhere to go
Wild grass shines deepest green
Leaning into
Sun and wind

CHORUS

Each grain of sand a sponge
Spread eagle to the sky

Thunder clouds rush by
Icy winds throw gales into horizontals
Laughing workers retreat from fields
Crowd into grumpy trucks
Wait for the storm to pass

Each grain of sand a sponge
Spread eagle to the sky (repeat)

PROPANE

October 17, 1998

Oklahoma City, Oklahoma

If you asked Wood if he enjoyed playing the propane convention he might
have lied, saying something about selling his soul, but it was a good time
and paid the bills for a few months. After a few unpleasant corporate

experiences, he settled into a regular show with a national propane association, who hired him to play most years. The crowd was always a festive and friendly group, who left their worries at home for a few days a year to make connections and party down with colleagues. At his first convention he sang a funny version of JJ Cale's "Cocaine," popularized by Eric Clapton. It was a hit with the crowd.

Wood and Margaret strolled around the convention grounds. They sat on a bench in front of a Ferris Wheel, taking in the scene.

A father walked toward him holding a baby and sat near them. His wife and son waved to him as they circled high above the convention. In another seat, two girls yelled, "Hi, daddy!" each time they passed. The man laughed and waved back. He wore boots, Wranglers, a checkered shirt, and an Oklahoma Sooners trucker hat.

Wood said, "You have a beautiful family."

The man smiled, "Thanks. They drive me batty but I wouldn't trade it for the world. How 'bout you? Got a wife and kids?"

"Nope, just her." He stroked Margaret's long ears, "I got all the family I need. Where are y'all from?"

"Not far, just over in Bethany." Looking up at the Ferris Wheel while he bounced the baby on his knee, the father returned to the topic. "Maybe she's all the family you need now, but what about when you're 60?"

This touched a nerve in Wood. As he was thinking of a response, the man's wife and children walked up. She looked at Wood and said, "Oh hey, you're the Cocaine guy." The husband looked back and forth at them, wondering how his wife knew "The cocaine guy."

Wood cleared up the confusion, "It's the name of a song I sing every year at the convention."

"Oh, you're that guy? Nice!"

"That's me. It was good talking to you. We're going to get ready for our set."

***

Wood took the stage to tepid applause. Conventions were different because the crowd wasn't there to see him; he was there to make the convention better – like the useless bags you get with your name tag, snacks between sessions, and pens that only work once. He played some of his acoustic numbers and poked fun at the current president of the association. Playing to the crowd, he told a few jokes in between songs, channeling his rural Hoosier accent.

"Any Sooners fans here?"

A few hundred people cheered, accompanied by a smattering of boos from Oklahoma State and Texas Longhorns fans. He knew his audience.

"You know why Jesus wasn't born in California? Because they couldn't find three wise men or a virgin!"

The crowd laughed and continued mingling with each other.

"Alright, let's get into some JJ Cale." He played the iconic guitar riff and the crowd cheered. He sang the altered lyrics, to laughter from the crowd.

> If you love to cook and you need that flame, propane
> If you barbecue, don't wanna mess with briquettes, propane

The whole crowd raised their drinks and joined in.

> She don't lie, she don't lie, she don't lie...
> PROPANE!

"Hey, God bless y'all and enjoy the rest of the convention!"

***

Wood called Rachel from the hotel. The dynamic had clearly shifted after they had slept together. She inquired about the gig.

"How did it go, baby?"

"It was great. The usual…I played some songs, made a few jokes, then sang Propane. Easy money."

"Good job! I'm proud of you. Did any drunk ladies hit on you? You know how they let loose when they go to a convention."

"Ummm…no. I just played the gig and went back to the hotel."

"So when are you coming back?"

"We're going to get an early start. The drive was longer than I thought it would be. This is a big country."

"It is! Listen, I have some great news. You got invited to play at an autumn music festival in Japan. One of the organizers saw you at the show in Italy and contacted us."

"I've always wanted to go to Japan. My high school friend Craig lives there. He's always bugging me to come visit."

"Can you give me his phone number? I'm trying to set up a few more shows since you're going to be there already, but I'm not making any progress."

"Yeah, I have it somewhere. He's an English teacher but I'm sure he has some connections. He's lived there about ten years now."

***

Wood and Margaret hit the road early the next morning. He drank a decent cup of coffee and confided in her.

"So Rachel and I finally slept together and it was very intimate, like we were meant to be together, but now she's asking me questions that she never asked me before. Of course drunk women flirted with me, it's a convention! Shit, give 'em enough chardonnay and they start hitting on each other. I was a good boy, but there's the rub…we're not even together, are we? So what if I did take a lady back to my room?"

Margaret looked over and shook her head in disgust. Wood did a double take, "Did you just shake your head at me? Just eat your Danish and stop judging!"

Wood drove in silence along Highway 40. There were only a few cars that early on a Sunday morning. Margaret began whining and barking and he pulled over to let her pee. Wood leaned against the front of the Blazer and laughed as she chased small lizards into their holes. He heard a noise and looked back to see an old Ford pickup approaching from behind, then turned around to see Margaret chase a lizard into the road. He heard the combination of skidding tires, a bone-crushing collision of metal on flesh, and Margaret's distinctive cry come together to form one sound that he could never unhear in the years that followed.

Margaret flew back to the edge of the road. The pickup careened as it skidded to the left, overcorrected to the right, nearly flipping over before coming to a stop in the middle of the highway. They slowly pulled over and an older couple jumped out and jogged over to Margaret. Wood was kneeling over her, in shock.

Wood stroked her face and body, knowing there was nothing he could do but be there with her. He tried to carry her off the road but she cried when he began to lift her. The old man said things about not seeing her and apologized, words that didn't register with Wood in this moment. The old lady put her arm on Wood's shoulder and cried with him. He lay down on the side of the road facing Margaret, their noses touching, telling her what a good girl she had always been and thanking her for loving him unconditionally. Margaret licked Wood's nose one last time, closed her eyes, and died beside Highway 40.

Wood didn't know how long he cried on the side of the road. The old man sat on the ground, leaning against Wood's Blazer, head down with his eyes closed. As Wood rose, they dusted him off and helped him load Margaret's limp body into the back of the Blazer on a blanket. They hugged him and apologized again. Wood thanked them and reassured them that there was nothing they could have done, knowing they would carry the guilt with them anyway.

"I noticed you have some tools in the back of your pickup. Do you have a shovel?"

THE BUR OAK

Wood's thoughts raced with things he should have done to prevent her death. The seat next to him was a gaping, silent void. He tried to think straight as he considered what to do with Margaret's body. He was eleven hours from Louisville and two more to Indianapolis. He felt a strong impulse to turn right on Highway 2 and retrace his steps, past Porum and the Whitefield grocery store, to the immense oak near Robbers Cave under whose protective canopy he and Margaret ate sandwiches and watched workers scurry from the thunderstorm. This time it was sunny and quiet and the long green grasses swayed in the breeze in the valley below.

He dug a deep hole, dropped to his knees, and bent down to lower Margaret's body into the grave. He placed the blanket over her, letting her head peak out. She appeared as though she were sleeping on his bed, relaxed and without worry.

"Margaret, I remember when I first got you from that disgusting kennel. You were all ears and smelled horrible. Remember when I gave you that first bath and all the fleas climbed to the top of your head? But you survived and you turned out to be my best friend. Uncle Jesse was right, you were the best roadie a band could have asked for, even though you never carried a damn thing or helped us fight off those hillbillies who jumped us in Appalachia. I promise I'll bring Rachel here to say her goodbyes. I want you to know that you are not alone here. You're on Choctaw land. Uncle Jesse's ancestors are going to play with you and take care of you. I'm sure they have dogs you can play with. Sweet Margaret, I will always hold you in my heart."

He took out his pocketknife and carved "Margaret" into the tree trunk. He rubbed his hands as he walked back to the Blazer, muttering, "I'm sorry I was never enough."

SECTION 4: DRIFTWOOD TOURS JAPAN

TOKYO METROPOLITAN HIROO HOSPITAL

November 23, 1998

He looked out through the gauze and saw Craig, the lawyer, the doctor, and the nurse surrounding him. He was still handcuffed to the bed.

The nurse said, "Okiteru mitai."

His friend said, "Wood, do you know where you are?"

His mouth was dry. He asked in a scratchy voice, "Tokyo?"

"That's right. Do you know who I am?"

"You're Craig from Park Tudor High."

"That's right." Patting him on the shoulder, Craig said, "You got beat up, then you were hit by a bus and had some head and neck trauma. Remember Nobunaga sensei and Nurse Nishimori? You've been in a medically induced coma for about two weeks. The swelling has gone down a lot and nothing major is broken so they decided to bring you back to consciousness. You're going to be in pain for a while, but we'll get you back to normal. Just get some sleep. I'll stop by tomorrow to check on you."

FRIGHTO RISKU

The sound of laughter stirred Wood from his sleep. The hospital smell of old people, formaldehyde, and ammonia was still in his nose. There were different people in the room this time and he didn't know how much time had passed since he spoke with Craig. A police officer and a man in a suit were speaking with the lawyer and Dr. Nobunaga. The doctor pointed to an X-ray of a head and explained as he moved his finger to different locations near the temple, behind the ear, and the jaw. He placed both hands around his head and expanded them quickly as he yelled, "Ba!" The police officer, detective, and Sophia all burst out laughing. They waved their arms and made similar explosion sounds. The lawyer approached the bed and explained as the police officer began unlocking the handcuffs as he laughed, shaking his head.

"Good news. They're removing the cuffs!"

He spoke slowly. "That's good. What was so funny?"

"Oh, it's just a play on words. I was trying to tell the detective that you're not a flight risk – that you won't flee the country. They weren't convinced until the doctor explained that the damage to your head was so severe that if you boarded a flight your brain would explode as soon as the plane got above 10,000 feet. You'd die of a massive brain hemorrhage before they even landed. Get it? Flight risk."

Dr. Nobunaga and the police left the room, laughing as they repeated, "Frighto risku!" down the hall.

Wood said dryly, "That's hilarious."

"Sorry, doctors, lawyers, and cops love dark comedy. That's the only way we stay sane."

"Why was I arrested in the first place?"

"You don't remember? You got in a bar fight and bit some lady, allegedly. That's assault and she's pressing charges. This is big."

"I bit her? Where?"

"At Gas Panic. Your first mistake was going to a bar full of drunken sailors in Roppongi."

"No, where on her body?"

"On her forearm. It's in the newspapers, 'Rock Star Bites Local Lady!'"

"Great. So why is the embassy involved?"

Sophia considered how to explain her involvement. "Well, you did great work for us in Estonia. I read the report. We want to make sure that the narrative is controlled. You're an American citizen and things have been very precarious. An sailor raped a woman on Okinawa recently – so you picked the worst time to get drunk and assault a Japanese lady."

"You know about Estonia? What ever happened to Galina?"

"The sniper? She formed a blues band. She's mellowed out a lot."

"Maybe I made a good impression on her."

Craig walked in, pointing behind him. "Your doctor was telling the nurses some hilarious story. What was that about?"

Wood said, "Don't ask" as he rubbed his wrists.

"Hey, the handcuffs are gone. Great!"

Sophia said, "Yes, thanks to my amazing legal work."

"And my head trauma."

Sophia went to her briefcase and took out a pen and legal pad. She sat at a small table. "Okay, guys, the arraignment is in a few days. Obviously, Wood can't attend and Craig wasn't charged with anything so I'll be there alone. Craig told me the basics of what happened that night, but now that you're both here I need the story from start to finish. No detail is too small. I'll decide what to share with the judge."

Craig spoke up, "I picked up Wood from Narita Airport and we dropped off his bags at the hotel. Then we went to get some ramen and caught up on old times. He said he wanted to see a bit of Tokyo so I took him to Roppongi. We went into Gas Panic and had a drink. At first it wasn't that crowded for a Friday night."

Sophia asked, "What time was this?"

"Pretty early…maybe 9:30 when we got there."

"What happened next?"

"I had a Guinness and Wood ordered a Jack and Coke. We were talking to these Australian ladies and their Japanese co-workers. Then I saw these teachers I used to work with – an Irish guy and a Kiwi lady from Christchurch. We talked for a while and I ordered another Guinness. Wood was still talking to the same people across the bar. Then about seven or eight sailors from the Yokosuka base walked in with a few Japanese ladies.

They were pretty chill but two of them were absolutely hammered and started yelling. My teacher friends and I went outside for a smoke. We were talking for about 10 minutes then I heard all hell break loose inside. People started running out of the bar and the bouncers were throwing people out. They wouldn't let me back in for a while. When I went in, Wood was on the floor, unconscious, and had blood on his face and down his shirt. I guess he got decked pretty good."

"Wood, what happened in Gas Panic while Craig was outside?"

Wood slurred, "I don't remember much. I remember a big blonde guy punching me. His fist looked really big at the very end."

"Was there a bar tab? That would prove how many drinks you had."

Craig said, "No, everyone pays with cash."

"What happened next?"

"I got Wood cleaned up and threw away his shirt. He was wearing a T-shirt underneath. He had a bloody nose and said he had pain in his neck and back. He was pretty woozy for a while. We took a taxi to a little izakaya I know called Rock Mother Bar. We stayed there and listened to music."

"You found him knocked unconscious, covered in blood, and the solution was to go to another bar."

"It seemed like the right thing to do at the time."

Sophia said, "If I remember correctly, you were there till dawn, right?"

"Correct. At dawn we were walking back to the train station and were about to cross the street. I was looking to my right, but I guess from living in the US, Wood was looking to his left. He stepped in front of a bus that came from his right. I tried to grab him but I was too late. Sorry, brother."

Wood closed his eyes and muttered. "Death comes from the right."

"What?" Sophia asked, ready to write it down.

"It's a voodoo thing. Nevermind. How did I survive getting hit by a bus?"

Craig explained, "It was coming to a stop so it wasn't going full speed, and you got hit by the mirror. That slammed you to the ground. The doctor said you have trauma on both sides of your head. They had to pick all of the gravel out of the left side of your face. That's why it looks like somebody shot you with a 12 gauge."

"I don't want to see myself."

"There was a public phone nearby so I ran and called 119. The bus driver also stopped and called it in on his radio. He was pretty shaken up. He was just starting his shift so there were no passengers on his bus."

Sophia finished writing. "The accident doesn't technically have any relation to the bar fight at Gas Panic, but hopefully we can milk some sympathy from this."

Wood spoke up, "So I'm going on trial?"

Sophia established expectations. "You bit a lady! The detective came and collected a bite imprint while you were knocked out. They'll use that to match it to the bite marks on the victim's arm. I'm a damn good lawyer, but if your dental records are on some lady, you ain't talkin' your way outta this shit!"

Wood grasped for a way out. "Can you try to get some music fans on the jury? All we need is one or two people to be on my side."

"There is no jury."

"What?"

Craig tried to reassure Wood. "There's no jury system here, buddy. It will be you, the lady who accused you, the two lawyers, and a judge. Maybe a few witnesses and that's it. On the positive side, you won't have the media circus that we have in the states. Having your trial all over the TV would probably work against you."

"What about the sailor who beat me up? Will he be there?"

Sophia gathered her things to leave. "He transferred back to San Diego. Unless you want to press charges against him for a bar fight, I recommend we keep him out of it. I'll let you know how the arraignment goes. Your case will go in front of Judge Kuronuma. She's tough but fair. Get some rest."

Wood looked around the room and tried to make sense of everything that had changed so dramatically in only a few weeks.

Craig said, "I'm sorry to bring more bad news, but I didn't want to keep it from you. I got a call from Rachel while you were in the coma. She said that your mother finally succumbed to her lung cancer. She died peacefully in her sleep. I'm very sorry."

Wood closed his eyes. "She had cancer?"

***

For the next three days Wood stayed in his room with no visitors. Nurse Nishimori showed him how to use the remote for the TV and brought him a few manga comics from the lobby. He watched The X Files in Japanese and a show where they pranked people in cruel, life-threatening ways. The host went to a campground and tied a rope around the foot of a man who was sleeping in his tent. The other end of the rope was tied to a horse that they slapped, dragging the screaming man through the campground. Wood said to himself, "That's how cowboys used to kill cattle rustlers." In another segment, a lady was strapped to the back of a killer whale as it performed a water park routine, jumping high above the water before twisting and landing on her. The camera cut to the studio audience as people laughed hysterically. A TV commercial showed Charlie Sheen in a jazz bar smoking a Parliament cigarette with a beautiful young lady. Another featured Jody Foster at an outdoor cafe flirting with a young man as she drank from a can of Pocari Sweat.

The hospital food was better than Wood expected. His favorite was a stew called nikujaga, which sounded like, "Mick Jagger." It had chunks of beef, carrots, and potato with a sauce he had never tasted before. He hid one of the chop sticks from Nurse Nishimori and used it to scratch his neck under his plastic brace.

***

Craig brought Wood some snacks from Lawson convenience store and a copy of Q, Wood's favorite music magazine. He leafed through it quickly, stopping to smile at a short article that caught his eye. "Check this out, Craig." He read haltingly.

> "While touring South America, The Featherdusters and supporting act, Kwicherbichin, temporarily suspended their tour after an angry mob in Sao Paolo, Brazil, tipped over their tour bus, due to what police chief Joao Almeira referred to as, 'Rude and insulting behaviour from The Featherdusters and excessive complaining from Kwicherbichin.' No major injuries were reported."

"Do you know them?"

Wood chuckled, then cringed in pain as he said, "I do. It finally caught up with them. I tried to help, but nobody listens to Wood."

"I listen to you, brother. Hopefully, they learned their lesson. I've been meaning to ask what it was like being in a coma. Do you remember anything?"

"Yeah, it was a long dream. I saw my whole life. Pretty crazy."

"That's wild. Anyway, I have a surprise for you." Craig went behind the curtain and came back with Wood's acoustic Martin. "Tada! I thought you could play some tunes to cheer yourself up. You can't get rusty. You'll be back on tour in no time."

Wood was touched. "Thanks, man. I missed this old girl. Come here, Martina."

He rubbed his hands along the neck and strings, resting it on his stomach to play. He formed his left fingers into the E position and strummed softly with his right thumb. He didn't change chords.

After a few minutes, Craig spoke up, "Try playing a song."

Wood continued to strum slowly with his thumb, looking down at his left hand.

"Do you need a guitar pic?"

"No, it's okay."

"Play Palace. I always loved that song."

Wood looked confused. "Palace? Who wrote it?"

Tears welled in Craig's eyes as his fears were confirmed. He leaned over the bed to hug Wood. "You did, brother. You wrote Palace. We're going to get this figured out. I'm here for you."

"Thanks, Craig."

Nurse Nishimori came into the room and began explaining the phone system to Craig, who was listening while looking at a piece of paper. He smiled and said, "Hai, wakarimashita. Arigatou."

Wood asked, "What are you doing?"

"We're going to use my international account to call Rachel. She's been dying to hear your voice." He entered a long number, a voice prompted him to put in a code and a security pin, then he entered Rachel's number in Louisville.

"Hello?"

Craig said, "Hi, Rachel. It's Craig. I have Wood here in the room with me. I'll let you two catch up." He handed the receiver to Wood and walked out with his fists raised above his head.

Wood tried to speak clearly. "Hi, baby." He heard a montage of sobbing, static, and words like "worried," "dead," "can't sleep," "home," and "love." After a few minutes the line cleared and Rachel pulled herself together.

She asked, "How are you feeling?"

"I feel great," he mumbled. "I don't sound great, but I think that's just the meds. I still have all my teeth and this neck brace keeps me from moving too much. The hospital staff have been nice. How are you?"

Rachel returned to crying, less dramatic this time, mixed with pertinent information about the trucking company and what she had read in the papers. She paused and said, "I'm so sorry about your mother."

"Thanks. Nobody knew she had cancer."

There was silence until Rachel said, "She told me that night I went out with her, but she made me promise not to tell you. She thought she had more time to break it to you. I'm sorry."

Wood was shocked but kept his composure. There was nothing to be done, no going back. "She shouldn't have put you in that position. I guess we'll never know why she didn't want me to know."

"When they put you in the coma your Uncle Freddie called saying she only had a few days to live. She passed the next day."

"Was there a funeral?"

"It was last Saturday and it was beautiful. A group of her girlfriends showed up in big black hats. Uncle Freddie and some of her friends spoke. I got up and shared how much she meant to you and the influence she had on your music and your work ethic. When I said that she played on a song for your upcoming album there were a lot of tears. There was a cute high school boy who talked about her as a piano teacher. He started taking lessons from her when he was five and he recently got accepted to Julliard. Another lady told the funny story about Charlotte, the Saudi Sheikh, and the filly she accidentally bought. Even Uncle Freddie laughed through his tears."

Wood used his blanket to wipe his eyes. "You'll have to tell me that story sometime. Rachel, you don't know how much it means to me that you drove to Indy to attend her memorial."

"It was my pleasure, baby. I know these calls are expensive and we're using Craig's account so I'll let you go. Let me know when the trial date is. I told my dad I want to be there to support you. We're trying to figure out who is going to run this crazy place while I'm gone."

THE ARRIVAL

The following day, Nurse Nishimori came in with a big smile. "Woodo-san...I have a very wonderful surprise for you! Can you guess my surprise?"

"Whiskey?"

She laughed and slapped his hand. She held up her arms toward the hallway, shaking her hands to announce a grand entrance. "Here is your...DAUGHTER!!!"

As Wood said, "I don't have a daughter" a young lady entered slowly. Nurse Nishimori looked back and forth at them. The girl, dressed in Vans, 501 jeans, and a black sweater, walked closer to his bed, half smiling and somewhat embarrassed. The three of them shot glances amongst themselves. Sensing a tense situation, Nurse Nishimori looked at her watch and announced, "Now...my break time!" She wisely fled the scene.

The silence continued until the girl said softly, "Nice to meet you."

He sat looking at her in utter confusion. She was tall and slim with black hair tied up in a ponytail. She looked familiar, though they hadn't met before. She held out a bag. "I brought you some snacks."

He ignored them. "What makes you think I'm your father?"

She put the snacks on a chair. "Because you are. My mother is Yvette. Do you remember her?"

Wood wondered if he should open Pandora's Box. Curiosity got the better of him. "I knew someone *named* Yvette years ago. Actually, I've known two or three."

"She went to Butler. She said you were classmates or something."

"How do I know you're really my daughter? You could be trying to get my money when I'm at my most vulnerable."

"My mother told me to ask if you remember Harold and Maude."

Wood looked around the room. His memories of Yvette - the excitement, the love, the beauty, the pain that was her - all came flooding back, twenty years later. He felt his face turn feverish with blood rushing through his veins and he became nauseous from the sudden change in his body's chemistry.

The girl noted the sweat and his face turning deep red. "Were Harold and Maude relatives of yours?"

He tried to control his breathing to calm himself. "No. They were characters in a movie we watched together."

"See, that's pretty specific."

"Yvette and I had a fling. Even if you really are her daughter, that doesn't mean *I'm* your father. I really don't want to hurt you or disparage your mother, but after the things that happened, I don't trust her. Let's just leave it at that."

"Okay, we'll leave it at that, but I don't know what else to tell you."

It was clear that this girl wasn't going to walk back out of his life so easily. With no other option but to cause a scene, he motioned to the chair. "Would you like to watch some strange TV with me?"

"Thanks."

He handed the remote to the young lady. As she shuffled through the channels, Wood drifted to memories of Yvette, for years blocked from his consciousness following the painful events of his junior year of high school.

SCHOLASTIC APTITUDE, PART II

1981

Wood's mother left town to meet her friends in Louisville in the days leading up to the Kentucky Derby. They had flown in from New York, London, L.A., and Dallas to drink mint juleps and catch up on their love lives, under the protective shade of immense hats. As Charlotte rushed out the door, she gave Wood some cash, the keys to the old Mercedes, and gestured vaguely at various meal options throughout the house. As she closed the door she yelled, "I'm sure you'll figure it out, Thurston!"

When Yvette showed up at her usual time on Saturday afternoon it was apparent that neither of them was the mood for academia. The tutorial quickly segued into a discussion about Wood as a person, as a high school student trying to navigate his way in the world. Yvette sympathized with him, "At first glance it appeared you had everything. Lots of shiny things, stability, freedom. But I look at you and I see a sadness staring back at me. I hear how your mother yells at her piano students. She's always running off somewhere and leaves you to live on pot pies and TV dinners."

"She's strict, but she's also an artist. Being an only child wouldn't be so bad if I was close with her, but we barely talk anymore, not about anything important anyway."

"That's sad. I fight all the time with my brothers, but we also laugh, we hug, we go places together. Do you have anyone to talk to when you're feeling down?"

"Not really."

They walked into the kitchen. Yvette opened the fridge and pulled out an open bottle of Gallo white zinfandel. Wood handed her two wine glasses and she filled them.

"This is a nice house. You mentioned that you're not wealthy, but it can't be cheap to have Waterford crystal and a signed Nagel."

"A signed what?"

Pointing to a painting, "Nagel! He's an amazing artist and you have a signed, limited-edition print." Yvette pointed to the bottom right corner. "Look right here, Wood. What does that say?"

Wood leaned in, "3 over 25."

"Yeah, that means there are only 25 of these prints, and your mom has the third one that came off the silk screen. And Nagel signed it himself! This thing could be worth a fortune someday."

"I've been walking by it for years. I had no idea."

Yvette continued absorbing the features of the room with its deep mahogany furniture, middle eastern rugs, and eclectic art. "Is this you in this photo?"

"Uh…yeah, that was a few years ago."

"Just hanging out in the Sistine Chapel. Who is that man standing with your mother?"

"I never found out. I remember he had a red convertible sports car and took us to dinner overlooking Rome. On the drive back to the hotel he and Mom got into this huge argument. I thought she only spoke a few words in Italian but she was giving him the business! We almost went over a cliff."

"Go Mrs. Underwood! She's such a badass." Yvette sat on the sofa, drinking her wine. Wood sat next to her.

"Well, young Thurston, sorry…Wood, you're one interesting dude."

"I've just been dragged along for the ride."

"Do you have a girlfriend at school?"

***

Wood snapped out of his daydream. The girl turned the channel to NHK news, which showed the front of Gas Panic, the bar Wood and Craig had visited in Roppongi. A photo of him onstage flashed across the screen and, though he couldn't understand, he sensed from the newscaster's tone that he had done something wrong. The last few seconds of the story showed an ambulance arriving at a hospital, sirens blaring.

The girl said, "Wait, was that you?"

"Yeah. I think that was more about my arrest than the bus accident."

"Holy fuck! You're on the news and shit!"

He understood that he was not in a position to tell this girl to stop yelling obscenities, but he didn't like what he was hearing. Her grandmother and Uncle Freddie would have been mortified to hear her speak.

Craig walked in and looked at the girl quizzically. Nurse Nishimori must have explained the arrival of a long-lost daughter. "Nice to meet you. I'm Craig, an old high school friend of Wood's." Though he was smiling, he gave off a hostile energy, like a drunk in a bar who calls you "pal."

She stood to shake his hand. "Hi. My name is Olivia. Everyone calls me Olive."

Craig smiled incredulously and tilted his head. "Wood, you never told me you had a daughter."

"That's because I just found out. Remember Yvette, my SAT tutor? Apparently, this is her daughter."

Craig began interrogating her about her name, place of birth, connections to Wood's family, which she answered with such confidence that it raised their suspicions further. Craig looked at Wood and threw his hands in the air.

Olive looked at Wood, tilted her head to the left, dropping it with a condescending lift of her eyebrows. "I've answered all your goddamned questions. I don't know how else to prove it to you."

It was Wood's mother looking back at him, scolding him from the grave. Any doubt that this girl shared DNA with her grandmother, Charlotte Underwood, vanished immediately.

Wood took in her features, seeing a version of himself in her young face. He exhaled and surrendered. "Welcome to the family."

Craig interjected, "Hold on! Not so fast. Let me do some research before you do something stupid." He looked at Olive, "No offense, but this isn't the first time someone has tried to rip off a rock star."

"You think I want your money? I just wanted to see my father before he died. Who the fuck are you? His boyfriend?"

Wood raised his hands. "Let's all just take a breath. Craig, I know you're trying to help, but she's my daughter."

"How do you know?"

"Just look at her! It's my mom. She's Charlotte."

Olive couldn't have known that her condescending head tilt with raised eyebrows sealed the deal.

Craig squinted then snapped into an understanding. "Damn. It's Mrs. Underwood in the flesh. Life is too weird." He shook his head, "I'm going to go get some snacks. I'll be back in a bit."

Olive sat and regained her composure.

Wood sighed, "Sorry about all that. He's the only friend I have here and this whole thing has been difficult. He's got the police grilling him with questions and he didn't do anything wrong."

Olive nodded, "He's a good friend."

"When did your mother tell you about me?"

"She mentioned something before but I didn't take her seriously. It's a sore spot for my stepdad. After your accident she sat me down and told me because she thought you were going to die. When I said I wanted to come here they both wigged out, but eventually they helped pay for my ticket. I'm twenty so there wasn't much they could do."

Wood sighed and closed his eyes for a moment.

Olive stood and said, "You must be exhausted so I'm going to let you get some rest. I'm staying at a little hotel nearby."

Wood smiled, "You know where to find me."

She stood for a moment, started to leave, then turned back. "Can I hug you?"

He lifted his arms slowly and she said, "I'll try not to break you" as she walked towards him.

He chuckled, "I'm like a good defense; I bend but I don't break." Olive closed her eyes and sighed as she hugged her father for the first time.

THE REMOVAL

A few days later, Dr. Nobunaga entered the room carrying a folder, accompanied by Nurse Nishimori. Craig translated for the doctor.

"He says you're doing much better and you are ready to start your physical rehabilitation. The specialists will help you with the pain in your neck, shoulders, and your back. Tell the doctor if this hurts, okay."

The doctor unfastened the neck brace and removed it from Wood's neck. The inner cloth lining of the brace was stained and reeked of sweat. Wood exhaled and moved his neck slightly, testing his mobility to identify when the pain transitioned from dull to excruciating, indicating the limits of his range. Dr. Nobunaga put up his hands, "Yukuri de ne."

"He said to take it slow."

Craig continued translating. "You will start your rehab tomorrow morning. The clinic is a few kilometers from here. You can come back here, but it is time to make plans to leave."

"How am I going to get there? Craig, you work, right?"

"Yeah, I'm working. Sorry."

Nurse Nishimori spoke up, "Ah yes, the bus driver will come in the morning to take you. We can help you to the lobby."

"What bus driver?"

She looked surprised by Wood's confusion. "The bus driver who hit you. He will take you to all of your rehabilitations." Dr. Nobunaga and Nurse Nishimori exited the room, leaving Craig and Olive with Wood.

Craig explained, "Showing remorse is very important in Japanese culture. Either the bus company or the insurance must think it's a good idea for the driver to help you."

Wood smiled, "Doesn't that show some fault on their part? He was just driving and I walked right in front of him. There was nothing he could do."

"It's not like in the west where apologizing automatically means you're accepting the blame."

Craig broached the uncomfortable reality of Wood's situation. "I need to find you an apartment, fast, because you can't stay here much longer and they confiscated your passport. You're not leaving Japan for a while." He pulled "The Japan Times," from his bag, the daily newspaper in English. He perused the classified ads in the back. "How big of a place do you need?"

Wood turned to Olive. "When are you heading home?"

"I don't need to be back in West Lafayette. I took the semester off."

The town's name could only mean one thing. Her new father asked slowly, "Do you go to Purdue?"

"Boiler up, y'all!"

He closed his eyes and wondered how much bad karma he had amassed to justify the cosmic revenge that was being exacted on him. He gathered himself, "You're welcome to move in with me. We can get an apartment with two rooms. I'll just be healing and waiting for the trial, whenever that is."

Olive replied, "Thanks. I'd like that. My credit card is maxed out."

PHYSICAL THERAPY

The following morning, Nurse Nishimori and an assistant helped Wood into a wheelchair and brought him downstairs. The lobby of the hospital was immense, with a crowd representing every expression of human malady possible. Wood saw a man of about 60 get out of a Toyota Camry and enter the lobby. He approached them, then threw himself to his knees, and bowed down on the linoleum floor in front of them, fully supplicated, yelling, "Gomennasai!" Wood strained his neck to look down and see him, feeling embarrassed by the driver's public display of remorse. People looked over, then returned to their illnesses.

Nurse Nishimori spoke to the man and they helped Wood get into the back seat of the Keio company car. They arrived at the rehab center and Wood was surprised when they walked in and were approached by a blind man holding a white cane. The man and the bus driver exchanged pleasantries. The bus driver sat down and read the Yomiuri Shinbun sports section while he waited for Wood.

The blind man felt for Wood's hand and carefully led him to a seat. He took a roller and began working it slowly over Wood's shoulders. The man looked up into nowhere as he massaged Wood's neck and upper back. It felt soothing, but Wood cringed in pain when he passed over his right shoulder blade. The man felt through his hospital gown then continued massaging.

Next, he led Wood to a station and sat him on a chair. He felt for a leather bridle connected to a metal cord. He put it around Wood's head, then took out a small cloth, folded it, and placed it between the strap and Wood's chin. Another strap wrapped around the back of his head. He put his hands on Wood's shoulders and smiled. He found the On button and started the machine. The cord slowly ticked as it pulled up on Wood's head, stretching his neck and reversing the trauma of the bus crash. Wood sighed as he experienced a combination of pain and tickling. It was a good pain and he let the full weight of his body relax to increase the stretch. He heard a few pops that sounded like cracking knuckles. The machine continued clicking as the cord loosened, letting him back down, then reversed and continued to pull up again. An elderly lady smiled at him and bowed slightly as she walked on a treadmill. A young man did stretches on a yoga mat across the room.

Next, the blind man removed the bridle and brought Wood to a massage table, putting him face down. He put oil on his hands that smelled of menthol and became hot as he massaged him, concentrating on pressure points this time. Sharp pains shot through Wood's body, then subsided as the man continued working in the oil before moving to another point. After twenty glorious minutes, he patted Wood on the back lightly and whispered, "Hai. Ijou desu."

They led each other back to the main table near the entrance. He took out Wood's paperwork and a little tube from his pocket that looked like lipstick. He removed the lid and stamped the paperwork, smiling and handing it back to Wood. The stamp was red and contained a circle with Japanese characters inside. Maybe that was his name.

"Hai. See you on Tuesday, Woodo-san!"

Wood got up the nerve to say, "Arigatou."

THE TRIAL DATE

Sophia Balmaceda arrived and removed some paperwork from her briefcase.

"Good news, your trial was supposed to be in six months but Judge Kuronuma is going on vacation so she scheduled us in March."

"That's still a long wait."

Her frustration showed, "You're not a rock star here and you're not in a position to make demands."

"I wasn't making demands."

"This case is going to be tough. The good news is that it's such a slam dunk for the prosecution that they put a rookie lawyer on it. This is only his third trial on his own. He wasn't very prepared at the arraignment and the judge was annoyed with him."

Sophia seemed capable, but she was young and a mystery to Wood. He asked about her background. "How did you end up being a lawyer for the embassy?"

"Both of my parents were in the foreign service – my dad is Peruvian and my mother is Japanese. I was born in New York so that makes me an American citizen. They told me to do *anything* but foreign service so I went to law school. Then I saw an opening as a government lawyer and I applied. So here I am."

"Are you trilingual?"

"Yes, although writing in Japanese is definitely the toughest for me."

Sophia was used to this kind of conversation with a client and sought to reassure him. "I'm not saying this to brag, but you're in good hands. I understand how things are done in Japan. I'm not going to give up just because the odds are against you. I want you to know that I'm rooting for you, Wood. That counts for something."

He was reassured. "I'm glad you're in my corner."

"I definitely am. Now that we know the dates, we can tell Rachel so she can come support you. I've been in touch with her."

"How do you know Rachel?"

Sophia made a ghoulish face, stared off into space, and whispered, "I come from the foreign service. We have eyes and ears *everywhere!*"

HOUSEWARMING

December 6, 1998

Shimokitazawa, Tokyo, Japan

Craig and Olive prepared the apartment he had found for them in Shimokitazawa. "Olive, you're going to love this neighborhood. There are universities nearby so you've got coffee shops and vintage clothing stores. There's a great club here called Jazz Haus Posy. Shimo has a young vibe, and you're still close to Shibuya and Harajuku. Jump on the Odakyu line and you're there.

Craig brought a few boxes of kitchen and bathroom items from his apartment and they went to the grocery store to buy fruits, veggies, a square contraption with clothespins to hang laundry, and clear plastic garbage bags. Olive added funny items to their little shopping cart, including gum called "Black Black" and "Naïve" hand lotion. Craig added bowls of instant ramen with James Brown on the label.

At the apartment, Craig reluctantly gave them his most prized possession as a housewarming gift. He carried the rolled carpet under his arm and pushed it across the living room floor with a flourish, revealing its unique beauty as it opened. "I bought this in Korea but my wife hates it, mainly because it's Korean."

Olive's eyes darted around the rug. "What the fuck am I looking at?"

The outside border was traditional Asian - elephants, bedazzled in jewels, linked by trunks and tails. The inside of the rug was cats and mice playing basketball. The mouse point guard dribbled downcourt from the left while the cats held out their paws in a 2-3 zone defense.

Olive tilted her head as she absorbed its message, "Um...thanks?"

Craig knelt and rubbed his hand along his rug, speaking to it solemnly. "We've been through a lot together. Take care of Olive and Wood for me."

As they unpacked groceries, Olive asked, "What's it like being an English teacher here?"

Craig laughed, "It's interesting. Most Japanese just want to expand their horizons and be able to order a meal in English when they go to Los Angeles or London. Some of them pick it up easily and others really struggle. The English teachers come from all over the world - obviously Great Britain, but also South Africa, Canada, the US, Australia, New Zealand, Jamaica. We even had a teacher from Fiji."

"Sounds like a fun group of friends."

"Oh yeah!" Craig checked his watch. "It's time to pick up Wood from the hospital."

***

As Craig helped Wood to the front door, Olive explained the ground rules for entering the apartment.

"Craig explained this to me and it's important. This little section here is the genkan, the entrance. This is where we remove our shoes."

Wood said, "Yes, I know we don't wear shoes in the house."

"Oh, it goes deeper than that! Your socks can't touch the genkan because then you'd be tracking all the filth inside." She demonstrated by gracefully exiting her shoes and stepping directly onto the tatami with a clean sock.

Craig said, "You nailed it, Olive!" He helped Wood remove his shoes.

Craig and Olive showed him around, proud of their efforts to make it a hospitable home. Wood was in a lot of pain, but to look at him, his injuries were difficult to discern. His neck brace was off and he walked gingerly through the apartment without a limp, shuffling his feet down the hallway. The scrapes on his face from the asphalt were nearly gone. In the bathroom he asked, "Why is the tub so short?"

Craig explained, "I prefer these. It's really deep so you pull up your knees and the water comes up to your neck. Be sure to wash off first in the shower so you're clean before you get in the bath.

"Maybe I'll just take a shower for now."

Olive relaxed on the floor in the living room. "Check this out. Each tatami mat is about the size of one person. The mats are a standard size, so you can tell how big a room is by how many tatamis it holds. Your bed is this thick blanket in the closet here. I'll get that set up for you."

Craig gave some parting information before heading home. "The hospital gave this address to the Keio bus driver. He'll come at 9:45 tomorrow morning to take you to therapy. I asked the landlady to give you the garbage schedule. That can get a little complicated. Just look at the neighbors' trash bags and copy them. Here's the number to make an international call on my account. Just put in that code and you can pay me back.

Wood gave him a hug, which hurt his shoulders and back. "I don't know what I would do without you, brother. I really don't."

THE CALL

The phone rang and Olive walked down the hall to answer it. "Moshi

moshi. It's your dime, don't waste it."

Wood couldn't make out who it was, but he made a mental note to remind Olive that her snarky line was no way to answer a telephone in a respectable family. He could hear the call escalate as he struggled to stand up and amble down the hall.

Olive said, "Maybe you're the one who needs an attitude adjustment."

Muffled talking.

"Then you should learn how to take care of your man!"

Muffled screaming.

"Bitch, I will drop you like a bad habit!"

Muffled psychotic screaming.

Olive's last line shuttled Wood straight back to junior high. "I don't start fights, I *finish* 'em!"

He wrestled the phone from Olive, gave her a look of disappointment, and raised a screaming Rachel to his ear.

"*...so unless you wanna end up hanging next to a beef carcass you'd better learn some manners, kid!*"

He paused and spoke calmly. "Hi, honey. It's Wood. It sounds like you've met my daughter." He could hear Rachel panting through the phone. She took a full thirty seconds to calm herself.

"That girl has a mouth on her. And her tone is like nails on a chalkboard. Jesus!"

"I will talk to her. I'm sorry about that."

"Craig called yesterday to tell me about her. I think he was trying to drop the bomb so you didn't have to. He also told me you're having trouble remembering your songs. How are you feeling?"

"Much better than before. They removed the neck brace and I'm walking around without assistance. I go to physical therapy every other day. They gave me some pain killers but they don't work."

"I have some heavy-duty stuff I take for my PMS. They're like horse pills. I'll bring some with me when I come to visit."

Wood's spirits lifted, "When are you coming?"

"This Saturday morning, Tokyo time. Craig's going to pick me up. I'll be there through the end of the trial then I have to come straight back."

"It could take a long time."

"I told daddy that I haven't taken a real vacation in years. He knows this is important and he likes you. There wasn't much he could say. I'm giving my niece a crash course on how to run this place. She's a sharp kid and her next semester doesn't start for a while. She's a Business major."

Wood exhaled, "I miss you. It'll be good to have you around after all this insanity."

"I'm nervous about flying, but I'll make it."

***

He hung up the phone and found Olive sitting on the sofa watching TV. He promised himself not to use foul language. If he was going to teach her some manners he had to be a good example, or at least not a hypocrite.

"Olive, turn that off, please. I want to talk to you."

"Hold on, it's almost over."

"Turn it off *now!*"

Olive instinctively blurted out, "You're not my dad!" then blushed at her error.

Wood walked over and pulled the TV cord out of the socket. The screen went dark.

"You flew to the other side of the world to tell me that I *am* your father. Now I know which line you've been using on your stepdad for the last 15 years. I've never met him but I already feel sorry for the guy. We're going to have some rules around here."

Olive shifted back and forth on the sofa, still holding the remote.

"What kind of rules?"

"Rules of decorum and basic etiquette. I don't know what expectations you had in your house, but what I just witnessed was appalling. There was absolutely no reason whatsoever to get in a shouting match with Rachel. She just called to see how we were doing."

"So I guess your parents were strict."

"It's a long story. My mother, your grandmother, lived by her own rules and I had a lot of freedom as a child. I mean, a *lot*. But when we left the house I was expected to comport myself in a way that didn't bring shame to the family. You know, exchange pleasantries, give a firm handshake and look someone in the eye, not cuss like a sailor. I mean, Jesus, where did you get that mouth?"

"My mom thinks it's important to express myself however I see fit."

Wood closed his eyes and shook his head in utter confusion. "And the way you see fit is to throw a tantrum like a twelve-year-old? Come on, you're in college. Your mom might think you should express yourself however you see fit, whatever that means, but the rest of the planet does *not* work that way. It just doesn't, Olive. That attitude isn't going to work when you have to talk to a professor, have a job interview, or get pulled over by a cop."

Olive had no reply. She looked around the room, trying to avoid eye contact. "Is Rachel pissed off?"

"She'll be here on Saturday so you can ask her yourself!"

Olive finally looked at her father. "What?"

"Yeah, you can give her an attitude adjustment and drop her like a bad habit."

"Hey, I didn't start the fight with her."

"Well now you can finish it, just like you said!"

THE FIRST GUITAR LESSON

Craig called that night. Olive answered in a quiet voice. "Moshi moshi. Underwood residence."

"Hi, Olive. It's Craig. Are you getting settled in over there?"

"Yes, I guess so. We just ate dinner. I went and grabbed some burgers from McDonalds. I asked for more ketchup and the girl went and talked to her manager. Then that manager found another manager, then they gave me one more packet. It was kinda funny."

Craig laughed. "Yeah, you'll have a lot of funny stories when you go home. Just try to see the humor in things and you'll be fine. Can I speak with your dad?"

"Yes, just a moment, please."

She handed Wood the phone and said, "It's Craig, your highness."

"Hey Craig, what's up?"

"I have a surprise for you. I'm sending over a guitar teacher to give you some lessons. My friend's daughter studied with him and he was very patient. He's in a cover band. I went to check them out and this dude was laying down some smoking solos. He's incredible."

"Ummm…okay. What's his name?"

"Atsushi."

"Like sushi?"

186

"No, the accent is on the A. *AT*sushi. Listen, he doesn't know who you are. He thinks you're some gaijin who wants to learn a bunch of famous rock songs."

"It's probably better that way. Thanks for doing this."

"You bet. He'll stop by tomorrow afternoon. His English isn't that great, but they say music is the universal language."

"I guess we'll find out if that's true."

***

The next afternoon, Olive opened the door and greeted Atsushi, who brought his guitar, a small amp, and a book bag. He was in his early twenties with shoulder length hair and wrist bands. He wore a Fence of Defense T-shirt. He removed his shoes and said, "Sumimasen" as he walked down the hall. Olive led him to the living room where Wood was seated with Martina, his acoustic. He greeted Atsushi, who said, "Nice to meet you" and began setting up his equipment.

He sat down and smiled, "Craig-san tell me you want to learn rock songs. Who do you like?" He counted on his fingers, "Eaguruzu, Pinku Floyd, Oasisu?"

"I am also in a cover band. We play Driftwood songs. The hits."

Atsushi looked confused and shook his head. "Why do you like Driftwood?"

"Umm…because he's cool."

Atsushi looked through his book bag and pulled out a Japanese/English dictionary. He said to himself, "Muno, muno, muno" until he found the word and showed it to Wood."

Wood read the word, "Incompetent."

Atsushi said, "Yes. Maybe we can practice song from good musician."

Wood felt a burning sensation in his neck and upper back. "I like Driftwood. I only want to learn his songs."

Defeated, Atsushi shook his head. "Okay. You are za bosu!"

"Thanks. I have his CD. Let's start with 'Palace.'"

THE GOMI DILEMNA

Olive walked back into the apartment looking dejected. She removed her shoes and yelled, "They left it there again!"

Wood studied the trash schedule, trying to make sense of the calendar. Two of the days were a different color. He assumed those were Saturday and Sunday, then wrote letters above each day in English. The instructions describing what should happen on each day looked like a sushi menu. A group of pictures denoted fire, food, batteries, a stereo, and a stack of magazines.

As Olive sat down he asked, "Why did you and Craig buy see-through trash bags? Buy black next time so they can't see what we're putting in there!"

"They only sell transparent bags! I looked out the window and the trash guys were investigating everything like FBI agents at a fucking crime scene. Sorry, at a crime scene. One of them took our broom though."

"That wasn't garbage! It was our only broom. He just wanted it for his house!"

KINOKUNIYA

Olive came home with a bag from Kinokuniya bookstore and yelled as she removed her shoes in the genkan. "I bought some goodies!" She pulled out a sketch pad and a box of pastels, a few stacks of flashcards with metal rings holding them together, a Japanese/English dictionary, and two copies of "Japanese for Busy People."

"What's all this?"

"I was thinking we could study Japanese together. I met this lady from the French embassy at the bookstore. She said this is the book all the gaijin buy when they first arrive. That's what we are, "gaijin." It will help with your cognitive recovery."

"Cognitive recovery. Okay." He thumbed through the book. "Wait, they have three alphabets? What are you getting me into?"

"They have hiragana…that's the main one. Then they use katakana for foreign words, and then there are thousands of kanji characters. We can just learn some phrases though."

"Yeah, I'd like to be able to interact with people around here."

"And we can make flashcards with the answers on the back. The French lady said that's how she learned. There's a section on ordering a pizza delivery. There's even a part about sorting garbage. It's called 'Gomi'."

"Be sure to highlight that."

"Check it out. These are the days of the week. Tuesday means 'Fire Day.' Maybe that's when we put out stuff that will burn."

Wood patted Olive on the back, "Good work. We'll give that a try on Tuesday."

Craig called and asked how things were going. Wood summarized the current chapter in his life, "Let's see…I'm going to physical therapy because I got hit by a bus, I forgot my own songs but I'm learning them from a guitar player who thinks they suck, I'm probably going to jail for assault, and my dead mother has been reincarnated in the form of my new daughter, a Purdue student who cusses like a sailor. But you know me, I'm not one to complain."

Craig laughed, "Keep your chin up."

"I would if I could move my head."

NIHONGO

Wood took a long walk around the neighborhood at dusk, noting the round mirrors that warned drivers of someone coming around the corner. He was walking without dragging his feet now. He walked inside the apartment and removed his shoes, making sure not to touch the genkan with his feet. He heard Olive yell, "Okaeri!" He walked into the living room. She was sitting on the ground filling out flash cards as she looked at Japanese for Busy People. "When someone comes home you're supposed to yell, 'Okaeri.'"

"What does that mean?"

"'Welcome home' or something. Look how many I've made so far?" She handed him a stack and he flipped through them, impressed by her diligence and penmanship.

"Good job, Olive. Looks like I need to catch up. You wanna divide and conquer?"

"How so?"

"Tell me a topic to look up and I'll make another stack. We can study each other's flashcards, too."

"Good idea." She picked up his book and found the chapter on garbage day, called Gomi No Hi. "Here. This oughta keep you busy for a while."

Wood grabbed the garbage pamphlet from the kitchen and found the corresponding kanji in the book. He wrote down important terms like "Moeru Gomi" on the front and "Burnable" on the back.

WHERE EVERYBODY KNOWS YOUR NAME, PART I

Wood went for a walk through the neighborhood while Olive watched TV. Shimokitazawa was hopping with young people in shops, laughing, and taking photos of each other. For some reason, everyone felt the need to make the peace sign. There was a young British couple trying to take their own photo with the nightlife in the background.

Wood asked, "Would you like me to take your photo?"

"Cheers, that would be great."

Wood focused the camera and pressed the button. "I think I got it."

The woman viewed the photo on the back of the camera and said, "It's a little out of focus." He watched her delete the photo and hand the camera back to him. "Could you take another, please?"

"What kind of camera is this?"

"It's digital. If you don't like the photo you just take another one."

"Where's the film?"

"You upload them to your computer." The woman looked a little embarrassed for him. He took another photo, making sure it was in focus.

He walked down a narrow alley and heard Patsy Cline blaring from a karaoke machine. Somebody was walking after midnight and falling to pieces at the same time. He opened the door and entered. Everyone looked surprised to see a gaijin walk in. Not many foreigners had found their way down that little alley, but this was Tokyo, after all. Anything could happen.

He ordered a Jack and Coke. The owner, a petite lady who looked to be in her forties, smiled and repeated his order, "Jacku Danieruzu to Coke, desune?"

Nodding, he replied, "Hai, kudasai."

She passed him the drink, motioning to a little table toward the back where he could observe the whole scene. A cute young lady came from behind the counter to bring some snacks to Wood, giving him a friendly smile. She had shoulder length, curly hair. "Hi. My name is Haruna." Pointing back at the owner, "She's my...nanteyuno...my father's sister."

"She's your *aunt*."

"Sou sou...my aunt."

"Hajimemashite. My name is Wood."

"Nice to meet you. Nihongo wakarimasuka?"

"No, sorry, not yet. I'm studying though!" He pulled a packet of flashcards from his breast pocket and showed her.

The door opened and a chubby man entered wearing a cheap suit, sunglasses, and gold jewelry. The whole crowd yelled, "Noguchi!" The owner asked him a question, he replied, and everyone laughed.

Next in was Kurihara, who had just arrived from the Post Office. Wood couldn't understand a word he said, but judging by the facial expressions of the others, his opinions didn't quite gel with their understanding of history or current events. He said something to Haruna and she frowned, shaking her fist in his face.

Finally, a tall, intellectual man with a receding hairline walked in and ordered a glass of red wine. Noticing a new face, and a foreign one at that, he walked over. "Welcome to our izakaya. Nice to meet you."

"I'm Wood. Nice to meet you, too. I like this place. It's very small and everyone is happy."

"Yes, very happy, like a family without the fights. Do you live in this neighborhood? Just visiting?"

"I've been living here for a few weeks. I like it."

"Are you here on business?"

"I was a musician. I think I still am. It's a long story. How about you?

"I am a psychiatrist."

"Are there a lot of psychiatrists in Japan?"

"Not enough! Everyone has the same philosophy. GAMAN!"

"What does that mean?"

"It means many things; persevere, don't complain, don't cry."

"I like that. I've been practicing my gaman for a while now."

"Are you here alone or with family?"

"I'm here with my daughter but she's only twenty. I wish she could see this place."

"The drinking age is twenty in Japan! Bring her with you next time."

FLASHBACK

The next evening, Olive and Wood sat in Agoos Café drinking coffee. He took a drink and said, "I don't understand why your mom kept everything from you."

"I just came over here because I wanted to see you before you died, but you never died."

"Thanks. What do you want to know?"

"Everything."

"If you can't take it then let me know right now."

"I've been trying to figure out what the hell happened my whole life. Obviously, my mom hasn't been much help."

"She gave you enough information to come find me. Give her credit for that."

"Was she one of your groupies?"

"Your Mother was my first love, in every way. I met her my junior year of high school."

"So you were high school sweethearts?"

Wood smiled and took a drink of his iced coffee. "Not even close." He looked at Olive and said, "Here's how you came into this world."

SCHOLASTIC APTITUDE, PART III

1981

Yvette asked, "Do you have a girlfriend at school?"

"I do fine but I don't want to be tied down. I enjoy my freedom and hanging out with friends, playing music." Wood couldn't admit that no girl that he desired would give him the time of day. It was always the same, when he showed interest in a girl she laughed in his face. When someone told him that a girl was interested in him, he rolled his eyes. Maybe knowing that someone was willing to date him lowered their stock, like Groucho Marx saying he would never join a club that would accept him as a member.

Wood couldn't believe that Yvette was still there, spending her precious time with him. "Are you going back to Butler? I'm sure there are plenty of dorm parties on a Saturday night."

"I'm not really into that scene. I don't have anywhere else to be. Want to watch a movie?"

"Yeah, I love movies!"

A tiny seed of what may be happening found its way into Wood's 17-year-old brain, but every fiber of his being told him he was wrong. She was just too bored to be anywhere else.

Although it was a nice spring evening, Wood built a roaring fire in the hopes that it would kindle some primal desire in her. She knelt next to him looking through their VHS tapes. More wine was essential. He looked through his mother's collection, settling on the oldest bottle with the longest name. 1971 Domaine de la Romanee-Conti Grand Cru, Cote de Nuits, France. He opened it to breathe while he made a Jiffy Pop, making sure not to burn it, walking on eggshells as if any error, any misspoken word, would launch the beautiful Yvette into the night, never to return.

As Wood entered with his feast of popcorn and French wine, Rachel asked, "What's Harold and Maude about?"

"That's the only movie that my mother and I both love. It's about an old lady and this awkward rich kid who become friends and start hanging out. The whole soundtrack is by Cat Stevens. Mom loves classical and jazz, but she makes an exception for his music."

Handing her the glass, "To us."

"Yeah, to us." They touched glasses then took a drink. She savored the wine for a moment. "Hmmm…pretty good. A little too dry for me but it gets the job done!"

They watched the quirky romance together. He laughed when Yvette laughed and mimicked her emotions during every scene. He glanced down to see when she was reaching for popcorn so his hand could collide with hers. When Maude was running from a CHP, spinning donuts with a tree in the back of the car, they yelled, "With a tree in the back of an El Camino!" They laughed when Harold chopped off his fake arm in front of his horrified first date. By the end of the movie they had drained the wine bottle. During the final scene, as Harold's Jaguar careened over the cliff and he began dancing with his banjo, Wood grabbed his acoustic guitar and sang along with "If You Want to Sing Out" by Cat Stevens. As the credits rolled, Yvette glanced over to watch Wood play and sing along. After the screen went black, she turned toward him, saying, "I'm pretty buzzed so I shouldn't drive right now."

"Yeah, you should stay until you sober up."

"Are you sure you don't have a girlfriend? I find it hard to believe that a handsome young man like yourself isn't taken."

"I swear it's true." He put the guitar down and turned to face her. This wasn't happening. Why would she ask him that?

"It's hot in here." She pulled off her Butler sweatshirt, took off her glasses, and ran her fingers through her hair. All that was between Wood and her breasts was a thin white t-shirt and no bra. Only a shy teenage boy could have this many clues and still not believe what was about to happen. Wood didn't move. He sat staring at her, unsure of what to do next. She waited for him to do something, anything, then reached over and touched his hand. She leaned over and kissed his forehead, then down the side of his face, stopping at his lips, their faces nearly touching. She could feel him trying to control his breathing.

Wood whispered, "I've never done this before."

"I know, baby. It's okay if you're nervous. Just relax. I don't bite." He gathered the nerve to kiss her on the lips. Sensing he was finally home free; he slid his hand under her shirt.

Yvette grabbed his hand and gently pulled it down, "Hold on. Not so fast."

"Sorry, I thought it was okay."

"You teenage boys get a hard on when a girl walks by. It's okay, just go slow. Enjoy it."

He put his hand on her cheek and kissed her lips slowly. "I love you."

"And *definitely* don't say that too soon!" She laughed and rolled her eyes, "You have a *lot* to learn! Lucky for you, I'm willing to teach you."

"But I love you. What's wrong with telling the truth?"

"Because women are like cats. Actually, men are too. If you run across the room to pounce on a cat... *'Rahhh!'* that thing is long gone. You will never hold anything when you scare it away. But if you sit back and maintain, eventually it will curl up in your lap."

She pushed him back against the sofa, straddled him and began kissing him again. She took his hand and put it under her shirt as she unbuttoned his pants and straddled him.

"I don't want to get you pregnant."

"It's okay. I'm on the pill. Just relax." She began grinding him, slowly at first, then faster as they kissed. Just as she felt him getting close, she slid off of him. "If you want it to last you need to know when to slow down. You don't want some future girlfriend telling all her friends that you lasted two minutes, do you?"

"I thought only boys talked about sex."

"Oh God, you are so naïve! High school girls talk about everything! They will know if you're well endowed – luckily you are. They'll know if you were sensual or just wanted to get laid. They'll know if you can last, everything."

"That's a lot of pressure."

"You better tell your friends with little weenies that they'd better figure out where that clit is, and fast. You boys with your locker room talk got nothing on us."

By now she was on him again. He held her hips, helping her to grind faster as she moaned, leaning her head back and closing her eyes until her body started shaking. She leaned forward, letting her long black hair fall on his face as she brought him to his first orgasm with a woman.

They fell asleep on the sofa. Wood went comatose, woke to feel Yvette's body against his, then slept again. At dawn he opened his eyes to see her getting dressed. Bending down for a kiss, she whispered, "This never happened, okay?"

***

That morning, Wood called his neighbor Wendy, a classmate he'd known since kindergarten. He had to tell *someone*. Wendy was shocked and told her best friend, because she had to, and the high school's well-oiled gossip machine hummed. By Thursday, even a few teachers knew that he had been "sleeping with a sexy Butler student." Wood's social standing skyrocketed, although it was not his intention for anyone but Wendy to know. Saying things like, "Sorry, I'm not a kiss-and-tell kinda guy" only added to his intrigue.

Questions were asked in the girls' locker room; "Did we get it all wrong?" "By the way, why do they call him 'Wood'?"

Oblivious to these hallway musings, Wood's brain could only dedicate itself to one thought – Yvette. He counted the hours until he would see her again. Any attempts at studying morphed into his writing her name in his diary. He wrote her full name then replaced her family name with Underwood to see what it would look like when they got married. He was dejected when he heard her voice on the answering machine cancelling their tutoring session, citing her papers and exams as the excuse. He listened to it repeatedly just to hear her sultry voice, ignoring the fact that it carried news that he did not want to hear. He considered erasing it. Each time his finger touched the Delete button, he pressed Play again.

At school, his announcement that he planned to "have a few friends over" while his mom was partying in Kentucky added airs of daring and social benevolence to his reputation. He wasn't throwing a party; he was just having a few friends over. It was something one would say while wearing a smoking jacket. "There's wine coolers in the fridge and a pony keg in the garage. No biggie."

It was important for Yvette to be there, for her presence to be known by at least a handful of classmates, for with any grand rumor comes the naysayers, speculating that perhaps she didn't even exist. Wood found her number and left a message about the party. "Hey, Yvette. I hope your exams went well. My Mom's still outta town so I'm gonna have a few friends over this Saturday. Bring a few people if you want."

The party started out slowly and was in danger of being a boring affair. He dispatched a friend to the local fast food parking lots to spread the news. Within an hour a huge crowd streamed in, many of them strangers. They drank through everything in sight and devoured snacks like locusts. With a good buzz now thoroughly installed, Wood worried about his ability to prevent the destruction of his own home.

"Hey, Wood, we need more booze! Where's the key to this bar?"

"Sorry, man, my mom took it with her."

They took the hinges off the doors, opening it slowly to reveal its contents, like an Egyptian tomb. There was a note in Charlotte's handwriting, "Thurston, I love you. Please don't do it." By this time the party was on autopilot, a sentient being unto its own, turning a deaf ear to Charlotte's requests, her son now a bystander.

The only reason to throw the party at all was to show off Yvette - yet she wasn't there. When Wood returned from kicking two lovers out of his mother's room, he saw her in the kitchen holding a beer. There were two Butler girls with her and some guy. Who the fuck was this asshole? The college boy took a pack of Charlotte's cigarettes from a carton above the fridge, lit a smoke and opened a bottle of beer by placing the cap just above the countertop and slamming his palm down on it. The cap rolled across the kitchen floor. The intruder left the cap there for someone else to pick up and took a swig of the beer he had stolen from Wood's fridge.

Wood fumed as he saw the college boy put his arm around Yvette, who glanced over to gauge Wood's reaction, then smirked and looked down. The high school kids were playing quarters. Yvette yelled, "You amateurs suck. Give me that quarter!" She sat down, held the coin up to the bridge of her nose. "The trick is to look forward, not down." She released the quarter and it glided down her perfect nose like a ski jumper, hit perpendicular to the table and bounced into the shot glass with a triumphant clink. Pointing at a guy wearing a football jersey, "Drink, motherfucker!" The room erupted in cheers.

"Beginner's luck!" called out a math nerd, immediately regretting it.

"Beginner's luck? Okay, these are for you, Clearasil!" Yvette placed the shot glass between them, clinking the quarter eight more times. The room laughed as he chugged beer after beer for the sin of harassing a college girl. Finally, slamming the quarter down on the table, Yvette yelled, "I'm bored. Next!"

She walked down the dark hallway and closed the bathroom door. Wood slipped out the door into the back yard, went around and entered through the side door, waiting in the hallway until she came out. As she exited, he touched her shoulder and motioned for her to follow him into his bedroom.

Wood was livid, "Who the hell is that guy? And why is he hanging all over you?"

"He's a friend from college. What do you care?"

"Because I love you. I throw this party and you bring some guy. Really? You're *my* girl."

Rachel looked confused, "Are you kidding me? I'm *nobody's* girl. Not yours, not his. I just felt sorry for you. All this puppy love bullshit is your own fault."

"Then why did you make love to me?"

Correcting his description, "We *had sex* because you were lonely and stressed. I knew it would be your first time and I wanted it to be special."

"It was special. I think about you constantly. It's painful. And now you bring this fucker to my party?"

"Well, I made a mistake." She opened the door, "I gotta get back to the party. Chad's going to come looking for me."

"Chad? You're dating a guy named after a country? Well, that's just perfect! Nobody will ever accuse you of being original."

Shaking her head as she left the room, "Whatever, kid."

That last word - "kid"- brought a new level of pain he didn't know existed. Wood paced around his room, steaming, dejected, confused, buzzed. Maybe she wouldn't think of him as a kid if she saw him take charge of the situation. He slipped around the back yard. As he approached the back door the glass shattered in front of him. He looked down to see a frozen burrito at his feet. He calmly entered, walked over to the console stereo, intentionally scratched the needle across Joy Division's Closer and screamed, "Party's over! Everyone, get the fuck out!" He scanned the room to see Yvette's reaction, but she and her friends had already gone. Wood's magnificent affirmation that this was, in fact, *his* party and *his* house went unwitnessed by its intended recipient.

The crowd made a few complaints, then began returning the burritos to the freezer and gathering their things. The aquarium castle relinquished its role as makeshift bong and was returned to its watery home. The last to leave was Wendy, his trusted neighbor and childhood friend. She kissed Wood on the cheek. "I'm sorry about Yvette. I'll come by in the morning to help you clean up this mess."

The last car's engine faded down the street and Wood stood alone in the quiet living room. He picked up a few bottles, put them back down, went to bed and cried.

***

Wendy was a true friend and specialized in post-party resurrections. She singlehandedly took on the bathroom, which alone canonized her in Wood's mind. Someone had projectile vomited, with the obvious goal of hitting everything but the toilet.

Returning to the living room 20 minutes later, Wendy was a changed person. "Well, that's done. Now the trick is to predict the questions your mother would ask if she were to walk in right now."

"Why is a moldy burrito in the fish tank?"

"Who stole my carton of cigarettes?"

"Why does this bourbon taste like Earl Grey?"

"Where's the cat?"

After two hours the house was as close to its previous state as they could make it. Future discoveries would hopefully be so bizarre that they couldn't be linked to the party. Years later, Wendy became a respected forensics expert, unraveling crime scenes for the FBI.

***

Wood settled back into school life. There were comments about the party for a few days until the students turned their attention to the next rager. Even Wood's friends, who cruelly reminded him that Yvette left the party with some college guy, had to admit that she existed, and that she was even more attractive than Wood had described.

All week he recited the things he would say to Yvette during their next tutoring session, but the time came and passed without her arrival. Given their argument, he wasn't entirely surprised. Wood sat in his room writing her name on the pages of his diary. His daydreams drifted from their lovemaking to thoughts of what she might be doing with Chad. He wondered why anyone would sign up for a lifetime of love, given the pain that caved in his chest.

UNCLE FREDDIE: THE FUN BUFFER

Wood's mother returned and resumed her life without noticing any evidence of a party. Yvette had disappeared. A month later, Uncle Freddie called to say he was coming to take Wood out for lunch. He was expecting to go to a nice restaurant but was surprised when he followed his uncle into the Freemasons Hall down near the city circle. They went into the bar and Uncle Freddie signed in Wood as his guest. He greeted the bartender. "Hi, Jimmy. This is my nephew, Thurston. We'll have two Macallans, please."

"Good to know you, Thurston. Have a seat wherever you like and I'll bring those over to you."

When Jimmy brought over their whiskey, Wood tried to refuse and order a Coke. Uncle Freddie spoke up, "Pay no heed, Jimmy. My nephew wants to be a man. A real man! He needs that whiskey!"

"It's just that..."

"Sure, you do! You want to drink your mother's whiskey, throw parties, let your friends destroy family heirlooms, and get a college girl pregnant!" Wood looked down at the table in shock, realizing the real reason they were there.

Jimmy walked behind the bar and performed one of his prized bartending skills; the ability to busy himself while others discussed cringeworthy topics.

Wood sat staring at the dark mahogany table between them. After an endless silence, feeling the heat from Uncle Freddie's stare, he whispered, "I can explain."

"Sometimes, in life, less is more. I was thinking we could play a game where you shut up and I speak for a while, if you don't mind."

"Yes, sir."

Uncle Freddie took a long drink of his Macallan and gathered his thoughts. "This...Yvette." He hissed the T when he said her name. "She called me a few days ago because I am the one who hired her, the one who pays for everything at your house, and I mean e-ver-y-thing. Not just for you, but for your mother. I don't discuss money out of respect for her unfortunate state of financial affairs. Your housing, clothes, insurance, car, Park Tudor, and hopefully your college tuition someday. Your mother is a piano teacher. Do you think that paid for your trip to Europe last year? I thought it would be healthy for you to see Europe's great museums, maybe take in some theatre, improve your French and Italian. It made me a better young man and it encouraged me to take my studies seriously upon my return, to take advantage of the wonderful opportunities that this life, that this *family*, had afforded me. Even as a young man I could grasp the good fortune of my life. One cannot learn about the great artists and musicians of Europe and not realize that they could have only accomplished it through great perseverance and tutelage! I wanted that for you because I know you haven't had a father around. I'm not saying that your childhood has been easy. Your mother can be quite demanding, and I've tried to be a buffer, if you will. A fun buffer! Did you not enjoy the skeet shooting? Remember the sailing lessons on Lake Max?"

After a long pause, Wood sensed it was his time to respond. "I loved it. I thought I expressed my thanks."

"I was hoping you would come back from Europe and apply yourself, truly *apply* yourself, but I soon realized that you slid back into your lazy behaviors, your music. I won't pretend that I wasn't disappointed when you quit the basketball team. You quit because some kid beat you out for starting forward? If one kid rolled an ankle, you'd be back on the court as a starter. You were the sixth man and we were damned proud of you. Anytime someone got tired or in foul trouble, who went in? Thurston did! Every rebound, every baseline jumper made your mother and me swell with pride. So you can understand how crestfallen we were when you quit. You never told us of your intentions. You just quit! You have been quite nonchalant in your betrayal of your own talents. Yes, your *betrayal* of God-given talent. You cannot deny that, Thurston." He pounded his index finger on the table.

"I understand, sir."

"Now, your grades have been unimpressive, as you are aware, and yet nobody can doubt your pure intelligence. Your *Underwood* intelligence. That is why I sought an SAT tutor for you. If you can get a great score, one that really raises the eyebrows, coupled with our family connections and perhaps a generous financial donation, well, the sky is the limit, as they say! So I interviewed a few tutors, knowing I had to find someone to really pique your interest. I found very smart tutors but when this, this YveTTe walked in I knew that she would keep you focused, based on beauty alone, and it turns out she aced the damned test! Truly a gem of a young lady, from a prominent Zionsville family, no less. But I never thought for a moment that you would end up sleeping with that little Jezebel!"

He took another long drink and lit a cigar, fiddling helplessly with his Zippo as he tried to calm himself. Jimmy the bartender shined glasses and held them up to the light for inspection.

"Does my mother know that...that Yvette is pregnant?"

"She does not, and she will *never* know. Before I sound too self-righteous, Thurston, I must admit that I have howled at the moon a few times in my younger days. Oh yes, *howled*. My friends and I got up to some tomfoolery, especially at Wabash! My dear fraternity brother, Henry, was quite the drunkard and skirt chaser. Oh, the things we did to Freshmen trying to rush our beloved fraternity! Well, Henry was able to straighten himself out and find his way in this world. He is the Dean of Admissions at a very prestigious liberal arts college now! Luckily, I avoided bringing shame to this family, delicately navigating life's twists and turns as they were presented to me, dodging bullets and grasping opportunities!"

Lowering his voice, Uncle Freddie tapped the table, "This pregnancy is not the end of the world, but it must be solved hastily."

By this time, Wood only wanted to know when he would see Yvette again. He was in love with her and, although a baby was not originally in his plans, he quickly envisioned a life with her and their child. His mind raced with images of a beautiful baby, who looked like him and whose mother was a sexy genius. Was it a girl? He didn't even know Yvette's phone number, had no idea how to contact her. Uncle Freddie's mention of a fine Zionsville family gave him a starting place, but how could he know she wanted to be found? Butler was just down the road. Maybe he could hang out there until she showed up. He awoke from his daydream with Uncle Freddie's chubby fingers snapping in front of his face.

"Sorry. What do you want me to do, Uncle Freddie?"

"It's done!" said Uncle Freddie emphatically. "You'll never see her again. I sent Yvette and her friend to my condo in carMELL. It's much easier to get this kind of problem solved in California. I gave her plenty of money to stay out of our lives for good. It's for the best, Thurston. All I want you to do is focus on your studies. I've already arranged for a new tutor to begin next week – an ugly lad with horrible breath. I can assure you there won't be any attraction this time. Jimmy, mix us an Old Fashioned. We're celebrating!"

"Coming right up, Mr. Underwood. What's the occasion?"

"My nephew has become a man."

***

Olive wiped the tears from her eyes with her sleeve and stared into her coffee.

"I knew I was supposed to be aborted. I just had this feeling from the time I understood what it was. Mom always came up with one story or another; that my father ran off or was killed in a car accident. One time she said that he was a famous musician and I just ignored it. When she read in the news that you got hit by that bus she sat me down and told me. We got in a big argument because I wanted to come here before you died. She thought it was a bad idea but gave me the money. I'm closer to my stepdad than my mother."

"I'm sorry you had to live through all that uncertainty, Olive. I knew it would be better to tell you the truth. And that *is* the truth, as far as I can remember. I'm sure it's distorted by my youth and broken heart, but I owe you my truth. Our truth."

"Why didn't she get the abortion?"

"I don't know, but I was ready to be your dad when I was seventeen, as insane as that sounds. Jesus, I would have been a horrible father!"

"I'm just wondering why she didn't go through with it. Your uncle gave her a lot of money, which I'm sure she did not return."

"I can't speak for her. Once she knows that you have all the details she'll be more willing to talk openly. The cat's out of the bag, as they say. Just remember that she may never be willing to share why she made her choices, and you have to respect that, okay?"

Olive knew that it was *not* okay, and that she would rake her mother over the coals in the years to come, but nodded and said, "I understand."

Wood reached into his coat pocket and pulled out an envelope. He slid it across the table, saying, "I've been meaning to give this to you. It should stay in the family."

Olive opened the envelope and pulled out a delicate gold necklace with a treble clef pendant. "Was this my mom's?"

"It was your grandmother's. Her name was Charlotte Marie Underwood. She died recently of lung cancer. In fact, the funeral was last week. She was a music major and had an affair with her professor. He gave her this necklace before he left town. I only found out recently. That's who my father was...professor Menders. Can you imagine buying an album from Thurston Menders?"

Charlotte massaged the pendant with her fingertip, inspecting it closely. "Did you know him?"

"He wasn't in my life, although I met him a few times. This tall man showed up at our house on my 5th birthday. Your grandma said he was my uncle from Chicago. I thought Uncle Freddie was my only uncle. I just remember sitting on his lap while he played piano. Then he showed up years later and grandma said they were going on a date – so I knew she was lying. I said, 'You're going on a date with your brother? Ewww!'"

Olive rolled her eyes, "Why do adults tell children so many lies? Then they can't even remember which lies they told!"

Wood sat back and spread his arms across the back of the booth. "Hell if I know. I guess they think they're protecting us."

THE GUN STREET GIRL IN TOKYO

Wood and Olive walked to Lawson to buy snacks. He brought no experience to his new parental conversations and had little guidance in his own childhood. Not knowing how to broach the conversation, he just said it. "I want you to go with Craig to pick up Rachel from Narita."

Olive walked in silence before asking, "Why aren't you going?"

"I talked with Craig about it. Narita is really far from Tokyo and jostling around in the car isn't good for my neck. I think it would be a nice gesture for you to be there."

"It might clear the air. I mean, she's not going to haul off and punch me in the middle of an airport."

"Not if she's jetlagged."

"So what's going on between you? Are you an item?"

"Rachel has been my manager for about six years now. There was always an attraction there, but nothing happened until recently."

"Do you love her?"

It was Wood's turn to walk in silence. "Yeah, I do. I've come to realize that I've been a better man since she's come into my life, as hard as that might appear sometimes."

"Have you told her?"

"I don't think so."

"You don't *think* so? What the fu...hell...heck does that mean?"

"We didn't become intimate until right before I came to Japan. The accident erased some memories. I think I would have remembered telling her I loved her."

"If that's how you feel, you should tell her when she gets here."

They walked into Lawson and bought a variety of snacks, including the classics like Doritos and Kit Kats blended with recent staples like hiyashi chuka, onigiri, and milk tea.

Olive asked, "What do you think Rachel would like?"

"She has a sweet tooth. Nothing too weird." Olive added some Meiji chocolate, Boss coffee, and strawberry pocky sticks.

When they got home she used her new art supplies to make an airport sign with Rachel's name on it with flowers and hearts. Neither Craig nor Olive had seen her before. Craig tried to give Olive some perspective on the way to the airport.

"Your father has been through a lot in the last few months. His bandmate left him. His dog got hit by a car. He walked in front of a bus, then his mother died while he was in a coma. Oh, and he might do time in a Japanese prison."

"He told me about my grandma the other day. What kind of dog did he have?"

"A Basset Hound named Margaret."

NARITA INTERNATIONAL AIRPORT

December 13, 1998

Olive held her sign, looking for a woman who might be Rachel, not sure what would happen once they met.

Rachel looked tired but smiled as she approached them. "You must be Craig and...Olive?"

"Yes," Olive said sheepishly. "I brought you some snacks. Let's go find your bags!"

As she walked behind Olive, Rachel was surprised at the change in dynamics. Was this the same girl who screamed at her over the phone? They put her bags in the trunk. Olive started to get into the front seat, then paused and offered it to Rachel, who looked surprised that Olive had tried to take it in the first place. By the time they made the long drive to Shimokitazawa, Rachel had been apprised of the latest developments, from the trial to physical therapy, garbage to guitar lessons.

When they walked in, Wood was clean shaven and dressed in a collared shirt. He almost appeared back to normal, and it made him feel like his old self.

Rachel gave Wood a kiss and a long hug. "I'm sorry about your Mom. She was a great lady."

"Thanks, baby. I didn't know she had cancer."

They showed her around the house. Craig stayed for a minute, then drove home.

Olive asked, "Are you hungry?"

"A little, thanks."

"We discovered hiyashi chuka. It's cold noodles with cucumber, tomatoes, ham, and a sauce. It sounds weird but it's *so* good. They only eat it in the summer."

"I'll give it a try. Thanks."

KNIGHT RIDER

That evening Olive explained their new linguistic competition to Rachel. "We made these flashcards to study Japanese vocab, then we watch Knight Rider reruns. You get a point if you know any of the words. I've been kicking his butt."

Wood said, "Get ready to go down, kiddo."

The show opened with David Hasselhoff driving KITT, his talking Pontiac

Trans Am, both speaking fluent Japanese.

KITT said, "Konnichiwa, Michael-san."

Olive yelled, "Konnichiwa. Hello!"

Hasselhoff, with his feathered hair, squinted as he scanned the horizon and explained this week's predicament. Wood yelled, "Watashitachi means we! Hidari is right! Bam!"

Olive said, "Hidari means left. Right is migi. I'm deducting a point!"

Rachel shook her head and laughed. "That car is fluent as hell!"

Olive said, "KITT is the shit!"

Wood turned to her, "Hey, watch your language."

She gave him her grandmother's condescending look and continued her linguistic domination until the end of the episode.

Wood looked over and Rachel was in a deep sleep. He helped her into his bedroom and they slept on the futon on the floor.

PHYSICAL THERAPY, PART II

The next morning Wood asked Rachel if she'd like to come to physical therapy with him.

"Yeah, I'd like to be there."

The bus driver knocked on the door and they came outside. He was surprised, pointed at Rachel, and asked, "Okusan desuka?"

Wood paused then nodded, "Hai, sou desu."

Getting into the car, Rachel asked, "What did he ask you?"

"If you were my wife."

She smiled, "Well okay!"

***

Rachel sat in the visitors' area while the bus driver stood outside smoking a cigarette. Wood received his initial massage. She didn't realize the employee was blind until she noticed his caution as he felt his way back to the main desk. Wood walked to the other side of the large room and sat at his favorite machine. He placed the leather bridle around his head and secured the strap firmly under his chin. He leaned over and pressed the On button. The machine began clicking as the cord pulled up on his head. As it reached the top, the leather strap began cutting into his jaw. Sharp pains shot through his neck and head. He had forgotten to place the soft cloth under his chin. He stood to grab the cloth, just out of his reach, and his foot knocked over the stool as he fell back. He choked loudly as he dangled from the cord with his feet flailing under him. The blind worker stood up and began turning quickly, trying to place the location of the choking sound. Rachel ran past him and grabbed Wood, placing the stool under him, and helping him to sit down. She found the power button and turned off the machine.

Wood grasped for air as he pulled off the bridle. "Thanks, baby! I was choking."

Rachel was shocked. "What the hell are these medieval contraptions? Holy shit, you could have broken your neck!" She sat next to Wood.

The employee arrived on the scene and smiled, "Okay, okay, okay." He began a deep tissue massage on Rachel's shoulders. It felt great and her tension began to subside.

Wood said, "Hey, not fair. He thinks you're me."

She closed her eyes and whispered, "Shhh...I deserve this."

***

Back at the apartment, Olive asked if she could use Craig's international account to call her mother. Wood found it and explained how to use it. As she dialed he realized what was happening. Olive was calling Yvette. *That* Yvette. The girl Uncle Freddie referred to as YveTTe, and she was calling her with Rachel sitting in the living room. He sat next to her on the sofa and turned up the TV volume. He could barely hear Olive's muffled words. In a silent panic he asked Rachel, "Wanna go for a walk? There are some cool shops nearby."

"Sure."

Just as they stood up, Olive leaned around the corner, "My mom wants to talk to you."

Wood looked at her, then at the receiver. "With me?"

"Yeah, you" as she held out the phone.

Rachel put her hand on his shoulder and said, "It's okay. Do what you have to do." She sat back down and continued watching TV. Olive handed him the phone and joined Rachel on the sofa. Rachel patted her on the thigh to reassure her.

He lifted the receiver to his ear, but could not speak. He heard, "Um…hello? Wood? It's Yvette. How are you feeling?"

"Hi. I'm feeling better. I'm going to physical therapy and starting to remember things." He shifted his weight back and forth, listening for her to say something. He was seventeen again, annoyed with himself for still being under her spell.

"So what happened to Olive?"

"What do you mean?"

Yvette said, "She stopped cussing at me."

"We had a heart-to-heart. I told her she needs to grow up and she changed her tune. I try to remind myself that she's been on an emotional roller coaster since she arrived."

"I'm sure she'll have some good stories. Thanks for watching out for her."

"We've been studying Japanese together. Rachel just arrived and they're getting along after a bumpy start."

"Let me guess, Olive was a smartass and Rachel wanted to kill her?"

Wood chuckled, "Something like that. We're all learning to be patient with each other."

"That's good. I was wondering when Olive is coming back."

"I have my trial next week. She said she'd like to be here to support me. I was thinking of buying a ticket for September 10th. How does that sound?"

"That sounds good. Are you coming back with Olive?"

"If I'm not in jail."

Yvette sighed. "Shit. Good luck. I'm rooting for you."

"Thanks." Wood looked into the living room at Olive. "So...we're parents."

"We are. I'm hoping we can make it work."

"I'm sure we can. I've heard good things about Eric. He seems like a good guy."

"He is. I'd like to meet Rachel soon."

"I'll tell her you said that." It had taken him twenty years to summon the nerve to say the next two words: "Goodbye, Yvette."

"Goodbye, Wood."

He walked into the living room. "I'm going to catch some air. Anybody want anything from the conveenie?"

Olive said, "I'll take a cold milk tea...please."

Rachel smiled, "I'm good, thanks."

***

Wood walked slowly to Lawson, trying in vain to think clearly. He bought Olive's drink, some donuts, and a magazine devoted entirely to wrist watches, then approached the front counter. He was getting more comfortable paying, as long as he could see the numbers on the register.

As he walked past the corner shrine he heard a screech. He turned his torso and saw the largest crow he had ever seen.

"Hey bud, you trying to tell me something?"

The crow cocked its head and stared at him. It screeched once more before taking flight, its wings rustling the leaves with their power as they beat downward.

Wood heard shouting as he approached the door of the apartment. He opened the door to hear Olive yell, "I can't just shut it off!" He stepped out of his shoes at the genkan and walked into the kitchen. Rachel passed him in the hall, shook her head, then walked into the bedroom, slamming the door behind her.

He looked at Olive and shrugged his shoulders. His inclination was to blame her immediately, but he had witnessed Rachel's temper firsthand.

Olive spoke loudly at first then began lowering her voice. "SHE SAID SHE wanted to clear the air about our phone call argument. I said I was sorry. She accepted my apology, but when I asked if she was going to apologize also she got offended. It spiraled from there."

Handing Olive her milk tea, Wood said, "I'll go talk to her, but I want to be clear that I don't plan to jump in the middle of every problem you two have in the future."

"I can handle myself."

"Can you? Handling yourself isn't just about shutting people down. You have a smart mouth, Olive. Unless you learn to speak to people more respectfully you'll have this problem everywhere you go. Coworkers, neighbors, relatives, you'll constantly be in conflict."

"I know. That's why I told her that I can't just shut it off, but I'm trying."

"Just pause for a split second before you speak to people. Think about the language you use, your body language, tone of voice, the VOLUME OF YOUR VOICE, okay?"

She whispered. "I'll try. I really will."

"That's all I ask."

He walked into the room and moaned as he lowered to a knee, then slowly sat on the tatami next to Rachel, who was flipping through Japanese Cosmopolitan with a vengeance. She paused on a Lancôme ad featuring Isabella Rossellini.

She shook her head, "That Olive gets on my last nerve."

"I know. It probably doesn't seem like it, but she's trying. Did she apologize to you?"

"Yes, she did. That says a lot. I'm still jet lagged and…all of this has been a lot to handle. I don't normally have such a short fuse. I shouldn't have blown up at her."

"I get it. Let's all try to give each other space. This apartment is pretty small. Let's go talk it out with her. I think she's embarrassed more than anything."

Rachel stood and helped Wood to his feet. The three walked through the neighborhood. Being outside helped the tension subside. The crow had returned to the shrine. Wood pointed up, "He tried to warn me not to go home, but I didn't listen. Sorry, brother."

THE FIFTH GUITAR LESSON

Atsushi was surprised by the progress Wood had made learning the unfortunate Driftwood catalogue. Even Wood was surprised at first, but he realized that while most of the songs escaped his mind, the muscle memory remained in his fingers, sometimes moving independent of his thoughts as he played along to his CD. Thankfully, he had always made a point of including the lyrics on his albums and they became more familiar to him upon each listen.

Atsushi still didn't know Wood's identity, but marveled at his misguided devotion to Driftwood. Wood had never included a photo of himself on any album cover. Rachel had finally convinced him to add his image to the upcoming album, but after being slammed into the asphalt the prospect was looking bleak.

Atsushi pulled the guitar strap over his head. "Woodo-san, what do you want to learn?"

"How about Take Me to the Trains."

"Okay, this song is easy. Do you know the song by The Featherdusters called Down the Track? Same song."

Wood took a deep breath and closed his eyes. "They are *not* the same song."

"Same song, same feeling, different words" Atsushi looked through his dictionary. "Driftwood did this." He pointed to the phrasal verb, "To rip off."

Wood's rage reached a level he had not felt in years. "I…Driftwood wrote the song first! His album came out first and *then* The Featherdusters did their rip-off a year later!"

Hearing an increase in volume, Olive peeked her head out of the kitchen and saw a large vein protruding from her father's forehead. She observed his attempt to regain his composure through deep breaths.

Atsushi was taken aback by the passion Wood displayed. "Hountou ni dai fan desu. You are very big fan."

"I just don't think it was fair. Driftwood took The Featherdusters to court but the judge, who knew *nothing* about music, said the songs were different!" He saw Atsushi and Olive staring at him with concern, then caught himself.

"I'm sorry, Atsushi. I know you're trying to help."

Atsushi smiled, "It's okay. Music gives us...passion. If someone say bad thing about The Verve I want to kill them." The rest of the practice went smoothly.

As Atsushi was leaving he noted the immense pile of garbage outside. Olive and Wood grabbed the pamphlet and begged him to help. Wood pleaded, "My friend Craig tried to explain it but we obviously don't understand."

They reviewed the validity of their garbage through the clear plastic bags. Atsushi said, "This is moeru gomi...to burn with fire...on Friday."

Wood protested, "It's full of paper! Why didn't they take it?"

Atsushi pointed inside the bag, "Because it has a newspaper."

Olive threw her arms in the air and yelled, "Newspapers burn!" She turned to catch a neighbor peeking at her. The curtains shuttered quickly and the shadowy figure retreated to the safety of an inner room.

Atsushi read their schedule and shook his head. "Sorry. Newspapers are for the second Tuesday each month. It's okay...I will make a garbage plan for you."

As Atsushi and Olive re-entered the house, Wood waved his arm in a wide swath over the pile, speaking to each trash bag. "Technically, *all* you bitches will burn. I should know, I'm the star of the propane convention."

WHERE EVERYBODY KNOWS YOUR NAME, PART II

Wood brought Rachel, Olive, and Atsushi to his izakaya to meet his new friends. The first thing they saw was a little Christmas tree with lights and decorations. Holly twisted around the posts of the bar and white lights offered a warm winter ambience. The owner and her niece wore red Santa hats and greeted them.

Rachel said, "I didn't know they celebrated Christmas here."

Atsushi explained, "Not for religion. We eat KFC on Christmas like you, maybe give a small present to girlfriend, something like that."

Rachel was confused. "We don't eat KFC on Christmas day."

Atsushi tilted his head to the side, "Hmm…maybe not in your part of the country."

"I'm from Kentucky."

Wood said, "*Anyway*, let me show you Japan's greatest invention, the Bottle Keep!" Pointing behind the bar, "Olive, see that bottle with a little tag hanging from it? That's *my* bottle of Jack. Mine! Nobody else can touch it."

"I don't understand."

"I bought that *bottle* and they *keep* it for me. If I come back here two years from now it will still be here waiting for me. Then I can pour some for my friends."

"That's pretty cool. Maybe they'll keep an old can of Coke next to it."

"Don't be a brat."

Wood was excited to have Atsushi there so he could translate for him. They made the rounds, chatting with Wood's new friends. Can you ask them why everyone is always angry at Kurihara-san? Maybe they don't like the post office.

Noguchi yelled, "Itsumo baka no koto wo itteru!"

Atsushi translated, "He always say stupid things."

"Aha. And what does Noguchi do for a living?"

Atsushi said, "I don't want to ask." He pointed to the tip of his pinky and motioned for him to look. Noguchi had a gold pinky ring on his knuckle and a nub. The rest of his pinky had been chopped off. The perm, shiny suit, and sunglasses completed the Yakuza look.

Wood whispered, "Mafia? Holy shit. I had no idea. He's a cool guy."

"Maybe cool guy, but don't borrow money from him."

Wood learned that the owner never drank because the bottle ruined her previous career. She enjoyed giving everyone a safe place to go. She explained, "Toki doki, minna, anatano namae mou shiteru na tokoro ni ikitaindesu."

Atsushi explained, "She said sometimes people want to go where everybody knows your name."

Wood yelled over the din, "Yes! That's true. And they're always glad you came."

Atsushi told the group, "Soshite, haeru toki ni, minna shiawase ni narimasu!"

This is where the analogy broke down as they all motioned to Kurihara, who sat blissfully ignorant, picking stains from his post office uniform.

"We have a TV show called Cheers. She's Sam, the flirtatious owner. Her tough niece is Carla, shaking her fist in everyone's face. Kurihara is Cliff, the postal carrier who talks nonsense. Chubby Noguchi is Norm, and that guy is Frasier, the psychiatrist." Wood smiled and wondered if every country had a bar full of Cheers characters.

It was karaoke time. Sakamoto-san handed the microphone to Kurihara, who took a deep breath and channeled Prince. In case the patrons had any remaining respect for him, he trawled them through an excruciating, eight-minute rendition of Purple Rain, pouring the frustrations of postal workers everywhere into each lyric. He interpreted the dead silence that followed the song as a good thing.

Wood came out of the bathroom and heard the opening of 'The Biting Wind,' his own song. Olive smiled, handing him the microphone. "Gotcha!"

By the end of the first verse the entire izakaya turned to look at him.

Haruna, easily the youngest there, asked, "Woodo-san wa...Driftwood desuka?

He shrugged, smiling, "Sou sou. I am Driftwood."

Atsushi was mortified and he remembered reading that Driftwood was still in Tokyo awaiting his trial. "Just a minute! You are this singer? I mean…Driftwood is you?"

Wood smiled, "Yeah. Sorry I didn't tell you."

Atsushi searched frantically through his little dictionary and pointed to a word. "This is…"

Wood squinted to read the word in the low light, "'Awkward!' Yeah, a little awkward, but that's okay, man. Not everyone has to be a fan. I learned a lot about my own music from you." He took Atsushi's dictionary and looked up "To appreciate" then pointed at him. "Atsushi read, "Kansha shiteimasu." Wood rubbed Atsushi's back and smiled at him. "I appreciate you." He raised a glass, "To Atsushi, the best guitar teacher ever!"

The owner brought a tray with Wood's bottle of Jack Daniels, cans of Coke, and four glasses. Wood poured drinks for everyone.

Olive protested, "Why does your glass have JAAAAAACK and Coke and mine is Jack and COOOOOOOKE?!"

"Because I'm your dad. It's my job to torment you."

"My mom taught me how to play quarters off my nose!" She gave him her condescending Charlotte look and retreated to another table with Atsushi, who bowed slightly in a preemptive apology.

Rachel stirred her drink and smiled, "That girl is a pistol. It's funny how you've slipped into this fatherly role."

"I'm flying blind! My role model was Uncle Freddie, a mysterious, elitist man with no children. I just do the opposite of the advice he would have given."

Rachel smiled, "I finally met Uncle Freddie at the funeral. You're right, he's eccentric, but he couldn't have been more gracious and he was really touched that I was there. He asked how you're feeling after the accident and said he'd like to get in touch with you. I think his sister's death gave him a different perspective."

Wood took a drink and pondered his relationship with Uncle Freddie. "I need to bury the hatchet with him. He tried to be there for me, but I disappointed him."

"He was bragging to people about his talented nephew. I don't think he feels the same as before."

"It only took four albums and a Grammy!"

Rachel laughed, "Family. Watcha gonna do? I've been meaning to talk to you about your music."

"I've learned a lot of my songs already. Who cares about the obscure tunes."

"True. I have some good news and some interesting news."

"Let's hear the interesting news first."

"Jesse is coming to Japan to support his album. He's bringing a full entourage with him and he's going to play with some local acts. It's a big production. I've talked to him a few times and we're on good terms. He asked about you."

"That is interesting. Sounds like he's doing well. Is Tommy from The Featherdusters coming?"

"No, they already had a falling-out. He has a new management team. I've heard of them. He's in good hands. He even has a girlfriend now, but he doesn't know a soul in Japan so I gave him your phone number."

Wood took it in. "I guess I'll have to swallow my pride and play host. What's his album called?"

"'This is Jesse.' It takes balls to go by one name, Prince, Cher, Madonna, Jesse!"

"Very true. What's the good news?"

"I've been talking to some bands about you producing their next album.

You would be there to guide the creative process, be a mentor, play on a few tracks here and there if they need you to."

"I've always wanted to produce someone's album. Which bands?"

"One is out of Bloomington - The Impossible Shapes. I listened to a few songs. They're raw but really good."

"Who else?"

"The Mysteries of Life. They have a great songwriter and a cellist."

"A cellist? Nice!"

"Maybe we could convince them to come down to Louisville. You could finish your album while you produce theirs. I think you have three songs recorded; 'Estonia, Estonia,' 'Lives Drag On,' and the one your mom played on, 'To Live Through You.'"

"I found the lyrics and chords to some new songs that I had written in my notebook. One was after my argument with Jesse called, 'When You Let Someone Be Who They Are' and a song on the road trip to Oklahoma called 'Spread Eagle to the Sky.' I've been working on a new song called 'Margaret, I was Never Enough.' That brings us to six."

Rachel's mixed her drink with the straw. Her voice quivered, "I miss that girl."

"She was a great dog. A great friend."

"We could get another Basset Hound puppy."

"Hmmm…maybe a different breed. There was only one Margaret." Wood looked over at Olive and Atsushi. They were laughing and flirting.

Rachel returned to the subject. "So if you started producing albums you wouldn't have to tour so much."

"That's true. I could finally settle down. I'll be 37 in a few months. How about you? Have you ever thought about settling down?"

"I'm married to my job at the trucking company and live with my dad in the same house I grew up in. I'm as settled down as anyone could be."

Wood looked around the izakaya then into Rachel's eyes. "I mean settling down with me."

For once, Rachel was speechless.

Wood continued, "You know I'm in love with you."

She looked down at the table and her eyes began welling with tears. "No, I don't know that because you never told me, you asshole. I love you, too."

"I'm sorry. How long have you been in love with me?"

"Since you showed up at the radio station with a Basset Hound puppy." Rachel laughed as she wiped her nose with a napkin. "There were times when I wondered if I just loved Margaret, though."

Olive saw Rachel crying. She caught her father's eye and put her hands up in the air, looking for an explanation. He motioned for them to come over.

Wood said, "It's all good. I just told Rachel that I love her."

Olive punched him in the arm and laughed, "It's about time! Life is too short for this bullshit. Now let's celebrate!"

Wood yelled, "Hey, watch your mouth" as he poured her another Coke with a capful of Jack.

They finished off Wood's bottle. He bought another bottle as a promise to the owner that someday he would return. She smiled as she wrote his name in Katakana and placed it in its own cubby hole high above the bar.

Wood and Rachel walked outside to see Olive and Atsushi making out under a tree. Wood called out, "Olive, we're heading home. You coming?" She jogged from under the shadows, wiping her lips on her sleeve. Atsushi approached, looking embarrassed. Wood put his arm around him. "Don't worry, Atsushi. It's cool. We love you."

Atsushi smiled and told them goodnight. As he walked to the station, he turned back to yell, "Arigatou, Driftwood! See you next week! Bye, Rachel!"

Rachel yelled, "Ja nay!" She turned and said, "He's a great kid. I wish I could stay longer to get to know all these people but I have a feeling the trucking company is falling apart."

Wood said, "No, it's cool. I get it."

Olive asked, "Are you coming back for the trial?"

"Yes, I'll definitely be here to support both of you."

Wood said, "Can we afford it?"

"Oh yeah. Il Masturbatore is the gift that keeps on giving. It's still selling in Europe."

NEW YEARS

December 31, 1998

Craig brought snacks, drinks, and long toshikobi soba noodles to help Wood and Olive celebrate the new year. "These noodles are extra-long for a long life. Here's some mochi, too. Careful, every year a bunch of old people choke on it and die."

Olive chuckled, "I guess the noodles and mochi balance each other out."

Wood was drinking a Sapporo while watching a singing show. He called out, "Hey, Craig, what's going on here?"

"That's the Kohaku singing competition. Every New Year the whole country stops to watch this show. It's the girls against the boys."

They ate noodles and drank beer as they watched groups like the Kinki Kids and Tube face off against Amuro Namie and Fuji Ayako, who sang enka in a kimono. Craig explained, "Enka is their country music. Three chords and the truth!"

Wood asked, "What's it about?"

"It's usually about lost romance, drinking, or your home village with references to nature, like snow falling on a mountain river, things like that."

"That's country."

A boy band took the stage with one of them singing lead. Olive said, "I'm rooting for the girls but that guy's pretty hot."

"That's Kimutaku. He's bigger than The Beatles here."

As the clock approached midnight they gathered pots and pans to make noise on the balcony. As they counted down the last 10 seconds, Craig whispered, "Check this out." As 1999 struck, he put his finger to his lips, "Shhhhhh." Olive and Wood held their pots still as they looked at him in confusion. "Listen." The neighborhood was cold, silent, utterly tranquil. A breeze whistled lightly through the leaves nearby. A low gong from a distant temple bell reached them through the frigid air as the monks rang in the new year. As the gongs continued, Olive closed her eyes and whispered, "That's the most beautiful New Years I've ever heard."

The following morning was relaxing. They drank coffee and watched an NHK documentary about snow cranes in Hokkaido, followed by a variety show that took the usual absurdity to new heights.

In the afternoon they took the train to visit Gotokuji Temple with Craig, in hopes that a visit would bring them good fortune in 1999. Hundreds of people walked from the station, speaking cheerfully in low tones. It was cold and windy with crows dotting a bright blue sky.

As they approached the temple Olive laughed, "What the hell?" There were hundreds of white statues of cats holding up one paw. "It's like they're about to testify in court."

Craig smiled, "Yeah, I thought you'd like this temple. It's my favorite. The legend goes that a few hundred years ago a feudal lord was passing by during a downpour and the temple's cat waved at him, like, 'Come on in, bro. It's warm in here.' Then the lord gave them a bunch of land or something."

Wood said, "I love it. We'll have to get a few souvenirs."

They approached a large incense burner billowing smoke throughout the courtyard. People stood around it waving the smoke toward them. Craig said, "Come on, Wood. Let's get you healed." He and Olive waved smoke toward Wood, then at themselves.

Finally, they approached a large rope that hung down from a bell. Craig demonstrated as he threw coins into a large wooden box with slats, "Make your offering, ring the bell, bow twice, clap your hands twice, pray for a few seconds, and bow once more."

Wood asked, "What do people pray for?"

"Good health, remembering their songs, not rotting in a Japanese prison…the usuals."

"Smartass."

ATSUSHI'S GIG

Wood returned home from his physical therapy feeling relaxed. The blind man used a few chiropractic and stretching techniques to summon a few loud cracks from his neck, back, and hips. Wood twisted his neck back and forth as he approached the door. As he took off his shoes at the genkan and removed his coat he heard voices from the living room. He walked in to see Olive and Atsushi on the sofa, drinking a Sapporo and watching TV. She had her hand on his knee and neither realized he was standing behind them. He cleared his throat loudly, so as not to witness anything he'd rather not see.

Olive said, "Okaeri!" while Atsushi jumped and bowed his head repeatedly in apologetic motions.

"Hey, Atsushi. Do we have a lesson?"

"Uh…no. Gomennasai."

"Don't apologize. You're welcome here anytime."

"No, it's okay, Wood. I have to go to band practice." He rifled through his book bag and pulled out a flyer, handing it to Wood while looking down to avoid eye contact. "Please come to my band show this Friday."

Wood looked it over. It was printed in Japanese with Atsushi's handwritten directions in English. He had even drawn a map on the back.

"We'll be there. Domo."

Atsushi gathered his things and exited quickly. Olive sat staring at the TV in silence. Her father sat on a chair as he thought of ways to break the tension. Without looking away, Olive said, "Just tell me what's on your mind."

"Okay, I think I'm a few years late for the birds-and-the-bees talk, right?"

"That would be correct. We're being safe, if that's what you're getting at."

"So I go to physical therapy and you start boning down like rabbits?"

"Gross!"

"Finally, we agree on something. Just be careful, please."

She sighed and rolled her eyes. "We are. I just told you that."

"Not just sexually. Be careful with your heart. We won't be here much longer." He rephrased with the correct pronouns. "*You* won't be here much longer. I might be sticking around for a while, depending on how this trial turns out."

"Don't worry. I like being around him but we're not getting attached to each other."

***

That Friday, Wood and Olive huddled together under a single umbrella as they left the train station, following Atsushi's directions past pachinko parlours and izakayas until they were officially lost in a labyrinth of tiny streets. A buzzed salaryman approached, singing to himself in a suit and loosened tie. Olive approached him, pointing to the flyer, "Cyotto sumimasen. Kono basho gozonjidesuka?" The man laughed and looked at the flyer. "Your Japanese very good. Come with me!" He circled back the way he had come and they followed him for a full ten minutes through winding alleyways until they arrived at a dark doorway with blaring music inside. He pointed and bowed from beneath his umbrella. Wood smiled, "Arigatou gozaimasu!"

Olive laughed, "I can't believe he walked us here. I guess he knew we'd never find it."

They opened the door and paid the cover charge of 800 yen each to a beautiful young lady with green hair and horn-rimmed glasses. She gave them each a drink ticket then retreated backstage as another person manned the door. Olive whispered, "She looks like a model."

They were the only gaijin in the dark club. Wood's experience sizing up crowd sizes told him there were about 200 people there. A punk band was on stage jumping around. The singer did a back bend and wailed into the microphone. After the song, the singer gave an extended and polite description that Wood and Olive surmised as the band's back story. They launched into another psychotic scream-fest, followed by another polite speech. They played their final song, bowed, and left the stage to a smattering of applause.

Olive went to the bar to grab their drinks as the next band took the stage. Wood had witnessed numerous theatrics over the years, mostly in his own shows, but he had yet to see a duo performing a bass solo accompanied by violent flower arranging. As the bassist closed his eyes and played lightning fast runs up and down the fretboard, his bandmate cut flowers and thrust them into a large vase, sometimes jumping and throwing them for a more dramatic ikebana experience. As the song ended, the rock florist bowed and saluted the crowd, like a matador after dispensing a bull. It was a glorious ten minutes – then they were gone. Only the flower arrangement remained onstage as evidence of the history that was made.

Olive returned and handed her father his drink. He asked as he took a swig, "Did you see that?!"

"Yeah, that was stupid."

"Hold on, not so fast. It takes a lot of guts to dream that up and make it work in front of a few hundred people. They could have taken the easy way out and played Oasis covers, but they stuck with their vision."

"And that vision was playing a bass solo at a flower shop."

"Fair enough."

Olive yelled, "There's Atsushi!" As the band took the stage, he put the flower arrangement on top of his amplifier and plugged in. His hair was thick with gel and blow dried high with dabs of green on the tips. The cute, green-haired girl who was working the door greeted the crowd, then began singing in a low, sultry voice. Atsushi played a slow, funky rhythm behind her as the bass and drums joined in. The crowd moved toward the stage. The vocalist looked out above the crowd, singing into the unknown. She was magnetic. Olive could barely see Atsushi as he started his guitar solo. The beautiful singer swayed as she played tambourine and watched Atsushi before returning to sing the chorus. He stood next to her and they sang into the same microphone.

Wood leaned over and yelled, "They have great chemistry!" He glanced at Olive, whose face revealed a sentiment both curious and homicidal. He corrected himself. "I mean, he's really locked in with the drummer. They just need a new singer. She's weird!" His words fell on deaf ears as she stared at the girl.

The next few songs were faster and heavily distorted. A mosh pit formed in front of the stage. Atsushi laughed as bodies slammed together, creating violent, dark silhouettes. A young man with a mohawk jumped onto the stage and fell backwards, crowd surfing toward them. The beautiful singer put her arm around Atsushi and sang as he played fast power chords, smiling.

Olive turned to her father and yelled, "I wanna go!"

"But it's just getting good!"

"I said I wanna go home!" She moved roughly through the crowd toward the exit, slamming her drink on the bar. People looked at her as she passed, then returned to watching the band. Wood followed her, apologizing by holding his hands together in prayer as he passed through the crowd. At the doorway he looked back to catch Atsushi shielding the lights from his eyes to see them leave. Confused, he shrugged his shoulders at Wood, who shook his head and mouthed, "Sorry" as he walked out to find Olive. The rain had stopped and she was already down the alley, stomping quickly through puddles. Wood caught up to her, turned her around, and bear hugged her as she cried into his chest. He rubbed her back and said, "I know. I know."

It wasn't a time to tell her there was probably nothing going on -- or that Atsushi would not have invited them if he had a reason to be "caught."

It was a time for a father to be there for his daughter as she cried in the alley.

THE TRIAL, DAY I

February 25, 1999

Wood, Rachel, Olive, Craig, and Sophia convened at the courthouse. They all dressed nicely. Wood wore a suit he had recently purchased with a non-aggressive baby blue tie. He visited the barber the day before and used gel in his hair. His face was clean shaven. They entered the court room and noticed the prosecuting attorney setting up his poster boards on a tripod. He took out a pointer and placed it on the table in front of him. The accuser wore a navy-blue skirt, a matching vest, and a light blue shirt with a pink silk scarf. Her sleeve was rolled up to reveal a bandage on her right forearm, most likely for dramatic effect. Wood looked at her closely to trigger any memories. Nothing.

The court reporter entered with a small stack of folders and a pointer of her own. Judge Kuronuma entered from the rear chamber with files and pointer in hand.

Sophia huddled them up and whispered, "Shit, I forgot my pointer! This is *not* good."

Olive, sensing that this was her moment to contribute, whispered, "On it!" and briskly walked out of the courtroom. She returned five minutes later with a retractable metal pointer and handed it to Sophia. The bottom of the antenna was bent with a Toyota logo in clear view.

Wood whispered, "You just ripped that off a car?!"

Sophia calmed everyone down. "I'll cover it with my hand. Good job, kid!"

The trial began in earnest and the judge inquired about Wood's need for a translator. Craig rattled off a number of "magazines" he had translated from Japanese into English, as proof of his fluency in Japanese, not mentioning that they were obscure manga comics. She accepted his offer to translate for Wood, on the condition that both attorneys agreed. Sophia and the young man across from her nodded approval as they reviewed their paperwork.

Olive took out her art supplies and sketched frantically with pastels.

The prosecutor called Wood to the witness stand. Since there was no jury he stood facing the judge while the young attorney grilled him with questions from the side. Craig believed that accurate translation involved mirroring the prosecutor's antics, tone of voice, and physical movements.

Craig translated, "You have a history of songs about violence, specifically biting, don't you?"

"What? No, I don't."

"Let the record show that the defendant wrote a song called Vampire Morning."

"Vampire Morning was off my first album. Come on, I was a kid. The opening song is called The Camaro!"

"And your most recent album has a song called The Biting Wind."

"Yes, it's about a storm."

The attorney walked a few feet away from Wood then whipped around, "Igurisu no Hull de, nani ga okurimashitaka?"

Craig strolled a few feet then whipped around, "What happened in Hull, England?"

Wood was rattled, "We played a show there. The crowd was drunk and violent. They attacked us and I was hit with a beer bottle. An Englishman punched me repeatedly. We stopped the show and I went back to the hotel."

"So you were violent?"

"Not really. I tried to defend myself but it didn't work out that way."

"Was your tooth bent from the punch?"

"Yes, it was."

The prosecutor picked up his pointer and walked confidently to his tripod, like a matador approaching a wounded bull. With a flourish he pulled away a sheet to show his poster, which displayed a mouthful of crooked human teeth.

"Let the record reflect that these dental images were captured by a detective while the defendant was in a coma."

One tooth in particular was pointing inward. The prosecutor pointed at the tooth, tapped with his pointer, then slowly turned around and pointed at Wood. He asked in a high voice in English, "Mista Underwood, is this your canine tooth?"

Craig began translating into Japanese then caught himself.

The prosecutor repeated, yelling this time, "IS THIS YOUR CANINE?!"

Wood closed his eyes. "Yes, I think it is."

The prosecutor smiled and removed the poster to reveal an identical poster behind it with the same set of teeth. This photo showed Wood's bite marks on the arm of the lady sitting nearby.

Knowing the trial hinged on this moment, the prosecutor paused, then pointed slowly to the same tooth and repeated himself in a lower voice, "Mista Underwood. Is *this* your canine on the victim's arm?"

Wood paused, looked at his attorney, then back at the prosecutor. "I don't know."

The prosecutor laughed, "Haha…you don't know? It is the exact same set of teeth, just on the victim's arm! Why don't you know?"

"Because I was hit by a bus and I don't remember anything. You see…"

With a violent waving of arms, the prosecutor and Craig screamed, "NO FURTHER QUESTIONS!"

***

That night, Wood reviewed Olive's courtroom pastel sketches and beamed with newfound fatherly pride. "These are amazing, kiddo! I'm so proud of you!" Rachel sat next to him and smiled, impressed and shaking her head.

The first sketch showed the prosecuting attorney using his pointer to antagonize Wood, nearly touching his face with the tip. Craig pointed back, holding the Toyota antenna like a cutlass, as if they were fencing over Wood, who buried his face in his hands. The next sketch featured Wood's lawyer prying open his mouth, pointing to his tooth while the judge checked the time on her wristwatch.

"Olive, I'm going to frame this last sketch! It has so much action!" It depicted their reenactment of the bus accident, a shameless and futile ploy for sympathy. Wood played his acoustic guitar and looked to his left, Craig approached him from his right holding a bus mirror. The prosecutor pounded on his desk, screaming an objection while the judge waved her arms to put a stop to the charade. A little cloud over the judge's head read, "Baka! Please stop!"

Olive walked in holding the Toyota antenna, pointing it at her father. "Sophia gave this to me as a souvenir of the trial."

Rachel laughed. "That was nice of her. Your thievery came through in the clutch!"

Wood took a shower then walked into the living room. As he was putting on a T-shirt, Olive glanced over and yelled, "What the fu…hell is that?"

"What?"

"Turn around." She lifted up his shirt and inspected his right shoulder blade. "Holy shit!"

Rachel said, "I saw it the other day but I thought he landed on something during the accident."

Olive grabbed her makeup mirror and positioned him so he could see his back in the bathroom mirror.

Wood squinted. "I can't make it out. What is it?"

"That's a bite mark. Clear as day! That lady bit you. That's why you bit her back! It must have been deep to turn into a scar. It's been a while since the bar fight."

Wood picked up the phone, "I'm calling my lawyer to tell her the good news!"

THE TRIAL, DAY II

March 4, 1999

Wood's lawyer pounded her stack of files for dramatic effect. "Your honor, I have received evidence *this very day* proving that the accuser is *lying!*" Sophia had used her "This-very-day" speech many times in her legal career and basked in the glory of knowing it was finally true.

She asked Wood to stand in front of the judge. He turned around and lifted up his shirt. She used her pointer to denote the specific bite marks. Craig translated for Wood. "Your honor, the defendant was being attacked by an American sailor. They were settling their disagreement as men do. The accuser came up from behind, put him in a head lock, then bit him in the back. He thought she was another sailor and simply bit back in self-defense."

The prosecuting attorney, clearly rattled, leaned over and whispered with the accuser, who spoke to him quietly while waving her arms. Sophia had them on the ropes and continued her assault.

"Your honor, if you ask the accuser to stand up, you'll see that the height of her mouth matches perfectly with this location on my client's back." She turned to the young lady, pointing at her, "You bit him, didn't you!" She walked closer, nearly touching her with the pointer. "DIDN'T YOU?!"

The woman began to cry, nodding her head. Her young lawyer scrambled for something to say. When his client cried out in English, "Yes! I bited Driftwood!" he threw his hands in the air and leaned back in his chair, shaking his head with his eyes closed.

Sophia said, "Let the record reflect that the accuser has admitted to biting my client. The defense rests."

***

After a short recess the court was called back to order. Craig leaned over and whispered his translation of Judge Kuronuma's verdict excitedly. "This is good! She said something about your brain not functioning correctly even before the accident. You bit the lady, she bit you. We don't know who bit first, but we do know that you were both in a horrible bar…like a cauldron of vice. Tokyo has many problems, like yakuza and chikan groping women on the trains…okay she's kinda riffing now. It is the opinion of this court that our time has been wasted by the accuser, and therefore I *am throwing out this case!* Please return the passport to the defendant so he may leave our great nation. This court is adjourned. I am late to my tee time!" Craig laughed, "I had a feeling she was a golfer!"

Wood buried his face in his hands and wept. Craig shouted, "Yes!" and high fived Sophia, then hugged Rachel, who was already sobbing. Olive leaned over the railing and hugged her father from behind. The accuser and her lawyer gathered their things and exited quietly.

The judge picked up a large stack of folders and retreated toward her chambers. Shaking her head, she glanced back at Team Driftwood, smiled, and said in perfect English, "Thanks for the entertainment, you dipshits."

SAKURA VIEWING PARTY

March 7, 1999

Yoyogi Koen

Olive and Atsushi staked out a place for their group on the grass at Yoyogi Park. She laughed as they walked by the rockabilly dancers with their Elvis hair, leather jackets, jeans, and black boots.

"I'm sorry I assumed that singer was your girlfriend. You could have told me she's married to the bass player."

"Sorry. We are all classmates from junior high school. She is like my sister."

She asked Atsushi as they spread out blankets and unpacked drinks, "Why are cherry blossoms so important? They're beautiful, but it seems deeper than just beauty."

Atsushi thought for a moment, "Hmmm…maybe for many things. We are happy because spring is coming. Also, sakura come and go very fast, like life."

Olive smelled the blossoms from a branch and smiled. "When did these picnics start?"

Atsushi shrugged and chuckled, "Maybe thousand years. Same party, just the snacks change. This year the sakura come early."

She motioned to two young men in suits holding down a large space next to them and whispered, "What's their story?"

"They are rookies from a company. They come to hold place before big bosses come." He asked, "Sumimasen…nanji ni tsuita no?"

"Asa no rokuji desu! Toshiba no Oguma desu. Yoroshiku onegaishimasu!"

He turned to Olive, "They come at six this morning for Toshiba company party."

Wood, Rachel, Craig, Jesse, and Gina walked single file through narrow paths between picnic blankets. There were thousands of people in the park. A group of musicians weaved through the crowd playing drums, tambourines, and flutes while dancers wearing ghoulish masks made gestures with their hands along with the music. Nearby, a man dressed as a scary demon pranced around on a stage. Women laughed as they held their babies up to him. The children screamed in horror as the demon rushed at them.

Jesse looked over and said, "Damn, those moms are hardcore!"

Craig laughed, "It keeps 'em in line!"

"Craig, Wood told me that you were his translator at the trial. You must be fluent in Japanese."

"Yeah, I'm thinking of doing more trial translation in the future. I think it pays pretty well, although this time was pro bono."

Wood interjected, "Craig was the most dramatic translator in legal history! This dude thought he had to *act out* everything the lawyer was doing!" Wood turned away then whipped around, "What happened in Hull, England?!"

Jesse laughed, "That's a valid question. What the hell *did* happen in Hull, England? That was a gig I'd rather forget. Everyone showered us with beer after we tried to sing a Housemartins tune. That guy clocked you pretty good."

Wood laughed, "Remember how my tooth was bent in? That was a big moment in the trial."

Craig and Olive pointed at Wood and yelled, "IS THIS YOUR CANINE?!"

Jesse nodded, "The doggy tooth came back to bite you." He looked up into the trees and saw a large crow staring down at him. "Everything's connected."

Craig asked, "Jesse, how are the preparations coming for your tour?"

"It's a little scary but I think we got all the kinks worked out on the last leg of the tour. Seattle was a great gig. We're going to play here in Tokyo at Akasaka Blitz. Then we're playing in Nagoya, Kyoto, and Osaka. I'm already lost."

Wood pointed at Atsushi, "Bring this dude. He knows his way around, he's a smokin' guitar player and a great guy."

Jesse said, "No shit? We have room on the bus if you're free. You know any of Wood's songs?"

Atsushi smiled, "I know many Driftwood songs. I write songs, too."

Wood laughed, "Don't get him started. I'm sure he'll tell how he feels about Driftwood on the bus."

After a few rounds of drinks Jesse was holding court on the blanket. "Olive, your father and me put Rachel through *hell!*"

Rachel concurred, "Like two brothers. Always fighting over the remote."

Jesse said, "He's very tricky when it comes to TV remotes. Rachel, are you coming to see the show?"

"No, sorry. I have to fly back to Kentucky. I've already been gone a long time. I'm afraid the trucking company is gonna fall apart if I stay much longer.

"That's okay. If we come through Louisville I'll let you know."

Jesse told Olive, "Your father is the most superstitious person I've ever met."

Wood defended himself, "The voodoo priestess was correct! She said I would be at death's door and that death would come from the right. It didn't make sense till that bus took me out. Boom!"

Jesse laughed, "Okay, I'll give her credit for that. She should have just told you to look both ways." Jesse turned to Olive. "One time we were playing a gig in Ann Arbor and I couldn't find your father anywhere. He was at the local fire department learning how to prepare for the Y2K doomsday. He showed up right before we had to go onstage."

"You won't be laughing this New Year's Eve when planes start falling out of the sky. I have boxes of freeze-dried astronaut food in my garage."

Olive was overwhelmed by the stories. She could never get back all of the lost years, but they shared experiences that other fathers and daughters would never have. She even had a new aunt and uncle.

Olive asked, "Gina, how did you meet my dad and Jesse?"

"Jesse and I were in the high school choir together in New Orleans. Then your father and Jesse came to play at our prison in Louisiana."

Olive said, "You work at a prison. Cool!"

Jesse and Wood laughed, "Well! It's complicated."

Gina laughed, "You two shut the hell up before I bitch slap you! I worked my *ass* off in that prison!" She counted on her fingers, laughing, "I served food in the cafeteeeria, mopped flooors, made license plaaates!"

Olive blushed and nodded, "Oh, I think I get it."

Gina continued, "Maybe this is the beer talking, but I want to tell you that your father is a great man. We had an inmate, a sweet young lady named Aliyah, not a mean bone in her body."

Wood was embarrassed, "Gina, please. You don't have to do this."

"Your daughter needs to know! I won't share the details, but Aliyah had horrible things done to her...unimaginable things. And she did *not* deserve to be in prison. And her ass wasn't getting out. *Ever!*" She pointed to Olive's father, "And this man paid for her to get a *real* lawyer. He never breathed a word to anyone, but Aliyah told us. Her retrial starts next month - in a *New Orleans* court, not out in the sticks. She won't get railroaded this time. There's been a lot of news coverage and everyone knows it was self-defense. Her uncle and his sleazy friends can't hide now, and it ain't gonna matter if the guy she shot was a church minister. He was also a rapist. And

Aliyah would have rotted in that prison for decades without Wood's help – so let's raise a glass. Kanpai!"

Olive took a drink, looking over her glass at her father, who looked down and wiped tears from his eyes as the others drank to him.

After some silence, Jesse said, "Is anyone else hungry?"

Olive said, "We can order a pizza. I have the number."

Wood added, "The pizza is pretty good but every time we call, the order takes a long time and it's always wrong."

Atsushi reached for the phone number. "I will call for you." He and Olive walked across the street to a green public phone. Atsushi dialed the number and began speaking. He was confused then burst out laughing. They walked back to the park together, laughing and gesturing.

Wood asked, "Did you order the pizza?"

Olive waved the piece of paper and explained, "Dad, this is the wrong number! We've been calling a Japanese family this whole time. They have been taking down our order and calling the pizza place for us. That's why it takes longer and it's always wrong."

"Oh my God! My faith in humanity is restored." Rachel raised her glass. "To Tokyo - a huge city full of good people. Kanpai!" She stood up. "Well, I need to head back to the apartment to finish packing." She started passing out bear hugs.

Wood held up his arms and Rachel pulled him up, aided by Jesse pushing from behind. Wood said, "Thanks for a great party, everyone. I'm going to go help Rachel pack."

Craig said, "Want me to come so we can leave to the airport from there?"

There was a pause, then Olive said with finger quotes, "Craig, I think they want to be alone when they 'pack'." Craig blushed.

Wood and Rachel walked away, shaking their heads. He called out, "Kids these days!"

THIS IS JESSE

March 10, 1999

Akasaka Blitz

Wood, Olive, Atsushi, and Craig stood on the side of the stage as the lights went down. A heavy and percussive thud sound came through the sound system with a slight echo. As a spotlight slowly beamed down on the corner of the stage, two men and two women wearing traditional Japanese yukata pounded mochi, one at a time, with large wooden mallets. They pounded a rhythm in 4/4 time as a second spotlight shown on Jesse, who was standing on a stack of amps holding a cigar box guitar. He began soloing with a slide over the rhythm of the pounding mallets. A minute later, the drums, bass, keyboards, and guitar came in together as the stage lights came up. Gina and another woman stood behind two microphones singing "Sweet Thang" by Shuggie Otis as the band played. It was slow and bluesy, always a gutsy way to start a show. Jesse jumped from the amp onto the stage below and the crowd cheered. They jammed, taking turns soloing, then transitioned to another great cover, "I Wish I Never Saw the Sunshine" by the Ronettes, which Gina sang at center stage. They flirted with each other before singing their choir duet, "If You Should Lose Me."

Wood smiled and told Olive, "They sang this when we played at the prison! They're great together." Wood was sure he would be jealous before the show, but an unexpected emotion welled within him - pride. Jesse's success was at least in part due to the avuncular guidance that Wood had shown him, and through all of the arguments, they remained friends. It was the same Jesse he remembered playing with on hundreds of stages, but more self-assured and in command of the situation.

Jesse played songs from his album, including the single that brought him to Japan, "Fréjus Café," which he had written after his conversation in the south of France with the lady from Alabama.

Atsushi said in between songs, "I will be back. Going to the bathroom."

Toward the end of the show Jesse said, "I have an old friend here tonight. Some people know him as Thurston, others know him as Driftwood, I just call him Wood, and he's right over there."

Wood walked out a few steps and waved to the crowd.

"People don't know this, but Wood is a big Carpenters fan. We always said we were going to cover this song, but we never got up the nerve to put it on an album. So I'm dedicating this to you, Wood, my brother from another mother. It's called, 'I Won't Last a Day Without You.'"

They played a distorted, psychedelic reggae version of the song that was fast enough to be danceable. Gina, Jesse, and the band sang the chorus:

> When there's no getting over that rainbow
> When my smallest of dreams won't come true
> I can take all the madness the world has to give
> But I won't last a day without you

After the song, Jesse said, "I also made a new friend named Atsushi!"

Atsushi walked onto the stage wearing his guitar and plugged in the cable from an amp.

Olive's excitement returned her to her old ways, "Holy shit! Atsushi's on stage! Fuck yeah!" She waved to him and he smiled back. He approached one of the microphones and translated Jesse's words into Japanese.

"We have a big surprise. You might have heard that Wood was in an accident. He almost died but he's getting back to normal and he's always in our prayers. We're going to play one of his songs and see if we can get him to come out and jam with us. But if he doesn't want to, we totally understand."

Atsushi started the opening to Take Me to the Trains and Jesse and the band joined in. They looked over at Wood.

Olive yelled over the distortion, "Go for it, dad!"

He walked out to applause, put on a guitar, and joined in with the band. After the second chorus, Jesse smiled and signaled for him to solo. Wood started slowly then added distortion as his fingers moved up the neck. Jesse twirled his finger in the air, signaling for the band to keep playing another round of measures. Wood closed his eyes and leaned back, head pointed upwards, smiling. As his solo came to an end he grinded the Fender's strings against the amplifier. A shriek of feedback came through the sound system and the crowd cheered. He signaled the band to end the song by thrusting his torso downward to the left. Wood took off the guitar and handed it to Jesse's guitar tech. He hugged Jesse, Atsushi, and Gina, then waved to the cheering crowd as he left the stage. Olive smiled and shook her head, taking in what she had just witnessed.

NARITA INTERNATIONAL AIRPORT

March 13, 1999

Wood pulled out his passport and looked through the stamps to pass the time. "I've always loved the stamps from different countries. They tell a story."

Olive looked over as he turned the pages. "Mine only has one stamp for Japan. We went to Mexico and Canada but you don't need a passport for those countries."

"I'm sure you'll see the world someday. So we're going straight to Chicago O'Hare, then we'll go through immigration, switch to the domestic terminal and on to Indy."

"My mom and Eric are going to meet me. I guess you'll get to see her after all these years. We can give you a ride to your house before we go to Zionsville."

"Thanks, but it's okay. Rachel's going to pick me up from the airport."

"That's cool. It will be good for everyone to finally meet."

Wood nodded his head. "I've been wanting to ask you something serious. How would you feel if I moved to Louisville to be near Rachel?"

"Why are you asking me?"

"Because you're my daughter and I want to be in your life. I need to include you and Rachel in these decisions from now on."

"I'm at Purdue most of the time anyway. We can talk on the phone and email. Which reminds me, you need a computer, mister!"

"I know, I know. I'll get one soon. I promise." He patted his guitar case. "At least I still have Martina." He opened the case, pulled out his guitar, and started strumming gently. Olive looked over, "Is that Cat Stevens?"

"Yeah, 'If You Want to Sing Out.' Know it?"

"That's my mom's favorite song. She played it on repeat when I was little."

Wood stopped playing and closed his eyes. "That's from Harold and Maude...the movie your mother and I watched together."

"The hint she gave me."

"Maybe that night meant more to her than I thought." They sang together, softly:

> Well, if you want to sing out, sing out
> And if you want to be free, be free
> Cuz there's a million things to be
> You know that there are
> And if you want to live high, live high
> And if you want to live low, live low
> Cuz there's a million ways to go
> You know that there are.

They heard a flight attendant speaking Japanese over the intercom say "Chicago." The passengers began forming a line. As Wood returned Martina to her guitar case, he said, "Olive, thank you for finding me – and for staying with me when I really needed you."

Olive stood and swung her gym bag, filled with snacks, bottles of saké, and souvenirs, over her shoulder. "You were a question mark for all those years. I never realized how lost I felt until I found you."

Wood struggled to stand. "Regardless of what the world throws at us, I'm glad you're in my life."

"Come on, dad, we're boarding." Olive pulled the two carry-on suitcases, leaning over to keep the gym bag on her shoulder, as Wood ambled beside her, carrying his guitar. She handed their boarding passes to the flight attendant and said, "My father's recovering from an accident. We'll need some help during the flight, please." The attendant smiled and nodded.

"Good job getting us upgraded to first class. Your grandma would be proud of you. My back and neck are killing me."

"You were jumping around the stage like Flea on shrooms! No more stage dives for you, old man. You probably reversed a month's worth of rehab."

Olive lifted the bags into the overhead bins then held her father as he sank gently into his seat. He groaned, "I'm not old. I just turned 37." She fastened his seat belt and adjusted the air vent over his head so he wouldn't catch a cold, then sat back in her seat and heaved a lengthy sigh.

When the flight attendant approached, Olive smiled. "Can I get two Jack and Cokes, please?" She turned to her father, "What are you having?" He was asleep. A tranquil smile revealed a sense of calm that Olive had not seen on her father's face before.

He was already home.

***

ARTISTS MENTIONED

FICTIONAL ARTISTS

Champagne Mane
Driftwood
Jesse
Kwicherbichin/Trippy Longstockings
Marisela
The Featherdusters
The Reluctant Hypocrites

REAL ARTISTS

Barbara Lynn
Bjork/The Sugarcubes
Cat Stevens/Yusuf Islam
Chalmette High School Fighting Owls Marching Band
Clyde Stubblefield
Culture Club
Debbie Harry/Blondie
Dolly Parton
Elton John
Eric Clapton
Fence of Defense
Flea
Fleetwood Mac
Gary Portnoy and Judy Hart-Angelo (Cheers theme)
Grandaddy
Hank Williams
Jaagup Kreem
James Brown
Jim Morrison
JJ Cale
John Lennon
John Lydon

Joy Division
KISS
Led Zeppelin
Lloyd Cole
Oasis
Patsy Cline
Peter Tosh
PJ Harvey
Policy
Prince
Radiohead
Rile 9 Collective
Roxy Music
Selena Quintanilla
Shuggie Otis
Stevie Nicks
Talk Talk
Terminaator
The Carpenters
The Cure
The Grateful Dead
The Hollies
The Housemartins
The Impossible Shapes
The Mysteries of Life
The Police
The Ronettes
The Sleepy Jackson
The Stone Roses
The Verve
Tom Waits (Gun Street Girl)
WAR
Wayne Hancock
Yanik Etienne
Zapp and Roger

BOOK CLUB SAMPLE QUESTIONS

1. How were Wood and Jesse influenced by the role models in their lives? In what ways did Wood and Jesse mentor each other?

2. What influence does Rachel have on Wood's career? How does their relationship change over time?

3. What is your view of Wood's mother, Charlotte Underwood? Do you think that Rachel and Wood see her in the same light?

4. How do you feel about the author's use of Margaret-the-Basset-Hound to provide insight into Wood's feelings about his own life?

5. How does Wood's view of the criminal justice system change after his visit to the women's prison in Louisiana?

6. Jesse would prefer that Wood and Rachel think he's using heavy drugs than come out as gay. What does this say about his view of society in the 90s? How does Wood react to finding out?

7. In what ways did Olive grow as the story progressed?

8. The author includes cover songs to give context to the story. Which songs do you feel had the strongest impact on the scene? Did you discover a new song that you like?

9. One of the story's themes is the proliferation of the internet in the 90's. How does this impact his public persona? How does Wood react to the changes in technology?

ABOUT THE AUTHOR

JP Lane played bass for Policy, Village Drums, and The Dancing Nancys. He travelled to Moscow and Kazakhstan following the breakup of the USSR. He taught English in Tokyo for four years, where he struggled with recycling. He holds a master's degree from Indiana University and lives in Sacramento, California with his wife, children, and a Basset Hound named Margaret Thatcher. He is the author of Painting the Grand Homes of California's Central Valley. The Driftwood Tour is his first novel.

SOCIAL MEDIA

Facebook: Art of JP Lane

Instagram: @artofjplane